ARRESTING DELIA

Borgo Press/Wildside Press Books
by S. Fowler Wright

ARRESTING DELIA

A Classic Crime Novel

by

S. FOWLER WRIGHT

WRITING AS "SYDNEY FOWLER"

The Borgo Press
An Imprint of Wildside Press

FIRST WILDSIDE EDITION

CONTENTS

CHAPTER ONE

MRS. KINGSLEY STARR, having been married something under four minutes, stood on the step of the Registrar's office in Princeton Street.

Her brother, who had married Kingsley's twin sister about three minutes earlier, had just handed his bride into a waiting taxi, which was disappearing in the direction of Victoria Station.

"Kingsley," Cora said, with a definite tone in the affectionate sweetness of her voice, "I'm not coming."

"Not—?" Kingsley looked his bewilderment.

"Not what I say, of course. I'm not coming to see them off."

"Well, I don't suppose they'll mind that overmuch.... What do you want us to do?"

"You're going to see them off and say how sorry I m that I'm not there."

"I'm not going without you."

"Oh, yes, you are. It's no use looking sulky like that. It's too soon to begin.... You can't let your twin sister go off without saying goodbye."

"I don't see that, any more than you. He's your brother as well."

"But not twins.... I've got to go back to the flat. I've just remembered I left a book...."

"I don't see that that...."

"But I do. If I didn't finish that book this afternoon, it wouldn't be any use being married at all. I couldn't concentrate at the right times...."

"There's...there's no catch?"

"Of course not. Kingsley, what a baby you are! It's just what I say. You'll go to Victoria and see them off, and pick me up at the flat in about an hour, or a bit more. Don't forget to bring the car round to the back. I can see it from the windows there, if I look. I shouldn't wonder if I come down."

"I'd rather come with you."

"That's because you're American. You want to get everything over in about a week. We're not in the same hurry in this country. When we once begin, we often stay married for quite a time."

"I wish you wouldn't always be talking that way. You know I...."

"I didn't think even an American'd begin grumbling at me before we got down the steps.... I suppose the charm's fading already...? Kingsley, I didn't mean anything really. We're not going to quarrel here. It isn't done.... But I hate standing on platforms, keeping on saying good-bye, and all cursing the train in our insides, because it's so slow to start.... And I really have forgotten that book, or...other things that don't matter to you. So if you'll just see them off and follow me up...."

As Cora spoke she waved her hand to a crawling taxi, and left her ten-minutes husband, sulky but subdued, to the solitary contemplation of his own car.

"I suppose I shall have to bring a book now," Cora reflected, with a slight frown, for she was a conscientious girl who knew that fibs should be disciplined. She was not actually tortured by desire to consume the concluding chapters of any volume of feminine fiction; and, in any case, after the inventory was taken.... She became aware that even her visit to her own flat might have a slight element of irregularity. Perhaps it would be better to call at the agent's first...? She interrupted her reflections to instruct the driver to stop at Hendersons, the estate agents in Kensington High Street.... "Yes, just opposite the post office...." It would make it a bit longer, but she had plenty of time.

Cora looked across a polished mahogany counter at a youth who tried not to show his surprise at her appearance there.

"I want you to let me have the keys of the flat for an hour or two. I want to get some papers that I forgot to bring."

"Yes, Miss...." The youth hesitated over the name, as well he might. She was to have been married that morning, and it was nearly gone.

"Mrs. Starr," she supplied to relieve his embarrassment.

But he still hesitated. Perhaps he hadn't been embarrassed about that. "Yes, madame," he said. "I'll tell Mr. Henderson."

The next moment she was conducted into the principal's private room.

"I don't think I need have troubled to see you," Cora said, somewhat annoyed at the formality of her reception. "I only wanted the boy to give me the keys of the flat for an hour or two."

"I'm afraid we...."

"I only want to get some papers we forgot, out of the bureau that's left locked in my brother's room.... You can send a clerk with me if you think...."

Mr. Henderson protested. "Oh, but, indeed, Mrs. Starr, it isn't that...." Cora, conscious of his glance at her left hand, only half-caught the following words, but she understood that he had surrendered the keys to the new tenants.

"I thought," she said, rather sharply, "that we hadn't let it to them till next Monday."

"But they cabled that they were on an earlier boat, and as the decorators had finished.... Of course, we shall charge them the extra week."

Cora and her brother had vacated their flat a fortnight before the date for which their marriages had been arranged, to allow of the thorough renovation which had been a condition of a letting which had been too good to refuse. A six-months' tenancy, during the most part of which period the flat would otherwise have remained vacant: the full figure for which they asked, and to be paid in advance: excellent bankers' reference: no children. Just an elderly Toronto lawyer and his wife, who wished to spend a few months in the home country. But their highly respectable Mount Street agents had stipulated that the flat should be vacated in time for it to be renovated throughout. The cost? That could easily be arranged. Their clients would contribute £50. How would that be? Mr. Henderson had thought it would be very well. Major Cattell-Pratt had thought the same. Cora, being a practical young woman, after a moment's pouting, had thought so too. Money had spoken as clearly as it always will.

"You think they'll be there now?"

"No, I don't. They scarcely could till tomorrow. I believe the boat docks at Southampton this evening. But we sent their agents the keys."

"That doesn't really matter," Cora answered, with a display of her natural frankness. "I've got another. I only thought I ought to let you know, as we'd put it into your charge."

"I don't see any reason you shouldn't call, if it's only to get something out of your own desk. You'd better ring first, of course. They're legally in occupation since yesterday, but I don't see that you need worry about that if they're not there."

"No, I don't suppose I shall overmuch. I'm sorry I troubled you."

"Not at all. It's a pleasure."

Mrs. Starr went out, and Mr. Henderson murmured "Lucky man" to himself as he resumed his work. He was thinking of Mr. Kingsley Starr. A very pretty bride; and one who had her wits about her, in spite of the innocent expression of those china-blue eyes, and the dimple in the small round chin. Mrs. Starr was not tall, and was very slightly—yes, *very* slightly inclined to plumpness. That was how he liked them himself (being tall and thin). Kingsley Starr was a lucky man.

CHAPTER TWO

QUITE INDIFFERENT TO any possible emotions which she might have aroused in Mr. Henderson's rather bony breast, and with a dimple that deepened as she reflected upon the probable sulkiness of her new possession, Mrs. Starr was driven rapidly to Knightsbridge. where she descended at the front entrance to Murdoch Mansions. "No," she said, as she paid the driver, "you needn't wait. I shan't want you again."

She had intended to ring, as is seemly when you call at a flat which you have let furnished since yesterday, but habit tells, and when she got to the door of No. 37 (fifth floor back), she automatically pushed her key into the lock and went in.

The door opened to a passage which went left-hand for a short distance, with the kitchen on the right, and then turned right, with rooms opening on either side.

Cora cast a critical glance upon the effects of clean paper and fresh paint as she walked briskly along the passage. She had been quite satisfied with the grey Wilton pile carpet which had covered it since she had come to live here with her brother five years ago—had thought the effect rather good—but this freshness of paint and paper did make it look rather shabby. She had determined in the five seconds before she reached the door of the lounge, that she would have a new carpet if they decided to keep the flat on after these people had left. She wondered whether the new decorating had made the other rooms look equally rotten. Perhaps she'd have a look round before she left.

She was at the bureau by this time, and unlocked it easily. It was the kind of lock that opens to three keys out of four, if they are about the right size. "Just like Ted," she remarked, as she took out an assortment of letters and other personal papers from the pigeon-holes, which she had accused him yesterday of having left, and been convinced by his half-hearted denial. "Of course, they wouldn't try to open it," he had answered indifferently, "and they wouldn't find much worth while, if they did." Just like a man. What did he know about the habits of Toronto lawyers, or the curiosities of Toronto lawyers' wives? And as to what might be there.... Well, she knew how careless Ted was.

So she carried her collection of papers into the kitchen, and sorted it over on the table there. After all, there wasn't much of any account. Ted had been right about that. But there were enough papers to be kept to make her handbag bulge more than it should, and she tore up the rest, and lifted the lid of the dustbin to drop them in—and stopped with it in her hand as she observed the débris of an obviously recent meal.

She looked down with a puzzled frown. Probably the painters and paper-hangers were accustomed to feed on the scene of action. But it didn't look quite what they would be likely to leave. And she felt sure that she had heard that they had finished on Saturday, Who else could have been having a meal here? It looked so *very* fresh, and yet— Well, there it was. Anyway, she couldn't bother about it now. She was very much mistaken if that wasn't the honk of Kingsley's horn in the street below. He hadn't lost much time. She threw the torn-up papers into the bin, put the lid on, and went back into the lounge. If you opened the window and leaned out sufficiently far, you could see a car in the street below.

Yes, Kingsley it was, in the ancient Morris-Cowley two-seater which she had helped him to drive when he had bought it a few months ago, and which was now destined to take them on a carefree honeymoon, exploring the beauties of the English country as the lure of an early spring and their whims might lead them. He looked up as she looked down, and she waved her hand as her head withdrew. He must interpret that as he would. She just wanted to swill that smear of dust off her hands in the bathroom basin and in two minutes she'd be down and away. She had other things in mind at that moment than a question of who fed in the flat, queer as it was.

There was a smudge of red paint on the edge of the basin...wet red paint...but would the painters have used red? And would it have stayed wet like that? And what else *could* it be?

Cora saw her face in the mirror which was hung over the basin, and was annoyed to see how frightened it looked. It was absurd to be afraid in your own flat—and with Kingsley honking below.

Yet a smear of—it *was* blood, and it was no use pretending to herself that she didn't know that—a smear of blood didn't come there of itself. Of course, a cut finger—it might have been done in opening that sardine tin that was in the dustbin now. But what right had anyone to have been—perhaps *to be* here at all?

It was all silliness, of course; with an absurdly simple explanation, which would make her laugh afterwards at the queer feeling of which she was conscious now. Suppose Ted had been here, and hadn't happened to mention it? Been here with George on the quiet? She didn't really believe that. Not that she wouldn't have believed it of George. George was a girl who might be equal to anything—anything nice, of course. Hadn't she just married Ted? But she couldn't believe that Ted would do anything of an unconventional kind. He took life too seriously for that. Besides, she could account for her brother's time during the last few days. Almost every hour...

Still, the idea gave her courage. The explanation was sure to be something simple. Something like that. And she wasn't going to be afraid of looking into her own rooms. She would just look round and see that everything was all right, and then go down to Kingsley, before he got too impatient and came up to her. She might worry for days if she were too cowardly to have a look round now.

Yet she stood in the passage for a long minute, gathering courage as she listened to the noises that were without, and the silence—the almost sinister silence—that was within. Then she told herself that she wasn't really going to search for any cause of that red smear on the basin's rim: she was just going to see how the new decorations looked. And she hadn't time to do more than that. She would just glance into the rooms and then go down.

Somewhat more self-assured by the idea that her real purpose was to look at the new wall-papers, and that she wouldn't have time to look under the beds, she walked down the passage, and opened the door of her own room.

CHAPTER THREE

CORA STOOD IN the doorway facing a young woman who sat on the side of the bed, and gazed at her with tragic eyes. A dark, brown-eyed girl with an oval face, which might never have shown much colour, but was now of an unnatural pallor.

"Perhaps you'll tell me," Cora asked, "what you're doing here?"

The girl rose uncertainly. "I'm not doing anything. I'm just going." She scarcely seemed conscious of what she said. After a pause she added: "But I suppose it's no use going now. I should be sure to get found. You'd better look at what's in the next room."

Cora had felt frightened of she knew not what as she had stood in the silent passage, but she had no fear of this evidently terrified girl. Still, as to the next room—she felt she'd like to know a little more about this one first. She said: "Never mind about the next room. What I want to know is who you are, and what you're doing in mine."

She was convinced, from the girl's manner, that she was not here with any authority from the new tenants. How, then, did she come at all into this locked flat, which might be entered at any moment by those who had a better right?

The girl looked at her for a moment in a silence of bewildered uncertainty—unless it were acting of unusual excellence and then said: "I'm Delia Russell.... I came because I.... I was asked. Taunton asked me, of course."

Cora felt no confidence in this explanation. She felt that Miss Russell, if such she were, was uncertain about the man's name. There had been a moment in which she had paused to invent or had hesitated to give it.

"Who is Mr. Taunton?" she asked.

"You'd better look in the next room."

"Very well. Come with me."

14

The girl drew back. "I'd—much rather not." There was terror in her voice and eyes.

"You mean," Cora said, with a sudden certainty, as she remembered that smear of blood on the basin's side: "you mean—someone's dead there?"

"Yes. Mr. Taunton."

"How did it happen?"

"He—got shot."

"Meaning you shot him?"

"Yes—no—of course not. He shot himself."

"What made him do that?"

The question reduced the girl to a frightened silence. She seemed to feel the necessity of explanation, but to be unable to think of a likely lie.

"I suppose he wanted to," she said at length. "How should I know, any more than you?"

Cora did not attempt an answer to this conundrum. It was pleasant to think that Kingsley might even now be coming impatiently up the stairs. She said: "Well, stay here. You'd better not try doing a bolt. Kings—my husband's probably coming up now."

She had remembered that the door of the opposite bedroom was somewhat further along the passage than that of her own. If she should go in there, though only for a moment, the girl might escape. In itself, she wouldn't have minded about that. She felt no particular ill-will toward her. But she didn't want to be left alone with a dead man, and have to do the explaining. Though there mightn't be any dead man in the case—just the nonsense or exaggeration of an obviously hysterical girl who had been caught in the wrong flat. It might be no more than a trick to get her into that room while the girl would bolt for the door.

But she didn't look as though she had any thought of bolting anywhere. She had the aspect of one who had been kicked by fate too hard to have any spirit left with which to kick back. Cora stood in the open doorway in a momentary indecision, looking at the door across the passage, which stood two or three inches open, and then back at the forlorn figure upon the bed's edge. The girl was not gazing at her. As Cora's eyes followed hers, she became subconsciously aware that the gas-fire was lighted, and that the little drawer under the slot-meter was slightly open. Then, as she was turning to cross the passage, there was a sharp, impatient ring of the door-bell, which brought Miss Russell to her feet with an exclamation of fear.

"It's only Kingsley," Cora assured her. "You needn't worry about him." And hoping that she was right, she went to open the door.

CHAPTER FOUR

"I THOUGHT YOU'D never—"

"Oh, Kingsley, I'm glad you've come!"

"Well, who did you expect...? I thought you'd never come down. If you can't find that book...."

"Never mind about that. There's a girl in my bedroom."

"I thought they weren't coming in till...."

"It's not them. She's got no business here. She says there's a dead man in the spare room."

"Well, is there?"

"I haven't looked."

"It's more likely a mouse."

"I don't think it's like that. There's some blood on the bathroom basin."

For the first time Mr. Kingsley Starr became serious. Up to that moment he had not cared how many girls might be in the flat so long as one came down to the waiting car. And as to talk of a dead man that nobody'd seen—well, that's how some women *do* talk. We all know that.

But he knew that Cora was very far from being a fool, and when the talk is of dead men, blood is an exhibit of a confirmatory kind. His hand went instinctively to the place where his gun ought to have been, had he not abandoned so absolutely the freedoms of Chickadee, as he said: "Well, it's no use talking here. We'd better see what the trouble is." He led the way down the passage with his usual briskness.

"This is Miss Russell," Cora said, as they stood at the open door of her bedroom. "At least, so she says. She doesn't seem very clear about anything else. She says there's a dead man in the spare room."

"Then you'd better stay here, and I'll see about hauling him out." Mr. Starr stepped briskly to the other door. He was a small, lean young man, of a manner which (except when he was being teased or bullied by the young woman whom he had so lately married) was alert and confident. In the assurance that his presence gave, Cora's curiosity overcame her previous hesitations, and she was close beside him as they looked upon the unpleasant spectacle of Mr. Taunton's end.

They saw the body of a middle-aged man, of a gross ungainly corpulence, lying on his back on the bed, with his head half on the pillow and his legs over the side. The dead face still had an expression as of a sudden startled protest. The lower jaw sagged somewhat, but was supported by the triple chins that hid the short thickness of the neck, and by the position in which the body lay. It was partly dressed, in a shirt and trousers, of which one brace was fastened and the other was loose.

A heavy army revolver, of an old pattern, lay on the floor about a yard from the place where the feet of the dead man projected from the side of the bed, its muzzle pointing from him toward the door. The bed around the lower part of his body was drenched in blood, and there was another wide patch which had spread from shoulder and neck.

The room showed no sign of a struggle. It was not disordered in any way. Cora, looking round, was aware that she was not reacting to the situation in the way in which she would have expected herself to do. Her thought was: "What an ugly brute!"

She saw his coat and vest on a chair. She saw a brush and comb on the dressing-table, and other evidences that he had made himself at home in that room, at which she had a natural annoyance that was much stronger than any horror of his abrupt and violent decease. With one quick feminine glance she knew that he had been its sole occupant. Miss Russell might have called as she said. But after that it was difficult to visualize what could have occurred.

Meanwhile Kingsley had been looking at other things with critical and experienced eyes. He looked at the attitude in which the man lay. Touching nothing, he considered the probable position of the wounds, from which he had died: the position of his right hand, which was thrown out somewhat toward the centre of the bed: the position of the weapon upon the floor. He said: "You'd better fetch her along."

Not without some persuasion, and something which approached a pull as the room was entered, Miss Russell came.

Kingsley looked at her with a keen but not unfriendly scrutiny. "Shoot this guy?" he inquired, with the reversion to his native idiom which was a tendency of his more active moods.

Miss Russell plainly hesitated in her reply. It was as though she were afraid to confess, or perhaps still in doubt as to what would be the most credible lie. Then she said: "No, of course not. He shot himself."

Kingsley looked unconvinced. "Well, it's for you to say." Then he looked at Cora. He saw that she shared the thought in his own mind. "Anyway," he added to her, "it looks like the soup for us."

The three stood silent for a long moment, Miss Russell's expression gaining slightly in confidence as she felt with a sure feminine instinct that her companions were not hostile to her. In some way, she felt that the situation was bringing them their own embarrassment: dimly she felt as though they might be making her cause their own. Then she knew that Kingsley was speaking to her again.

"If he shot himself, and this is his own gun, I reckon you can't do better than face it out, and the sooner we call a cop the better it's going to be for you.... But if you're not so sure that they'll lap up that tale, and you reckon a getaway's the best chance—well, if you don't need to say you've seen us, we've no need to have seen you. We hadn't any need to come to this room."

Miss Russell did not react to this exhortation in any very definite way. She repealed weakly, as though self-conscious that it was an unconvincing tale: "I didn't shoot him. I tell you he shot himself."

"Well, you've got to make your own tale, and I don't say it isn't wise to think it out a bit first.... But I'll put you wise to one thing, for your own good. If this guy shot himself—and I wouldn't say but what he made a good guess at what he's worth if he did—there'll be his finger-marks on that gun, however it got over to where it is, which it couldn't unless he did it with his left hand.

"But if he didn't do it himself, there'll be the finger-marks of the dame who did, and it won't do anyone any harm if it has a good wipe... But if there's nothing on it but his, they'll be best left as they are." As he said this, he pulled out his hand-kerchief, and watched her as he stooped slowly toward the gun. She said nothing, but there was no displeasure on her face as she saw him pick up the revolver in the handkerchief, and carefully wipe it clean.

He noticed, as he did so, that there was only one chamber discharged, and looked thoughtfully at the signs of injury that the dead man showed, though he made no effort to investigate what they might be. He put the revolver in the dead hand, and then looked at her sharply to ask: "Left or right?" She looked bewildered at first, and then said: "I don't know. Right, I suppose. I tell you I don't know him at all."

"Have it your own way." He took the revolver again by the barrel in his handkerchiefed hand, and put it back on the floor, though much nearer than it had been before.

"It's no good," he said, with an evident dissatisfaction in his voice. "You won't make any cop believe that. I reckon you'd better clear."

He looked at the girl who seemed so incapable of any exertion or decision on her own behalf with a feeling that was half inquiry and half contempt. "Shouldn't have said she'd have killed a bluebottle," he thought, "but you never know." He asked: "Got anywhere to go to? How's the till?"

"I've no money, if you mean that."

Mr. Starr considered again. He produced five one-pound notes. "Then you'd better take these. Know Hammersmith Broadway? Well, you'd better take a look at my car. If it's there in an hour's time, it'll mean you're to step in. If not, it will just mean that we've changed our minds, and you'll have to go your own way."

He led her to the window, and pointed to an old two-seater car on the other side of the street, far below. It was just possible to see it without leaning out. "You'd better take a good look, but I don't want to be seen looking out with you."

That might be prudence, but the risk did not seem considerable. They were higher than the top of the opposite buildings. No one was looking up from below.

Miss Russell came back from the window. "I suppose I ought to thank you," she said, in a more normal and more animated voice than she had used previously. "I do thank you very much, whether you meet me or not. There aren't many who would have taken it like this—especially when I haven't told you the truth."

"You needn't thank us for that," Kingsley replied easily, "we don't want to be hindered here. You see we only got married this morning. And besides, we've been through it ourselves."

"Been through it?" the girl asked vaguely; but Mr. Starr offered no further explanation. He may not have felt that it was quite the best time and place for discursive confidences. She added, with a belated appreciation of the earlier part of his explanation: "I am sorry. It must seem a dreadful nuisance to you. Hadn't I better go now?"

"No. You'd better stay where you are till we've quit. You can come out when you like after you've seen the car start.... Come on, Cora, there's no use in losing more time."

With no further words, Mr. and Mrs. Starr left the flat together.

CHAPTER FIVE

"I NEVER THOUGHT," Cora remarked cheerfully, as they sat at lunch five minutes later in the restaurant of the Palace Hotel, "I never thought that I should have a dull life with you."

"If you think this is anything to do with me—" Kingsley protested, rather sulkily.

"Of course I don't. It's just luck. But you must agree it's a bit queer."

Kingsley did not deny that. It was his own thought. It was only a few months since he and his sister George (now married to Cora's brother, and watching the recession of the English coast from the deck of a Channel steamer), had been involved in the fatal shooting of a gentleman of the name of Bulfwin, and though he had been no more than an American crook, the bumping off of whom in his own country should have been a minor detail in a good day's work, yet there had been some very anxious weeks before they had been able to feel that the laws of evidence (as they are interpreted by the British mind) had combined with Cora's ingenuity to divert the pursuing shadow of the indignant law.

Still, a habit of association with assassinated gentlemen in deserted rooms— It was an idea which could be appreciated between them without words. To have gone to the police with the simple, truthful, unconvincing tale that Cora had come unexpectedly to her own flat, and found it encumbered by the presence of a dead man and a frightened girl— Well, the police might have said: "Thanks very much. It was very good of you to come on the scene when you did, and to let us know." Or they might have taken it in quite a different way. At the best, there was the probability of some more or less involuntary detention, of the taking of statements, of questioning at Scotland Yard. At the worst, might not the police say: "You got away with it once, though we seldom had a clearer case than came into our hands when it was too late to use it against you, but if you think you're going to get away with it a second time—!" Not knowing what had happened, it was difficult to guess how easy or how difficult it might be to prove that that recently-discharged revolver had not been in Kingsley's hands when the trigger fell. Between him and Miss Russell, it was easy to see on which side of the balance of probabilities the scale would tilt. Of course, if they knew the truth— But, without that, it would seem that they were doing no more than to attempt concealment with an unconvincing denial. It would have been so different if it had been the first time!

"I can't think," Cora said at last, after they had digested the position in a mutual silence, "why you told her to meet us at Hammersmith."

"Well, she mayn't come."

"But if she does?"

"Well, we needn't be there."

"But you didn't mean that."

"I wasn't sure. I wanted time to think—and to talk it over."

"It seems to me that the less we see of her the better."

"Or the police."

"Yes, I see that."

"It seems this way to me," Kingsley explained after an interval of silence, "if they get that young woman, and she says nothing about us, we've no more to worry about. But could you trust her for that? If she squeals, as she most likely will, about our being there, and won't say anything else except that she thinks that he shot himself—which you can take it from me that he didn't do—you can't tell where it might end.

"If we give her a lift now, we might dump her somewhere where she wouldn't be over-easy to catch, and, if she were caught at last, she could keep her mouth shut about two things as well as one.

"It isn't only that. We might get her to tell us the truth, and we'd know better where we can pull out.... And it gives the cops some time to find out what it all means while we're clear away. I don't know how you feel, but I don't want to be locked up while they're finding out that they've got the wrong man—if they ever would."

"It wasn't quite what we'd planned," Cora admitted, with a cheerfulness which suggested that she did not think the danger to be beyond avoidance. "I suppose we'd better give her a lift.... The worst is, we'll be a bit jammed, and that makes people look. It's a lucky thing that she's slim.... And if we're going to do that, it's about time that we made a move."

CHAPTER SIX

THE CAR MOVED slowly through the crowded Hammersmith traffic, and stopped opposite a tobacconist's shop.

"You'd better go in, and be a good time trying to buy some cigarettes that they don't keep. You'll be all right about that if you ask for the Chickadee brands. If she doesn't turn up by when you come out—well, she'll be too late."

Kingsley agreed about that. "We're not going to stay here till the cops stare at the car."

Cora was left at the steering-wheel, to exercise the female faculty which can observe the dresses of a hundred women around and behind without movement of eye or neck. For a few moments she watched vainly for the red beret and two-piece nigger-brown costume, with every detail of which (including the little darn under the left elbow) she had become familiar an hour ago.

She was deciding, with some mental relief, that she was destined to complete the day without a measure of female society in excess of that which is customary for such an occasion—for even the exciting experience through which she had passed did not entirely obliterate the fact that she had gone through a wedding ceremony a few hours ago—when she became aware that the remembered dress was emerging from the door of a tea-shop only a few yards away. Without pause or hesitation, it approached the car, and, as Cora leaned sideways to open the door, it stepped in and sat down be side her. Almost at the same moment, Kingsley came out of the tobacconist's, where he had been a difficult but finally remunerative customer, wedged himself promptly and without comment beside the young woman who was separating him from his six-hours' bride, and Cora turned the car into the stream of traffic, unregarded by the passing crowd.

She was clear of the congestion of Hammersmith, and in the comparative quietude of the Richmond Road, when she addressed her companion: "Is there anywhere you'd particularly like to go?"

Miss Russell, still pale, but more self-possessed than she had been previously, continued to gaze forward into vacancy as she answered: "No. I don't think so. Wherever you're going, of course—"

"But we're not going anywhere."

The reply stirred her to a faint surprise, a flicker of animation. She looked at Cora, to say: "Not going—? I beg your pardon."

Cora thought, with approval, that she would be an exceptionally pretty girl under more favourable circumstances. Not one, she decided also, who was likely to make a habit of shooting corpulent gentlemen in abandoned flats, however necessary or desirable she might have found it in the present instance.

Kingsley was first to explain: "You see, we thought we'd go where we liked, without planning anything first."

The girl did not appear dissatisfied at this programme. She may have thought that those who do not themselves know where they are going may not be easy to trace. "It doesn't matter," she said, "to me." And then, after a moment's further thought: "But I don't know that I should care to be put down in a small place. Not where people talk. And I don't want to be a nuisance. I know you can't want me here.... I thought a seaside place might be best.... I could take a train somewhere, if you put me down."

Mr. Starr considered this, and decided that she might not be quite such a fool as her first behaviour had appeared to indicate. Certainly, a seaside place would be the easiest for a solitary girl to take temporary lodging without exciting curiosity, or being invited to explain her antecedents.

"There's no need to drop you for that," he said, looking across to Cora, who gave a nod of assent. She had the same thought as he: "Not such a fool as she looked." She said: "South's the word," and considered her imperfect knowledge of Sussex. But they would be sure to get somewhere, if she kept due south. You can't miss the English Channel, and the best roads lead to the larger towns.

After a time she said: "We'll go through Kingston and Surbiton. I think that gets us on the Dorking road. I'm not sure beyond there. Brighton, more likely than not: but we're sure of a seaside town."

"Plenty of time?" Kingsley queried.

"Lots."

So there was, but Cora's foot pressed the accelerator all the same. She didn't want this young woman on her hands all night.

It was 7:15 P.M. when they entered the outskirts of Worthing, and pulled up at a suburban tram-stop for Delia to alight. They had decided that it would be best for her to enter the town separately and find a solitary lodging. Inclination may have supported judgment in the formation of this programme. Other motives of prudence or curiosity may have prompted Cora's suggestion that they should meet on the beach next morning. "There'll be seats along the front somewhere, for sure," she said confidently. "We'll look out for you between eleven and twelve. Anyone can sit down on the same seat.... You'll find five pounds won't go far here.... You'll have to pay something in advance, having no luggage, more likely than not.... We can talk it all over then."

Miss Russell agreed to that. But she decided in a mind which was now functioning more efficiently than it had done a few hours earlier, that she would not be such a fool as to present herself anywhere without the customary suitcase. You can easily buy one before 7:30 P.M. in a seaside town.

CHAPTER SEVEN

COMFORTABLY SETTLED AT the Beach Hotel, and under the delusion that is customary under such circumstances that they were not recognized as being newly married—a fact which was obvious to every member of the staff, for the unmarried couples invariably arrived at the weekend, and usually left on the following Tuesday morning—the Starrs contrived to enjoy themselves in appropriate ways, only punctuated by unpleasant moments of anticipation as the morning papers were opened, and by occasions when Kingsley would stroll off by himself, while Cora talked to a dark girl wearing a red beret, who happened to share her seat on the promenade.

This condition continued until the afternoon of the fifth day, when, as they came out of the subdued light of a Cinema, where they had been entertained with the *Mystery of the Frightened Lady*, to the glare of the sunlit street, they were confronted by the posters of the afternoon papers, announcing respectively:

LONDON MONEYLENDER FOUND SHOT

and

TRAGIC MYSTERY OF LONDON FLAT

from which it was quite easy to conclude that the attention of the London police had been directed to the manner of Mr. Taunton's end.

"The curtain," Kingsley remarked, not without a note of cheerfulness in his voice, "appears to be rung up." He looked at Cora and observed that her face was clouded with an expression of anxiety.

"I'm not worrying about ourselves," she assured him, as he bought a paper, and resisted an indiscreet impulse to obtain a copy of the rival organ also, "I should think we're quite safe by now. I was thinking of that poor girl."

27

Kingsley thought rather differently about that. He thought that the security of all of them depended about equally upon the "poor girl" not being connected with Mr. Taunton's decease. If she got caught, he was sceptical about her capacity to flounder out without pulling him in, but he felt that it would be a mistake to discuss it there.

"You'd better not begin thinking," he said reasonably, "till we've read the account. It's a bit soon to look excited before you know it's your flat. We'll go somewhere and get some tea."

Cora felt the rebuke. She said: "It's all right about tea, but I want to buy something first."

With a self-control which has rarely been equalled in the records of feminine heroism, she bought two pairs of stockings, about the shade of which she was by no means easy to please, while Kingsley, with the folded paper under his arm, was waiting outside the shop.

It was only when they were seated at a table from which the waitress withdrew that Kingsley read the first details of the discovered tragedy, while Cora poured tea with a steady hand.

He passed the paper over to her as he received the cup. "It looks rather like your flat," he remarked with a sufficient excitement, and in a voice which might easily be audible to those at surrounding tables.

"So now I can register the appropriate emotions," she retorted in a lower tone, and with a smile which would have misled anyone who had been observing them, as she took the paper and commenced to read the account. Really, there was not much there beyond what they already knew. The discovery had been made that morning, and only allowed time for some first hurried telephoned particulars before the paper had gone to press. Paucity of facts was obscured by the size of type in which the news was given.

The tragedy had taken place at 37 Murdoch Mansions. There was no ambiguity about that: "from which the owners are understood to be absent on holiday for an indefinite period." No names were given. The Press moved warily among facts which it had not yet had time to verify. Important people may live in Knightsbridge flats. "The police are reticent, but it is understood that, from the nature of the wounds, and other circumstances, they are disinclined to accept the theory of suicide."

It appeared that the investigation had been undertaken in consequence of a communication which had been received at Scotland Yard from a firm of house agents in Mount Street, whose suspicions had been aroused regarding the circumstances under which they had negotiated a tenancy of the flat. Inspector Cleveland had the matter in hand.

"I think," Cora remarked, as she handed the paper back, "I'd better ring up Hendersons."

Kingsley looked his surprise. They had agreed that, if or when the crime should become public knowledge, they would ring up Scotland Yard at once. Hendersons would be sure to tell the police that Cora had visited the flat after it had been handed over to them, and at a time when the decorators had left. She should have been the last to enter it until the new tenants took possession. The police would be sure to want to interview her, and it would be much best that she should not wait for them to hunt her down. Besides, it was much better that she should go up to Town than that they should come poking round here, with Delia sometimes sitting on the next bench.

"I thought we'd agreed—" Kingsley began.

Cora rarely troubled him to complete a sentence. Now she interrupted with: "So we had, but we haven't now." Finding him to be subdued to a proper silence by that retort, she condescended to explanation.

"Can't you see that we were supposing that it would not be found out when the new tenants came on the scene, and be nothing to do with them? Hadn't we agreed that this man Taunton must have got possession somehow without anyone knowing, and felt sure he wouldn't be disturbed, as we were all getting married that day? But if these Mount Street people knew there was something wrong, it must have been something a bit fishy about the tenants themselves, and Hendersons shouldn't have let it to such people at all. It's a very annoying thing, and it's natural I should ring them up. I don't know how much the flat has been damaged, and I don't even know for sure whether they've paid the six months' rent in advance, though I expect they have, and Ted may."

"It's really Ted's flat, not yours?"

"There's no difference in that, especially with Ted being away."

"No, I suppose not." He saw that it might be the best course.

"Of course it is," she said confidently. "If I talk to Hendersons I shall find out all that they know, and they won't be wanting to get things out of me, like the police would."

"Well, let's get somewhere and find a booth."

"We'll do that best at the hotel. It doesn't matter who knows." She got up with the word. Kingsley left the paper upon the table, and as they regained the street he bought a copy of a later issue of its competitor. Opening it in the privacy of their own room, they gained no further information than was contained in the following paragraph, which appeared in the late news column:

> Major Edward Cattell-Pratt, the permanent tenant of 37 Murdoch Mansions who is at present in Paris, in answer to a telephone call this afternoon, stated that he let the flat about a fortnight ago to tenants of undoubted respectability. He had no previous knowledge of Mr. Cavendish Taunton, who could have no legitimate business in the flat as far as he was aware. He was unable to throw any light on the tragedy.

"Won't Ted be wild?" Cora remarked, as she digested this paragraph. "I hope they told him it was only in the spare bedroom, but I don't suppose they had that much sense. He'd hate to have anyone making a mess of his... Well, I suppose I'd better find out what Hendersons have got to say for themselves." She picked up the receiver and asked the hotel operator to get her Kensington 3984.

CHAPTER EIGHT

MR. HENDERSON WAS apologetic, but emphatic that the fault was not his. He had had Major Cattell-Pratt on the telephone from Paris half an hour earlier, and believed he had fully satisfied him of this already.

The fault rested entirely with Messrs. Thom and Porter, the Mount Street agents, who, it was only right to say, had assumed a very proper attitude, and accepted full responsibility. There was no doubt that they had been grossly deceived. The flat had really been taken for the use of Mr. Taunton, for what purpose he could not undertake to say.

But really he did not know that the affair would be so unsatisfactory. That was, from a financial standpoint. Of course, apart from that, he could quite understand how Mrs. Starr felt. It was an unpleasant thing to happen in anyone's own flat. But he hoped he was right in thinking that neither Mrs. Starr nor the Major had intended to make any regular use of it in future. Apart from that, he had the half-year's rent in hand. He had received the £50 toward the cost of renovation. Thom and Porter had suggested that Taunton's estate would be liable for any damage which might have been occasioned in the room in which the—death—had occurred.

Cora noticed the pause on the word, and interrupted him to say that she couldn't imagine why the man should have wished to commit suicide in her rooms. Why didn't he choose his own?

Mr. Henderson said it wasn't certain that it was suicide. He thought the police were more inclined to the murder theory. But he really couldn't say much about it. No doubt, it would all come out at the inquest. The inquest would be held tomorrow afternoon.

Cora, hearing that, felt a sudden doubt of whether it would not be a mistake to return to London as promptly as she had resolved to do. She had made up her mind what she was going to say, and she would much rather say it to Inspector Cleveland in his own room, than in the publicity of the Coroner's Court. But this was not a thought which she was likely to confide to Mr. Henderson, and as she was silent he resumed the explanation which her question had interrupted.

He had been speaking of the damage to the flat. Thom and Porter thought that it could probably be charged to Taunton's estate. He was not sure about that. (He did not elaborate his doubt, the subject being unpleasant for discussion with such a young lady as Mrs. Starr, but he saw a possible legal difficulty in setting up the proposition that a man is liable for damage caused by an involuntary distribution of his own blood.) Still, if Taunton were shown to be in illegal possession of the flat— And, in any case, it was of little practical importance to the Major or Mrs. Starr, Thom and Porter having accepted responsibility.

He supposed—he need scarcely ask—that Mrs. Starr had noticed nothing irregular—nothing that suggested that the flat was already in occupation—when she had called that morning? Or perhaps she had not had time to call, after all?

Cora said: Yes, she had looked in. She had seen some food in the dustbin which had puzzled her, looking so fresh, but it went out of her mind afterwards. She hadn't been there long. Mr. Starr had called for her almost as soon as she arrived.

But she had noticed nothing more serious than that? Cora countered with another question: Was it likely that she would have come away, if she had?

There was one question he might ask, as he knew the police were anxious to know—but, by the way, could he give them Mrs. Starr's address, as he thought they might like her own account of the state of the flat when she had called? He was sure they wouldn't wish to trouble her more than necessary.

Cora said: yes, of course; though she was afraid, if they were depending on any help she could give, they wouldn't get very far. But what was the question he had been going to ask?

Oh, about the keys! Of course, Mrs. Starr still had the one she had mentioned to him—the one with which she had entered the flat herself? And was it the only one beside the two which had been handed over to Thom and Porter, and which had been found, still tied together, in the dead man's pocket?

Cora said that there had never been more than three keys, as far as she knew. She still had her own. It was a point on which she could speak with sincerity.

Mr. Henderson was about to say that he hoped that she was having a good holiday, and how did she like Worthing? And how was

Mr. Starr? And he hoped she wouldn't let this unfortunate incident trouble her mind, when the call, which had been extended more than once already, was abruptly terminated.

Cora laid down the receiver with the remark: "I've learnt a bit, though not much. They don't seem to think it's suicide—"

"No, I didn't reckon they would."

"And they're puzzled somehow about the keys. They can't know much about what happened, for they don't know for a fact that I called at all. At least, Mr. Henderson didn't. I suppose Inspector Cleveland will be ringing up in about ten minutes. You heard what I said.... I wonder whether we'd better go out."

CHAPTER NINE

INSPECTOR CLEVELAND DID not ring up. He received the address of Mr. and Mrs. Starr from Mr. Henderson with considerable relief, for he had wished to have some conversation with Cora before the inquest, and his first efforts to trace the newly-married couple had been unsuccessful, being based on a knowledge of the fact that they had started with a vague intention of exploring the West of England, and knowing nothing of the event which had caused them to deviate to the nearer coast.

He had not anticipated that he would gain anything of value from this conversation, but he had better reason than he had thought necessary to communicate to Mr. Henderson for supposing that Cora had actually been in the flat on the morning, of her marriage, and it was an obvious routine to interview her under such circumstances. Naturally, he did not wish to fail at an operation which should be so simple as the tracing of these two people, who could have no thought of running away, and who were touring England in a car of which he not only knew the number, but could give a description from his own knowledge. Certainly, it would not have been many further hours before he would have located them.

Having the address, and learning that they were scarcely more than fifty miles away, he decided that he would not content himself with a telephone call, which might be unsatisfactory, nor ask her to interrupt her holiday to come back to London, probably to no sufficient purpose: he would go down to Worthing in the morning, and if she could give any information of unexpected value—well, she could come back with him, and be in time for the inquest in the afternoon.

He did not expect to be regarded as an unwelcome visitor, for he had known Cora for many years, and her brother was his intimate friend. If he were less friendly with Mr. Starr, it did not alter the fact that he had once done him a good turn of the first magnitude, and had felt obliged to tender his resignation at Scotland Yard (though it had not been accepted) in consequence.

Certainly, he did not suspect either Cora or her husband of being implicated in the murder (for he rejected the possibility of suicide) in any way. What he wanted was to fix; the time of the tragedy. That would narrow his inquiries, and might become evidence of a vital kind when he should have arrested the criminal, which he had little doubt that, with sufficient patience, he should be able to do.

But he did not call it an easy case. It was not that there was any difficulty in suggesting a possible motive for the murder, or even a possible criminal. The trouble was that there were so many—and might be others to which, at present, he had no clue. So far, his suspicions were most strongly directed toward a man who had been released from prison about three weeks ago, and who had good cause (or at least he had said so when in the dock) to hate Isaac Marks— which was the name by which Cavendish Taunton was known at police headquarters. But that was no more than a bare suspicion. He had no evidence to identify him with the crime. Of course, if he could connect him with the weapon in any way... But he had learnt the importance of approaching these investigations with an open mind.

It was a few minutes before ten next morning when he put up his motorcycle in the garage of the Beach Hotel. He inquired for Mrs. Starr, and her husband received him in the hotel lounge.

He felt, with a sensitiveness which had become abnormal by practice, that Kingsley was not pleased to see him, but that might easily e explained by the memories which his presence brought.

Mrs. Starr, it appeared, was out shopping. After that, she was not coming back. Kingsley said that he was proposing to join her on the Esplanade. But that was to be at 11:30. Perhaps the Inspector would like a drink?

The Inspector said that he never drank before noon. He was anxious to see Mrs. Starr as soon as possible. He must be back in London for the inquest in the afternoon. Perhaps the best way would be to have a look round for her. Kingsley said he would come along. He would much rather have kept the Inspector there. He knew that the most probable place in which Cora would be found during the next hour would be a seat on the sea front with a young lady in a red beret beside her.

Assuming that Miss Russell would have read of the discovery of the crime—if such it were—in the newspapers, Cora had wished to warn her that she had given her own address for communication

35

to the police on the previous evening, and to suggest that they should meet, if at all, with an added caution during the next few days. Beyond this, she may have had things to say of which Kingsley was not aware, for Miss Russell had given her a degree of confidence which even he had not been invited to share.

Kingsley said he would come out with the Inspector and help in running his wife to earth. The Inspector was suitably grateful, but declined, saying that he could get over the ground more quickly on his bike. Kingsley could not object to that. He said that there would be plenty of time to find her, and get back to London for the afternoon. Was the Inspector sure that he wouldn't like a drink first?

Inspector Cleveland, altering his mind, compromised on a lemonade. Kingsley ordered two. They sat down together.

CHAPTER TEN

EVEN AMONG FRIENDS, Inspector Cleveland was not randomly garrulous. If he gave information, it was because he thought it would suit his purpose to do so, or that he might obtain more in exchange.

But he had no cause to suspect Mr. Starr of any complicity in the present crime, nor of any possible motive for concealing or aiding those who were responsible for it. It appeared to him that Isaac Marks had obtained possession of that flat with such elaborate and peculiar secrecy with the object of meeting those whom he would not encounter in a more open way, and that they had reacted to his advances (whatever those might be) in an unpleasantly unexpected manner. Or he might have gone into hiding there from a danger which he had cause to dread, and which had yet pursued him successfully.

Neither proposition was rendered improbable by the record of Isaac Marks. He had been a black-mailer in earlier years, and that disreputable and dangerous profession had brought him the means of setting up as a money-lender. He had commenced that business after a short term of imprisonment on a minor count of an indictment concerning which a gullible jury had found him not guilty of the more serious issues. After that warning, he appeared to have abandoned blackmail for a more legal if not more reputable occupation. Neither is it one that induces friendship with its reluctant clients. The Inspector recognized that Isaac Marks had come to a natural end. Had he known that Kingsley had walked out of the flat after the tragedy had occurred, and leaving a young woman there whom he had subsequently picked up in Hammersmith, he might have considered that a new and profitable line of inquiry was opening before him. Having no suspicion of this, he was only concerned to gather the stray crumbs of contributory evidence with which Cora might be able to supply him. And there might be no harm in just having Mr. Starr's version of what this was going to be.

"Oh, yes," he said readily, "it was murder right enough. They'll call Sir Lionel Tipshift to prove that. It's just wasting a big fee, but it's the usual thing. Anyone could tell it wasn't suicide, with a child's sense.... The bullet must have been fired from about four or five feet distance. It must have hit him just as he was about to rise. He'd got his legs half off the bed, and may have lifted his head, but he was still lying on his back, as he may have been asleep, or just resting. The bullet went the whole length of his body, and came out near the back of his neck."

"So one was about enough?"

"Yes. There was only one shot. It was a heavy, old-fashioned army revolver."

So that was it. It was a point over which Kingsley had been puzzling ever since he had looked down on the dead man. He had thought that he must have been shot at least twice, and yet the revolver had been discharged from one chamber only. The bullet must have travelled almost from end to end of his body in a slightly downward direction, and the wound bled freely at both ends. No use theorizing about suicide in face of that. He asked: "Any fingermarks on the gun?"

"Not as many as we should like," the Inspector answered cautiously. "But I wouldn't say it won't help."

Kingsley saw that he had gone far enough. He must avoid giving any impression that he was trying to pump the Inspector, for whose abilities he had some respect. He said: "I'm afraid Cora won't be much help."

"You can never be sure of that. We have to piece the facts together, bit after bit, and it may be the least of all that shows us how they all fall into place. There's one thing I want to know that you might be able to help me to check. I want to know just what time it was when Cora got to the flat."

"I don't think I could tell you that. I know when I fetched her away. You see, she went to Hendersons first, when she left me."

"Yes, so I understood.... Well, I dare say she'll know.... I suppose you didn't go over the flat yourself enough to see whether anything had been disturbed?"

Kingsley observed to himself that the Inspector was assuming that he had gone up, unless he knew from some other source, but he was too wary to show any sign of that.

"No," he answered, with an apparent readiness, "I can't say I did. If Cora told me what she saw in the dustbin—which she didn't do till next day—I might have looked a bit more. All I wanted then was to get her away, and I wouldn't say but what she was willing to come."

There was as much truth in that statement as the circumstances allowed, and to the Inspector's mind, it sounded a likely tale.

"But she'd better tell you what she saw in her own way," Kingsley added. It was well enough to be getting all the information he could, but he didn't intend that the Inspector should have the opportunity of finding discrepancies in a twice-told tale. And now he knew that there had only been one shot, he saw the added probability that it came from Miss Russell's hand. Thinking of two shots, and of a weapon which had disappeared, he had felt that there had been others there before Cora came on the scene. But that point was explained now.

"Well," the Inspector was saying, "I'd better get on the move.... See you later, more likely than not."

"Yes. I'll be strolling round."

The Inspector went for his bike.

Kingsley followed a few minutes later, and it is perhaps not very surprising that he was the first to find Cora, as he knew better where to look. She was seated about where he expected, and the red beret was not more than two feet away. He made a third on the seat.

He was conscious that he was not warmly received. The conversation which he had interrupted was not resumed, and there seemed to be no disposition to commence another. He thought that he would rouse the interest of his companions sufficiently when he said: "Cleveland's come down to see you before the inquest. He's looking round for you on his bike. We'd best break apart now."

Cora frowned slightly, but did not seem greatly perturbed. She did not feel in any great dread of Inspector Cleveland, whom she had known from childhood. Besides, it was an expected thing. But she made no motion to rise

"I'm not so sure about that," she said doubtfully. "It's what we were talking over when you came up. But we hadn't quite made up our minds.... I wish you'd get me some cigarettes."

Kingsley looked at his wife with some astonishment, and a possible mutiny in his eyes, but he had learnt that there were moments when Cora knew her own mind, and would not be easy to turn. He had met them before, and had found that it had been the more pleasant course not to oppose them, and perhaps the more profitable also. He looked beyond her to the dark oval of Delia's face. It was troubled enough, but showed no disinclination to yield submission to

Cora's guidance. He got up with: "Well, it won't have been my fault if we all hang in a row."

"Don't be beastly," Cora said, with an unusual sharpness in her voice. "If you'll only go off and get those cigarettes, no one's going to hang anywhere."

Kingsley went, feeling a good deal less sure about that. He felt that the Inspector was equally confident of bringing matters to a different end. He had been foiled once before, but that made it about a hundred times less likely that he would be foiled again. Kingsley had sound realization of the improbability of his being concerned, however distantly, in a series of murders in which the murderers would not be brought to trial. All the same, if Cora decided to take the reins, it might only end in a bigger smash if he should attempt to snatch them. He strolled off obediently to purchase the cigarettes.

CHAPTER ELEVEN

KINGSLEY DID NOT hurry back from his purchase, feeling that the warmth of his first reception had not been sufficient to encourage such an exertion, and realizing that Cora, whether for good or evil, was resolved to play the game in her own way. But he returned in sufficient time to observe the Inspector approaching at a greater distance, but much more rapidly, from the opposite direction.

The two girls were seated as before, making it evident that they had resolved to face Inspector Cleveland together. It was natural that Kingsley should conclude that he was to be told some tale, whether true or false, as to Miss Russell's part in the murder, and he had a moment of regret that he had offered that lemonade and allowed opportunity for the conversation that had resulted. If the programme were to be one of open confession, he had made a bad preparation by denying any knowledge of what had occurred.

Not allowing himself to worry overmuch about that which it was too late to alter, and concealing some inward irritation: behind a carefree demeanour, he joined the little group who were now shaking hands with a satisfactory aspect of affability, and was in time to hear Miss Russell introduced with feminine calmness as "a friend we've made down here at least, not exactly made, we met at the flat once before."

The Inspector did not appear to accept the introduction with more than perfunctory politeness, or interest. He did not start at the name as being that of a criminal he already pursued. Kingsley was inclined to strengthen his opinion that whatever improprieties of violence Delia Russell might have committed in his wife's flat, she did not belong to that numerous class of the community who may be sufficiently grouped together as being "known to the police".

The preliminaries of politeness over, the Inspector said promptly that he was sorry to be a nuisance, but his time was rather short before he must be returning to London, and if Mrs. Starr would give him half an hour?

"You needn't worry about that," Cora said in her sweetest manner, "you're not a nuisance at all. We're all dying to hear about it. I was just saying to Delia before you arrived that I hoped it wouldn't be long before you turned up. I'd have given anything to have heard Ted when you told him what a mess there had been. He always says it's bad manners to swear on the phone."

Inspector Cleveland replied more seriously: "I think, Mrs. Starr, if you wouldn't mind—"

"Why not 'Cora' as usual?"

"If you could give me half an hour for a quiet talk...? I've got to be back in London for the afternoon."

"I thought at least you might stay for lunch, now you are here."

"I'm afraid I can't. You see, the inquest's at four."

"Then there's plenty of time for an early lunch before you start.... I'll tell you what. We can't all sit in a row and talk here. We'll go somewhere where we can have something to eat, and talk comfortably. I'll tell you all I can, but I'm afraid you won't get any clues out of me, unless an empty sardine-tin does the trick."

With no perceptible pause of hesitation, Inspector Cleveland said politely that that would do for him, if it wasn't too early for them, and receiving the necessary assurances of a common hunger, they left the seat beside which they had been standing as this conversation proceeded, and walked up to the town together.

He would have preferred, rather from habit than judgment, to take Cora's statement in a more formal way. Had she been a stranger to him, he would have proceeded by the vague intimidation of an invitation to the police station in the first instance, where she would have been expected to sign a version of her narrative transformed into the official jargon which is supposed to be used by all classes of the community when they impart information to the police. But he could hardly proceed with such formality in the case of his friend's sister, and one whose connection with the crime was of so vague and preliminary a kind. He reflected in a shrewd mind that there could be no harm in letting her talk before her companions. It was unlikely that she had any information to give which required secrecy, and it was almost certain that she would have told it already, possibly ten times over, to her husband and her female friend. Should it afterwards appear desirable, he could take a more formal statement, or even invite her to accompany him back to London, where she could give evidence if required.

He walked beside her to the Imperial, while she chatted cheerfully on indifferent subjects. Kingsley followed with Miss Russell in an unusual silence. His first idea that there was to be a programme of complete confession had been substantially altered as the conversation proceeded. Being mystified, he felt that silence was his safest attitude. He had no doubt that Delia knew a good deal more than himself, but he was too discreet to question her with the Inspector a short and varying distance before them. He looked at her with an observant curiosity. She showed an aspect of aloof serenity, but he thought that it was only by a conscious effort that she was able to do so. He remarked that there might be rain before night, to which she agreed.

Entering the Imperial in advance of his companions, the Inspector took control of the position. He ordered a private room and a light lunch.

CHAPTER TWELVE

"I UNDERSTAND," THE Inspector began, when the waiter withdrew, and the conversation could be both private and uninterrupted, "that you had occasion to go to the flat, which you had not visited for about a fortnight previously, on the morning of your wedding, and immediately after the ceremony, and that Mr. Starr subsequently called for you in his car, and you left together. Mr. Henderson has told us that you called to inform him of your intention, in new of the fact that the flat was actually let to a tenant at the time."

"No, I didn't know that till I called."

"Then, why—?"

"Because I knew the inventory had been taken, and it was in Mr. Henderson's charge, and I wasn't sure that I ought to go there without mentioning it. I thought the new tenants weren't coming in for another week."

"Then you did know it was let?"

"Yes, if you mean that way."

"I said let, not occupied. But it doesn't really matter. What I want to know is when you got there, and what condition the flat was in."

"You want to know when I got there, not when we left?"

"Yes. We know within five minutes when you left. You were seen to leave by a porter who was due on duty, and who was coming up the street at the time. But, unfortunately, it's not that we want to know. It's when you arrived."

"Is it really important?"

"It may be. Very."

Seeing that the Inspector did not propose to enlighten her further until he had her reply, Cora turned her mind to the required calculation.

"It must have been about half-past eleven."

"Not before?"

"Not much, anyway."

"Would 10:55 be a possible time?"

"No. I'm sure it wouldn't."

"Do you remember whether you met anyone as you went up?"

"No, I don't think I did."

"Nobody coming out of the flat on the floor below? The one with the door by the stairs?"

"No. I don't think so. Why?"

"Because a lady was seen to go up to the flat shortly before eleven—or, at least, it couldn't be later than that. And, of course, if it were you there is nothing more to investigate in that direction. We were inclined to assume that it was you at first, but there is a difficulty about the time. The lady who saw someone go past her door left by taxi to catch the 11:10 A.M. at Paddington for the Welsh coast. She is not sure how long it was before she left that she saw this lady. It was when she opened the door to a man hawking bootlaces. But it must have been before eleven. You see the importance of this. If it is certain that it could not have been you, there must have been a woman—presumably an acquaintance of Taunton's—who had access to the flat."

"But Mr. Henderson said that he had both the keys in his own pocket."

"Yes, but we don't know how long they'd been there. Besides, he might have been there that morning and let her in. The first question is, could it possibly have been you that the woman saw?"

Cora was not naturally an untruthful girl. Besides, she could see no use in a lie which calculation would inevitably destroy. The time when she left the Registrar's could be proved within a very few minutes. She said frankly: "If it was before eleven, I don't see how it could."

"So I thought, but I preferred to be quite sure. As a matter of fact, the description isn't like you in the least. But there's not much in that. Descriptions seldom are, unless they've read them in the papers first."

"She only saw the girl, not the man?"

"No. It's a curious thing that no one saw Taunton at all, either entering or leaving. The porters did not even know that the flat had been entered at all since the painters left, though the one who saw you in the street naturally assumed that you had been there."

Kingsley, having ears for the conversation, and eyes to spare for Miss Russell, who was seated opposite to him, and on the Inspector's right—Cora being on his other side—was glad to observe that his attention was so directed that he did not see the look of relief which passed over the paleness of her face, which had visibly increased as this conversation proceeded.

"The other point," the Inspector went on, "is whether you saw any signs that the flat was already in occupation. You see, it was several days after you were there that the discovery was made, and we don't even know (apart from any information you can give us) whether the murder may not have occurred before you were there. Sir Lionel gives his opinion that death had taken place not more than four days before. Dr. Foulkes—the police surgeon who first inspected the body—thinks it was longer. How far did you look over the flat?"

"I went into the kitchen, and the lounge and my own bedroom."

"You didn't go all over the flat?"

"No. I hadn't any reason to."

"You might have wished to see how the new decorations looked. But if you didn't, there's no more to be said. Could you absolutely swear that there was no one else in the flat while you were there?"

"No, I couldn't swear that. It all seemed very quiet. But I didn't go into every room. I didn't go into Ted's bedroom."

"Nor the one at the back? The one opposite yours? You couldn't swear as a fact that the man might not have, been lying there dead at the time?"

"No, I couldn't swear that."

Cora's answers were clear and serious now. The touch of flippancy, which had faintly annoyed the Inspector during their earlier conversation was entirely gone. He thought what a good witness she would make.

Her own thought was a gratified wonder at the way in which his questions had been worded, as though to save her from the need of lying. But would he believe that she had not done so, if he should learn more of the truth, in a few days' time, as she knew that he would be likely to do?

Apart from that, she had realized for the first time, as she replied to his questions, that there really might have been others in the flat at the time. She had assumed that there had been no one but themselves and Delia and the dead man. But Ted's bedroom might have held half a dozen others for all she—or perhaps Delia—knew. Still—the sound of that shot— No, she had no doubt that it had been empty—but she couldn't say that she knew.

"Do you mind telling me," the Inspector was asking, "not that it's likely to be of any direct importance, but so that I may have a clear account, just why you went to the flat?"

"Because I hate seeing people go off by train."

"It doesn't sound a very clear reason for doing that."

"No, I suppose not. I might have got out of it other ways. It wasn't only that either. I thought Ted had been careless about leaving papers about, and he said he hadn't, and I thought I'd see for myself."

"That wasn't what you told me," Kingsley interjected, in a slightly indignant bewilderment. "You said you'd got to go for a book."

Cora's natural dimple took its accustomed place for the first time during this conversation, as she answered: "Well, then, that's what it must have been. It wasn't likely I'd want to give Ted away about something he said he hadn't done, and I only guessed that he had."

"And you found these papers?" the Inspector suggested, "and tore them up?"

"Yes, those that didn't matter to anyone. I brought the others away."

"Nothing whatever to do with Taunton, or this case, in whatever way?"

"Oh, no. Nothing at all. They were mostly letters to other agents about letting the flat. We'd offered it for a bit less than the rent we'd got, and I thought they'd been left in the wrong place."

"And when you tore up those that didn't matter, you threw them into the dustbin?"

"Yes, and that's when I saw the sardine-tin, and some crusts and things that looked fresh."

"They weren't very fresh when we found them. You're sure they were fresh then?"

"Yes. The crusts looked quite new."

The Inspector's questions ceased. He pondered Cora's replies, and saw that they helped him little upon the road of investigation which he must pursue relentlessly, as he had done so often before, to its certain and sombre end. Only one point was confirmed, of which he had had little doubt previously. It was not Cora who had been seen going up the final flight of stairs that led to No. 37.

"Have I been any use?" Cora asked, when she thought that the silence had continued long enough to need breaking.

"Not very much," the Inspector admitted. "But you can never tell till you see how a case ends."

"I suppose you think it was the woman?" The question came from Delia, and the Inspector looked round in some surprise. He was more conscious of her than he had been previously. A dark, very pretty girl, whose lips smiled; but he had heard note of tension in her voice, to which he was too familiar in his investigations. The note of a sharp anxiety for others, if not themselves. He was not surprised to see that the question came from a girl who looked to be of an emotional disposition. One who would imagine such a tragedy when it was discussed before her, till she seemed to see and feel with those who had been in actual contact with its fears or horrors.

"No," he said noncommittally, "I shouldn't say that. It was more like a man's work. But you never know. There was a woman who cut a man's head half off with a fireman's shovel. Quite a quiet sort, she seemed, too. The sort that anyone'd trust to hold the baby.... But I wouldn't say it was she. More likely she'd be his fancy girl. But I'd give something to find her, all the same. She'd be likely to know a bit more than I've heard here."

Cora asked: "I suppose, if it was she, she wouldn't get off if she'd had the best reason to kill him that ever was?"

"Oh, I wouldn't go that far. There's such a thing as justifiable homicide. If it had been to save her own life, or her own honour, and there'd been no other way.... But it doesn't look like a case of that kind.... It look's like a man's work. The trouble is," he explained, with a somewhat unusual expansiveness—but, after all, what was he giving away but what everyone knew or guessed?—"that he was the sort who made too many enemies to make it easy to fix on one. There was a man let out of gaol two or three weeks ago—" But he pulled himself up sharply at that point, remembering that he had no right to voice his own suspicions outside the official precincts, even in regard to a man who was a gaol-bird already.

Besides, such theories are so often wrong. A detective's, like a doctor's, reputation for wisdom is based upon capacity for silence rather than speech.

With a feeling that he might already have talked rather too freely, even among friends, though it might not have been easy to decide what his indiscretion had been, he got up to go. ...

The evening papers announced that, after some more or less normal evidence had been given as to the finding of the body, and the cause of death, the coroner had adjourned the inquest for fourteen days.

CHAPTER THIRTEEN

"I DON'T AGREE in the least," Cora said, stubbornly. "There was no risk at all. It wasn't as though it had been a man. Women know when to talk and when not to.... It was really the safest way. He'd never think that we'd got anything to hide about Delia, bringing her along as we did."

"She seemed nervous enough to me to give the show away every time she spoke."

"And how often was that? I told you girls know when to keep still. Besides, you only thought that because of what you knew. Inspector Cleveland only thought what a nice, quiet girl she was, with better manners than mine."

"Well, if you think that was reason enough—"

"I didn't say that was the reason at all. She may have wanted to hear what he'd got to say. You can't wonder at that. Anyway, it went off just about as well as it could, so it's rather late to make a fuss now."

"But suppose he finds out in the end? It won't make him any pleasanter to deal with, knowing how he's been cheeked."

"Oh, I don't know. It'll depend on how he finds out. Quite a lot."

It was Thursday evening when this conversation occurred, and on Saturday morning Inspector Cleveland received a note to say that Mrs. Starr would like to see him about the Taunton murder case, and would call at Scotland Yard at twelve-thirty.

She kept the appointment as punctually as any woman could be expected to do, having taken the precaution to get some lunch after arriving in London on the sound presumption that she might have a rather long interview before her. She was received with the politeness which is usual at the Headquarters of crime investigation, and was only a little disconcerted on being shown, not into Inspector Cleveland's room, with which she had an established familiarity, but into that of Superintendent Withers, and finding herself in the company of both those gentlemen, with the addition of her brother, Major Edward Cattell-Pratt, whom she was very pleased to see.

"Hullo, Ted!" she said, when she had shaken hands with the two police officers, as she kissed him affectionately, "what on earth brought you here? And where's George Eliot? You don't mean you've left her in Paris? What a joke! I did think it would last longer than that."

Major Cattell-Pratt, who could best endure his sister's teasing when there were no others present to observe the operation, and who was aware that Cora's love for George was not yet a plant of full growth, replied, rather stiffly, that he had only flown over from Paris yesterday about this infernal murder, and should have been returning today if Cleveland hadn't told him of the note he had had from her this morning.

"I don't see," she said, "what you'd got to bother about, when I'd got the whole thing in hand."

"I didn't know that you had. And I'd rather you mixed yourself up with a—" He was almost saying "another murder" but felt the impolicy of bringing old recollections to the official mind, and altered his sentence to "an affair of this kind as little as possible." He went on to explain that a legal question had arisen with Mr. Taunton's executors in relation to the possession of the flat, the rent having been paid in advance, and he had come over to settle it personally, as he had wished to get the wretches cleared out as quickly as possible.

"If you can throw any light on this murder, Mrs. Starr, apart from such information as you have already given," Superintendent Withers interposed, "we should be glad to hear it." He thought it time to come to the point, for he objected to missing his meals as much as Cora, and, unlike her, he had not got his lunch in the right place. He was a rather heavy man, quiet and slow of voice and manner, and of a delusive mildness. Cora was not under any delusion, for she knew the reputation he held. Neither was she in any fear of him, for he was a man she liked, and she had a confident belief that he liked her.

"Well, I thought you'd like to know how it all happened," she said, smiling. "So I came up."

She was not without some nervousness as to the probable result of the programme that she had undertaken, but it was not sufficient to prevent her enjoyment of the effect of this statement. Even the Superintendent seemed surprised.

"Do you mean," he asked, "that you can tell us who committed the crime?"

"I don't know that you ought to call it a crime. I don't suppose you will when you know more than you do now. And, anyway, you couldn't say that he was much loss…. If you'd seen how he looked lying there…."

She hadn't meant to say that. Not, anyway (so to speak), before she began. It had slipped out, as things would, in her experience, if you don t watch all the time.

"Do you mean to tell us—?" Inspector Cleveland began, and "Look here, Cora, don't you think—?" came from the Major before the Superintendent's hand motioned them to silence, and his slow voice began.

"I think, perhaps," he said quietly, "you'd better leave this to me…. You understand, I am sure, Mrs. Starr, that this is a serious matter. We have already had an informal account of your connection with it. Do you mean us to understand that statement was untrue?"

"No, of course not. I answered every question quite truthfully. I don't say Inspector Cleveland's very good at examining, but you can't blame me for that." She felt just a little mean as she made this remark, and might have felt more so if it had not occurred to her that it was all his fault for getting her into a roomful like this. Why hadn't he seen her alone?

"Perhaps he trusted you as a friend," the Inspector suggested, and after that she had no doubt of how she felt.

"I suppose," she conceded, "it was rather mean to have said that. But when you're asked whether you can swear that the man wasn't there, when you know you'd seen him with your own eyes, what can you say except 'no'?"

"One moment." The Superintendent paused on his words. He had his duty to do, but he could not entirely forget that they were all friends in that room. Neither did he forget that that friendship had been used to procure what had been very near to an evasion of justice once before. Such things cannot happen twice.

"I have already asked you not to forget," he went on slowly, "that this is a serious matter. There is at present no accusation or suspicion against yourself of any kind. There is therefore no occasion to caution you in any way. You are proposing to make an entirely voluntary statement, as I understand it, in the interests of justice now…. You appear, from what you have said already, to have had some knowledge which you might well have communicated earlier, and which it was almost certainly your duty to do…. You are, I suppose, aware that there is such a thing as being an accessory after the event?"

Superintendent Withers paused in some uncertainty as to whether he might not have said too much in warning already. He added: "If you have no complicity in the crime—which I should find it hard to believe you can scarcely act more wisely than by giving us a full and frank narrative of all you know in relation to it, whatever reticence you may have exercised previously."

Cora opened wide eyes of astonishment upon him. "Well, of all the ways of taking it!" she said indignantly. "(Don't fidget, Ted; anyone'd think to look at you that I was just going to say I saw you do it.) Why, I've just got her to confess the whole thing—not that I think 'confess' is quite the right word, but you know what I mean— and you call it being an accessory after the fact!"

"I haven't called it anything so far," the Superintendent answered, in a rather different voice, "because I don't know what it is that you're going to say. I can quite believe that you may have given us very valuable help, which we shall be glad to have.... I think, perhaps, we'd better say nothing more till we've had the whole tale in your own way... No, Cleveland, we won't take anything down yet. We'll just hear the tale and see where it leaves us."

It was Cora's turn to be silent for a moment, not being quite sure where to begin, but when she did she went straight to the centre of the subject with the simple statement: "What I've got to tell you is that Delia Russell shot him about half-an-hour before got to the flat."

The Superintendent pondered this statement. He looked at Inspector Cleveland as he said: "The girl that woman saw going up." And then to Cora: "Have you brought the lady along?"

"No. She thought I'd better explain it first."

"And where is she now?"

"She's at Worthing, of course. Inspector Cleveland knows that. I introduced her to him, but he didn't seem interested."

Superintendent Withers looked at the disconcerted Inspector with eyes in which there was a twinkle of humour. "I'm afraid these ladies—" he suggested, leaving the sentence unfinished. Then his face changed to a graver expression, as he recollected that the matter was too serious for a jesting tone. He turned to Cora again as he said: "You cannot speak to this from your own knowledge, if it occurred before you got to the flat. You can only tell us what you have heard. Have you had any account from this woman of how or why she committed the crime?"

"She didn't mean to shoot him at all. She doesn't understand guns. She picked it up, and it went off."

"Where did she pick it up from?"

"From the dressing-table."

"Does she say that it was his gun?"

"So she supposes. It wasn't hers."

"Why did she pick it up?"

"Because he said things to frighten her. She wanted to make him stay where he was while she got out of the flat."

"Why did she go there at all?"

"Because he wrote her to."

"Did she know him before?"

"Yes. At least, I don't say she didn't. It isn't much to the point. She doesn't seem to want to talk about that."

"I'm afraid she'll have to alter her mind. At least, she will if she wants to get off with that tale.... Cleveland, you'd better go back with Mrs. Starr, and take a statement from this young woman, if she's still in the right mood. You can use your own discretion beyond that. I expect, one way or another, you'll find it necessary to bring her along."

"You're not going to do anything beastly?" Cora queried anxiously.

"We have our duty to perform, Mrs. Starr. You can trust us not to go beyond that."

"But if he frightened her, wasn't it the right thing to do?"

"There may possibly have been some excuse. I couldn't go beyond that till I know more. It isn't a very probable tale."

"But if she was the only one there, I don't see how you can contradict what she says."

"It is a difficulty we often meet, but we sometimes get over it."

"I supposed you'd want a statement from her before you'd be satisfied that there's nothing but what's best left alone. But you needn't go down to Worthing to get that. I've brought it along."

Cora produced a single sheet of folded foolscap, and laid it on the Superintendent's table. He opened it sufficiently to glance at its contents, but without settling to read it.

"Very well," he said casually, "we'll have a look at this when we've had lunch, and then we'll decide what to do.... We won't keep you longer, Mrs. Starr, now. I expect we're all getting a bit peckish. But there's just one thing I should like to know first. Was this Miss Russell a stranger to you, or did you know her before?"

"I never heard of her until I found her in my bedroom that morning, and the dead man in the other room."

"Then how comes it that she is with you at Worthing? I understand that you were alone with your husband when you left the flat."

"I picked her up in Hammersmith."

"Why?"

"I thought I'd like to know a bit more about what had happened."

"Then your husband knew about it as well as you?"

"Kingsley'd gone to buy some cigarettes. It's no use trying to bring him into this. I was alone in the car."

"But I suppose he saw she was there when he came back?"

"He knew she was having a lift. We put her down when we got to Worthing."

"And met her again?"

"Yes. On the beach. I don't know where she's staying now. Not the proper address."

"Well, we must look into it all in our own way. It looks as though we may have to thank you for some valuable assistance, I don't mind telling you, Mrs. Starr, that our own inquiries were pointing in another direction. It just shows how easy it is to go wrong. Can you give me this young woman's London address? Well, never mind. I dare say we shall have it soon enough."

He shook hands genially both with Cora and her brother, and steered them adroitly to the door, taking no notice of the obvious dissatisfaction in Cora's eyes.

"I thought, Cleveland," he said, as the heavy door closed, "it might be just as well to leave her guessing as to what our next move might be. She's an attractive girl, but I never met anyone quite so innocent as she can look when she likes. All the same, if this thing happened as she said, she's given the young woman good advice to put up her own tale before we get on her track." Then, with a sudden change of tone, he asked abruptly: "Do you think it did?"

"No," the Inspector answered with decision, "I can't say I do."

"Well, I've got my own doubts. It sounds likely enough on some points and a bit shaky on others. But we must hear what the young woman has got to say. You'd better come with me to lunch and we'll read this over.... You know Mrs. Starr got the best of you once, Cleveland. It mustn't happen again,"

CHAPTER FOURTEEN

SUPERINTENDENT WITHERS PASSED the document across the table. "Mrs. Starr's writing?" he queried.

Inspector Cleveland said not. He was sure of that.

"Well, that proves nothing. Probably copied out. It's a bit like her wording here and there." He smiled somewhat at a phrasing which was sometimes almost of the official pattern, and sometimes had the effect of parody. "Written, anyway, by someone who knows the ropes—but not well."

"Cora knows a bit. Her brother being with us the time he was."

"Yes, I should say Mrs. Starr worded this, whoever wrote it out. But it may be no worse for that. It's plain enough as far as it goes.... The question is how far it'll fit the facts.... If it won't, she's just hanging herself, with Mrs. Starr's help.... How does it strike you?"

"I should say it's about half truth and half lies. But I shouldn't call it a hanging case. You haven't seen the girl yet. It'll be an acquittal, or about five years where she belongs."

"You mean she's a good-looker?"

"She's a bit better than that. Looks quiet and well bred.... You'd need a jury of women to hang her sort.... If we prove it's murder, they'll bring in manslaughter, with a recommendation; and if we only try for manslaughter, they'll let her go."

"Well you haven't got to worry about that, Cleveland. You've only got to get the facts and be sure your witnesses won't let you down.... And I can trust you for that." He picked up the document which Cora had provided for his information, and glanced over it once again.

> I, Delia Russell, aged 23, spinster, of 16 Standish Gardens S.W.7, am making this statement of my free will, and do so solemnly and sincerely declare that on the morning of Tuesday, April 16th, 193-, I received a letter from Mr. Cavendish Taunton, asking me to

call upon him at 10.30 A.M. on the following day, at 37 Murdock Mansions, W.12, which it would be to my advantage to do.

I went accordingly at or about the above mentioned time on the morning of the above mentioned day. The flat was at the top of the building. Mr. Taunton let me in himself. He had no coat or waistcoat on, and I thought from his manner he had been drinking. He took me along the passage to a room at the far end. It was very quiet, and I thought we were alone in the flat. When we entered the room I found that it was a bedroom. He was very rude and I said I thought I had better go. He said: "Oh, no you don't." I saw a pistol on the dressing-table. I don't know anything about pistols or how they go off. I was frightened, and picked it up. I meant to frighten him so that he would let me go. I never handled a pistol before. I pointed it at him, and told him to stay where he was, and it went off.

After that I went into the next room. I was too frightened to go away. I waited there till Mrs. Starr came.

I did not mean to kill him. It was an accident.

Dated this 26th day of April, 193-.

DELIA RUSSELL

"I wouldn't say it's all lies," he said thoughtfully. "But there's a lot of truth that's not here. There are three things you might bear in mind when you get her for a quiet talk. The one is that Marks didn't take that flat for the sake of being rude to Delia Russell. The next is that she's a bit vague as to what his rudeness was. Just didn't like to say? Well, you might be right about that. You've seen her, and I haven't. But if she can't be more explicit when she really tries, you can call the whole tale a fake, and just run her in without wasting any more time. The other point is that before she wrote 'Cavendish Taunton' she began to write 'Isaac Marks', and then thought that she'd better not."

"There have been both names in the press."

"Yes, I know. There mayn't be much in it. But she'd be most likely to start writing the name by which she thought of the man.

We'd like to know how long she'd known him and on what footing...but I don't need to tell you how to handle a case like this."

"Well," the Inspector admitted, "if I don't know now, it's about time I did. But it's always easiest to go wrong. I'm in two minds now whether to get down to Worthing at once—if I let out a bit I could beat the rail, and get there before Mrs. Starr could be up to anything fresh. But I haven't got the young woman's address there. I shouldn't find her at once in a place that size, unless I went to ask the Starrs first—though, for that matter, she said she didn't know the address herself.... I'm more inclined to go first to this London address that she has given us, and see what's to be found out there When it comes to checking up on her tale, I'd like to know a bit more for myself than I do now."

"She ought to keep till the morning, if you're there first thing," the Superintendent agreed. She's not likely to bolt after writing this. You might see how the land lies, and put a good man or two on anything worth following up."

Having his own opinion confirmed, Inspector Cleveland was in no doubt that that would be the best way. It was not a case in which there was likely to be any difficulty in making an arrest. Nor, for that matter, in getting the first remand. Till he was in a better position to complete his case—till he could see his way to check that statement, and sort out the lies which it was almost certain to contain somewhat better than he could now—well, she might be just as well where she was.

Anyway, he would make a few inquiries first, and see her tomorrow. Probably, when he'd heard what she'd got to say, he'd be able to charge her at once, and bring her up to London in time to have her in Court on Monday morning. There'd be no time lost about that....

And while this conversation proceeded, Cora, seated opposite to her brother, and putting away a second lunch without any visible discomfort resulting, was finding some difficulty in persuading him that she had followed the allied paths of wisdom and rectitude since they parted at the Registrar's door about a week ago.

She was not (as we have observed before) a natural liar; and there was a strong affection between them, and (with its inevitable limitations) a mutual confidence. But she felt now, with a sound judgment, that there were some parts of the truth which must be used, if at all, with a very rigid economy; and, being so handled, it may often be found that a little will go quite a long way. She did not think that Ted would betray her under any probable circumstances, but she saw that a full disclosure of all that was in her own mind would disturb and embarrass his own with a silly masculine idea that it was his legal duty to do so, and would surely lead to a long and useless argument, and a vain attempt to persuade her to a different course of conduct, either from that on which she had embarked already, or that which was designing itself in the rear of her mind since she had felt an instinct of dissatisfaction at the manner in which Superintendent Withers had shown her the way out.

"You know," she said, that I always did hate seeing people off by train."

The Major did not dispute that, but he felt that it was not the real point at issue. He was a slow thinker, and Cora's methods of argument always confused him, so that silence was his usual refuge. But he felt that speech was a duty here. Why cannot women be reasonable? He said with truth that he hadn't said anything about that.

"Well, then, there you are. It wasn't my fault that there was such a mess-up when I got to the flat."

"I can't see why you didn't inform the police at once. It was the obvious thing to do."

"And be kept there all night, as likely as not? And suppose they'd said Kingsley had done it instead of that silly girl? You ought to know what the police are."

"But they wouldn't have said that. There was no reason they should. And there was the girl's own tale."

"But we hadn't got that then. It's taken days to get that. If she'd been worried then, before she'd had time to think, she might have said anything. She said he'd shot himself. She couldn't have made anyone believe that."

"But if she said he'd shot himself, it wouldn't have made the police think that Kingsley had done it. If he'd done it, she wouldn't have thought of saying that, and they'd have seen she was telling lies, and guessed that she must have done it herself."

The Major felt a glow of self-appreciation at the success of this mental effort. It really was a sound point. But it appeared that Cora hadn't brains enough to appreciate it at its full value.

"You don't seem to be able to see anything. When anyone's shot anyone once, the police always think it's them that's most likely to do it again, however necessary it might have been."

Ted might seem slow to those of more agile wits, but he had no difficulty in understanding this somewhat involved and ungrammatical sentence. He was stirred to retort that he had opposed her marriage to a man of such habits, and that this sequel showed how sound his judgment had been, but stopped himself, only just in time, with the recollection that he had married Kingsley's sister, and that she also had been concerned in the earlier homicide. He had better not say that. But it was an exasperating and amazing thing that Cora should be able to draw him into these difficulties, although he talked sense all the time, which she seldom did.

Abandoning discussion of events that it was too late to alter, he said weakly: "Well, perhaps there's not much harm done as it's turned out, but if they'd got on her track before you got that confession from her, it might have been rather an awkward mess. If you'll have the sense to leave it alone now—"

That being the course of wisdom which Cora did not propose to take, and being conscious of the difficulty of discussing possible future developments without the mendacity which she had been endeavouring to avoid, she changed the subject with the abrupt query: "Why didn't you bring George along?"

It appeared that George, who had good nerves for most of the risks of life, was shy of the air. She had a particular objection to being burnt to death, which she regarded as a probable result of cultivating that method of travel. Also, there had been the question of expense. It seemed a good deal to incur for so short a time. He should have gone back this morning had he not heard that Cora was coming to town.

"Won't she be wild when she knows you've stayed about me," Cora commented, without appearing at all distressed at the prospect, and then: "Was it really that she didn't want to come, or can't she get back with that photo?"

The Major understood the allusion to the deficiencies of George's passport photograph, concerning which Cora had suggested previously that it would be rather a joke if he got her out of England, and then couldn't get her back, but he felt unable to think of any better reply than to remark that he wondered that Kingsley hadn't come up with her to town.

"Oh," she said, "that's quite different. He'd have come quick enough if I'd said the word. Besides he's...." She checked herself abruptly, and then added, after an interval of unusual silence: "I wonder whether I hadn't better send him a wire."

She was so quiet after that, during the hour that elapsed before her brother saw her off at Waterloo, that he reflected with satisfaction that matrimony appeared to have already done something in reduction of her natural levity. He went with her to the telegraph office before she left, and she made no secret of the simple message which she despatched: "Shall not be back before seven don't wait love Cora." So she wrote it at first, but when she found that it would be more than twelve words, she altered "be back" to "return" and struck out the love.

"I told him," Cora remarked, "that I should probably be back for tea."

CHAPTER FIFTEEN

INSPECTOR CLEVELAND HAD learnt to believe nothing without verification. He was quite prepared to find that there was no such place as Standish Gardens in London, or that No. 16 had been empty for the past six months. But the directory assured him that it was a genuine address, and supplied the information that the house was occupied by Mrs. Rebecca Greenwater, or, at least, had been so when it was prepared for publication.

Pondering upon the singularity of English surnames, and with a mind vacant for the reception of anything he might hear or see, the Inspector crossed Coniston Avenue, and entered Standish Gardens at the southern end. He observed two short rows of dilapidated residences of a dreary sameness, with a railed triangle of evergreens at the further end, which must be the gardens themselves. The houses were high and narrow, and probably more spacious than their exteriors indicated. They had been "highly respectable" in their younger days, and though no one would be likely to describe them in that manner today, the respectability must have continued, or the name of Standish Gardens would have had a more familiar sound.

Boarding-houses, of course. No. 35 was at his right hand. Alternate numbers. No. 16 would be about half-way along on the other side. It must be about there that a man was standing at the door talking to a woman who did not invite him to enter. He turned away, came down the steps, and walked quickly toward the Inspector's end of the road. Inspector Cleveland had learned to take the chances that came. He crossed over to the other pavement, and advanced to meet a young man somewhat taller than himself, of an athletic walk and build but not with the appearance of one who worked with his hands. The Inspector's rapid glance summarized him as one who was probably engaged in a professional office—and who was now in an infernally bad temper.

"Excuse me," he said, sinking his official manner to one of a politeness which was equally natural, "could you tell me if there is a Miss Russell—Miss Delia Russell—living about here?"

There had been a moment when it had seemed probable that he would be pushed aside without the courtesy of a reply, but the name of Russell was spoken just in time to arrest the young man's attention. As he heard it, he stopped abruptly.

"Yes," he said eagerly, "Call you—" and then he checked himself, looking in suspicion—or was it fear?—at the Inspector's impassive demeanour.

The Inspector, having learnt the value of patience, said nothing. After an awkward silence, the necessity of answering the question more explicitly became unavoidable. The young man said: "Miss Russell lives along here, but I'm afraid you won't find her at home."

"No? If you've just been inquiring, I suppose it's no use for me to try." They walked side by side to the end of the road, where they paused again. The Inspector saw that the young man was on the point of asking something about which he hesitated. He waited silently. It was best that it should come without any prompting from him.

"I suppose...I suppose there's nothing wrong?"

"About Miss Russell?"

"Yes."

"Have you any reason for thinking there is?"

"She's—been away for some days."

"So I understood."

"Do you know where she is now?"

"Not exactly. That was one reason why I was inquiring here. I believe she's at the seaside."

"If you would let me know how I could get in touch with her, I should be greatly obliged."

"I don't know that I could do that."

"I thought it was one of the regular duties of the police to trace people under such circumstances."

"Under what circumstances?"

"When they don't come home, and anyone's worried about what might have happened to them."

"Have you reported Miss Russell's absence at the police station?"

"No. But I was intending to do so if she were not back tonight."

"Would you mind telling me what reason you have for thinking that Miss Russell is in any trouble?"

For the first time there was hesitation in the reply. The Inspector felt sure that it was less than the truth when it came: "She wouldn't have gone away without letting me know."

"I'm afraid we should need something more definite than that. In the first place, we should need to know by what right you inquire. Are you related to Miss Russell?"

"No. We are engaged to be married."

Inspector Cleveland, in spite of his occupation, was not deficient in natural sympathies. Being a good judge of his fellow-men, he had no doubt that he heard the truth, though he felt that there might be other things in this young man's mind that he would be glad to know. He had often found before this that the frankest method was also the most satisfactory in its results, and he felt a strong inclination to test it upon this occasion. He said: "Can you give me any evidence of that? At present, I don't even know who you are."

The young man produced a card. The Inspector learnt that he was talking to E. Burdett Wilson, the secretary of an archaeological society of which he remembered hearing before, and which was of a presumptive respectability. Having provided the card, Mr. Wilson continued to search his pockets. He produced a number of letters, somewhat the worse for wear. He looked at two or three, and finally selected one which he was least unwilling for the Inspector to see.

He handed it over with the remark: "I think that will show you that I have some right to inquire." Inspector Cleveland looked at the side of the folded letter which was toward him with some minuteness, but did not open or turn it.

"Yes," he said, "I think that's sufficient. I'm afraid I must give you some rather bad news, if you don't know anything about it already. We have received a document at Scotland Yard, purporting to be a statement by Miss Russell, admitting her responsibility for the death of Cavendish Taunton."

"But I thought he was found shot."

"Yes. The statement says that she shot him."

"But that's absurd! I don't believe Delia ever handled a gun in her life."

"So the statement says."

"I should say it's a hoax, more likely than not."

"I scarcely think that. The writing is certainly the same as that of the letter you just produced."

"You mean that was why—" There was a sudden anger in Mr. Wilson's voice, which gave way as the Inspector answered: "Not at all. I didn't ask you to show the letters. If the statement was really sent to us by Miss Russell—"

"Yes, I'm sorry. I see that. I thought I'd been tricked for a moment, and no one likes to think that.... But Delia didn't shoot anybody, all the same"

"The awkward fact about that is that she says she did."

"Can you tell me how I could get to see her?"

"Not immediately. This is the only address she gave. But we know the direction through which it came.... If you will call at Scotland Yard on Monday morning, I may be able to tell you more."

"You're not going to arrest her on this absurd charge?"

"I didn't mention a charge at all. We have, at present, only her own statement which asserts some justification for what she did. If we conclude that it is substantially true, we may be satisfied to call her at the adjourned inquest, and leave the matter to the decision of the coroner's jury. But I can't say much about that until I've had a much fuller account from her than the statement gives."

"Anyway, you wouldn't do anything before Monday?"

"I can't promise that. It depends mainly upon herself. But there are one or two points I should like to know a bit more about, and if you'll help me as far as you Can, I'll let you know how things are going any time you like to call at the Yard."

"You'll let me have Delia's address?"

"If she makes no objection, which isn't likely, from what you say."

"I won't answer any questions to make trouble for her."

"I'm not asking you to—not if she's told the truth so far. You may be doing her a good turn. Do you know whether she knew Taunton before she went to see him on the morning that he was shot?"

Mr. Wilson became silent. Not being a fool, he saw that the issue was not so simple as the Inspector's words might suggest. He had good reason for supposing that Delia, whatever she might have written, would have left some important matters unsaid, and if she were to be condemned for any inaccuracy or omission that might be discovered subsequently—well, he must be very wary, indeed. He saw also that for Delia and him to be questioned separately was a method of examination more likely to be satisfactory to the Inspector than the other parties concerned.

On the other hand, he did not wish to give the impression that there was anything that either he or Delia wished to conceal.

"I'd like," he said at last, "to give you any help I can. But, honestly, I'm not sure that I could tell you much that would be helpful. But I'm sure Delia didn't shoot him. She wouldn't shoot anyone. It's absurd. I'll give you all the help I can, but I don't think you ought to keep me in the dark if I do that. Can I see this statement you've got? I could tell you whether it's her writing for certain, and you don't really know that yet. It may be just a hoax."

"It isn't that." Inspector Cleveland hesitated, and decided to grant the request. He had never doubted that Delia Russell's statement was a genuine document, and the comparison with the writing of the letter had been no more than a matter of the careful routine by which he always proceeded, but he wanted this man to talk, and verification of handwriting would be a good enough official reason for letting him see the document. Its facts were so meagre that he was really giving very little away.

"You can come along and see it now, if you've got time," he said at last.

Mr. Wilson said that time was of no consequence. They got into a taxi together.

CHAPTER SIXTEEN

KINGSLEY READ THE telegram, whistled, and went out. He strolled along the sea-front until he observed the red beret in its usual location, and sat down beside it.

"Cora," he said casually, addressing the tide in a voice which was unlikely to attract the attention of any human loiterers, "asked me to let you know if she wired. She says 'don't wait'."

As he said this, he heard a sound suggestive of a gasp or a suppressed sob. He looked at his companion to observe a face which had recovered whatever of outward serenity it might have lost for a moment. "I'm afraid," he said, "that wasn't what you wanted to hear.... I know I'm not being let in on this deal, but if there's anything I could do to help...."

"Oh, I don't know...I suppose not...I've just got to get away.... No, Cora said she wanted you to keep out of this."

There was a conflict in her own mind as she spoke. She knew that Cora was being a good friend to her, and was doing what few would. And there had been one condition attached to this assistance—that Kingsley should not be drawn in. But Delia was one of those rather numerous women who find it difficult to have confidence in their own sex. If only Edward were here! Failing Edward, if only there were a man to consult. She did not think in that type. If there were only a MAN!

And she was scarcely more disposed to confide in him than he was to accept her confidence. So far, Cora had had her way; Kingsley understood her anxiety that he should not be involved in the circumstances of this second homicide, and had a reliance upon her abilities, if not her discretion, which he could not expect Delia to share. But he thought she might at least have let him know the nature of the game she was playing. He had little doubt that he could take care of himself, and he might be able to give essential help. If he were to agree not to interfere, at any rate he ought to know.

He had said this, with some picturesque vigour when Cora had told him that she was going to London this morning, and a quarrel had only been averted by her promptness in putting her travelling-clock ten minutes forward when he was out of the room, and then saying that she couldn't stay for another word. It appeared that she objected to being seen off at the station as strongly as witnessing the departure of others. "Ted makes me about mad, always coming to see me off, and I don't want you to start doing that. We'd better begin the way we mean to go on.... But you can help me if you'll listen a moment, and be quiet. If I send you a wire that says 'don't wait', I want you to let Delia know at once. Just those two words. The rest won't matter at all." So she had said, and here he was, with the blind obedience which she had assumed so easily. But he had come with the intention of learning a bit more if he could.

He was so far from guessing the truth that he supposed no more than that Delia had confided whatever had happened in the flat, and how the murder had occurred, and that Cora was assisting her in some way to hide her connection with it, or the murderer from the police. It was plain enough from the message he had delivered, and the exclamation it had caused, that these plans were not going well; which was an added reason why he should understand more than he did now. He said: "You mean you've got to clear out of here?"

"Yes. I expect I ought to be going now."

"How do you mean to go?"

"By train, I suppose."

"Car's the best for a start, if you don't want following...I suppose there isn't much of that twenty dollars left now?"

"Oh, I shall manage. I ought to let you have that five pounds back. I can get money if I write for it. I've got some in the Bank."

"And get run in when you go to collect? That's a silly idea. I'll let you have a few bills. You can pay them back when it's safe. You needn't fret about that. I've got piles."

"But you won't know my address."

"I'm not so sure about that. If you really need to lie quiet for a time, I might have an idea.... Now you just go back to the place where you've put up, and check out there, and about when it's getting dusk you get on the tram you came in on that night we arrived, and walk away a bit on the same road, and look out for my car that'll come crawling behind, and hop in, and I'll bring you some cash, and give you a few miles start, and perhaps then we'll talk a bit more."

Having said this, he got up, without waiting for her to reply, and strolled away.

CHAPTER SEVENTEEN

IT WAS SOMEWHAT later than her telegram had indicated when Cora re-entered the Beach Hotel, and asked casually at the reception-counter if Mr. Starr were in.

"No, madame," the young man whom she addressed replied politely, "I don't think he is now."

"I suppose he got my telegram this afternoon?"

"Yes, madame. He went out almost immediately afterwards."

That was satisfactory. She didn't want it to appear that there was any secret about that telegram. But he needn't have stayed out all this time, as though she'd given him permission to disappear for ever! It was an excess of realism which she did not appreciate. Nature, rather than diplomacy, prompted the exclamation which followed: "And you're sure he's been out ever since?"

"No, madame," the clerk replied with precision. "He came in, and went out again, about an hour ago. I think he's taken the car." The petulant frown which this information brought—for a tired and worried Cora had arrived in a confident assumption of her husband's welcome had scarcely time to form before it disappeared at the sound of Kingsley's voice behind her.

"Hullo, Cora," he said cheerfully. "Glad you're back. How about going out for a good run? It's going to be a fine night, with a good moon coming up in about an hour."

"I'm afraid I'm a bit too tired for that," she said dubiously.

"Well, come and have a bite of something and talk it over."

"Thanks, but I had dinner on the train."

"Didn't know they served it that early. Well, come upstairs anyway, and we'll talk it over."

They went up to their own room together.

They had scarcely shut the door upon that secure privacy before Cora asked "I suppose you gave her my message?"

"You can bet on that."

"And did she say she was going?" I suppose you don't know whether she's gone yet?"

"Not so far as she might. She's about five miles away, seated on a dead tree."

"Seated on—? It sounds silly. Why's she doing that?"

"It isn't as silly as it would be to stand till we get back."

"Till we get where? I wish you'd tell me sensibly what she's done. It isn't a joke at all. You'd know that if you'd been with me today."

"I've got an idea of that from what I've got out of Delia. But if you won't tell me, you can't complain that I don't know.... Look here, Cora, you'd better cough up what the trouble is."

Cora had been coming to much the same opinion, as she had reflected upon the position in the dining-car. She had felt somewhat depressed by the conviction that Superintendent Withers had not taken her friendly assistance to the police quite in the right way, and by a worrying doubt as to whether that telegram hadn't been a mistake. Her despondency had not been sufficient to prevent her adding a substantial dinner to the two lunches which had preceded it, but it had made her realize that it would be very comforting to talk matters over with Kingsley, whose energetic optimism might be of vital assistance to her own activities.

"Perhaps I will, if you'll tell me first what you mean about Delia and a dead tree."

"I mean she's waiting outside the town for us to pick her up and run her somewhere where she'll be safe. I'd have taken her straight on, but I thought I ought to come back for you.... We're just going a moonlight run."

"And I suppose I said the wrong thing? But I really do feel rather done in."

"No, I don't think you did. I'm dragging you out, and you don't much want to go.... It. couldn't sound much better than that."

"Very well. I reckon I look the part."

"You can go to sleep when we get in."

"Jammed like that? I'm more likely to be the one at the wheel. ... Kingsley, I'm not really cross, but it's not a wise thing to do. Not for us to take her away. If you knew all that I do—"

"I know a bit. I think it's silly to go at all."

"Then you don't know everything. But it's silly for us to be going out at the same time. Where do you propose that we put her down?"

"I thought of taking her home."

"What a mad idea! After the way that you and George used it before. It's about the first place that Inspector Cleveland will turn inside out."

"I know it sounds that way, but are you sure that he would? He needn't think we're hiding her at all, if we go ahead in the right way; and if he does he might think it's the last place we should choose, just because of what did happen before. Honestly, Cora, if we *didn't* put her there, should you expect him to turn up to look?"

"No," she said doubtfully, as that view of the matter penetrated her mind, "I don't quite know that I should."

"And you must see this. If she hides at all, it won't do for her to get found in a couple of days."

"No. Of course she'll have to say that she got frightened and lost her nerve. Lots of girls would do that. But it wouldn't do, all the same."

"Then have you got any better idea?"

"I had one at lunch today. That was why I half-hoped she wouldn't have gone before I got back. You know what a ghastly blur George's passport photo is?"

"Yes. We said that if it would do for her it would do for any-one."

"Not exactly that. It wouldn't do for me. But it might pass Delia well enough. Suppose I got Ted to fly over again, and take her back?"

"I didn't know he'd been over once."

"Well, he has. He's here now. I can't tell you everything in the first word. The question is whether it isn't a good idea?"

"It sounds crazy to me. That's just how people get caught. Bolting on to airplanes and ships. It's like a cow running into a butcher's shop."

"I wish you wouldn't have such beastly ideas. It's safer than Cheshurst Hall. And it's the same reason for both. Nobody'd ever suspect Ted. They know him at Croydon, and if he says she's his wife.... And if they arrived at the last moment, they don't worry much about the passports; not with people they know. I tell you *no-body'd* suspect Ted. It wouldn't even cross Inspector Cleveland's mind. He thinks he knows him too well."

"And suppose he's right about that?"

"Well, then it won't happen at all. But you needn't think about that. You can leave Ted to me."

"So I should. You know he wouldn't cross the road for me, unless it were the wrong way. Will you come now? We shall be late enough at the best. Don't talk about where we're going. I've got an idea about that. All we've got to say now is that we're off for a moonlight run."

Cora said "Righto" in a more cheerful tone than she had used previously. It was rather nice to feel that she and Kingsley were handling the matter together, and perhaps it would be better to tell him a bit more; but how much was still a point which she must think over. After all, she had better not let him drive. She could always think best when she had the wheel in her hands. ...

Kingsley said at the counter that he was afraid they might be a bit late. They were going out for a moonlight run. Oh, anywhere—just where they happened to find themselves. But they didn't want to be locked out. The hotel, he was assured, was always open to its guests. There was no danger of that. The night-porter would let them in.

Kingsley said he hadn't known. He wasn't one to stay up late as a rule. The clerk, looking after the receding couple, remarked to his companion that he didn't blame him for that.

CHAPTER EIGHTEEN

DELIA SAT ON a tree-trunk. It seemed to her that she sat there for a long time. She did not think of moving, for Kingsley's promise to return had been as definite as his warning that he could not tell her how soon he would be able to do it. Apart from that, she had nowhere to go.

But she felt chilled as the hours passed, and wished (not for the first time) that she had clad herself rather more warmly when she had set out to shoot, or shall we say to visit, Mr. Taunton?—but even that is assuming more than we know. Let us say that she wished she had been more warmly clad when she entered Mr. Taunton's flat. It is true that she had had the use of Kingsley's five pounds since then (her own pocket had been utterly empty), but she had had a suitcase to buy and quite a lot of toilet articles that she must have, because it would have looked so queer if she hadn't, and she had kept in hand enough to pay for lodging and board for the first week, and a bit more, so there had been nothing to waste out of that. Now she felt cold and wished—a good many things that it was too late to alter now, though she was unworried by self-reproach. for she couldn't see how she could have done differently, except that she might have tried to walk home when she knew that Mr. Marks was dead, instead of waiting for that shilling in the gas-meter that wouldn't fall. But even that might be turning out best as it was. Only she did wish that Mr. Starr wouldn't be much longer.

And the moon rose, large and round and yellow in the southeast sky, and showed through the branches, and then over the trees, and at last she heard the long hoot and the two short ones which had been the signal agreed, and rose, and took up the suitcase, which was quite heavy enough although its contents had been procured at such moderate cost, and came out on to the deserted moon-lit road.

Cora's cheerful voice greeted her approach. "I should think you got about fed up waiting there and half-frozen as well. But I've brought plenty of rugs. There'd have been a bit more room for ourselves if I'd brought one or two less.... Kingsley, that case'll go on at the back.... No, don't sit on that. That's the ham-sandwiches.... We had to stop a bit to fill up the tank, and tighten up a bit here and there. The old car isn't used to being up all night, though I won't say it's the first time. But she'd have a fit if she knew what she's got to get through before morning. You'll see her move when she gets warmed up to the work.... No, I'm not feeling tired a bit now. I suppose it's the night air. I'll go ahead for an hour and then you can have her for the same time."

Kingsley said that would do for him.

They agreed that the moon was a good thing. It not only lit the way. It gave them a general sense of direction, which it might at times be useful to have. They had an excellent map, which they had borrowed at the hotel, but it was more interested in Hampshire than Kent. They had chatted about roads at the garage where they had filled up, but it had been the beauty of the country between Worthing and Southampton that had engaged their minds at that time. It was too late to regret that now!

"I don't know much about this island," Kingsley admitted, "and I used to think that anyone couldn't go out at night without falling over the edge. That was how they taught us at Chickadee. But if we don't bear a bit more to the right—"

"It's the road to Dorking," Cora said firmly, "and it's a good road, and it can't be more than fifty miles, if we go through there."

"And how much less if we don't?"

"Anything from five to ten, for all I know. But if we get to Dorking I know the road."

"Well, have it your own way. But when you think we'll get back—"

"It's when you think we will get back. It's not my idea at all. But it's no good getting lost. It's not as though we wanted to ask the way." Kingsley saw that there was sense in that. He said: "Have it your own way," once again, but in a more satisfactory tone than before. And after all, they didn't go through Dorking; for when they got to Horsham they found a signpost to Reigate there, and as the road from Dorking would take them by that way, it was obviously quicker to go direct, as they did, and made such speed that, whether it were forty miles or fifty that their tyres had covered, it was less than an hour after midnight when they passed through the village of Little Hempstill, where not even a dog barked, and turned into the long lane which led at its winding leisure to the back entrance of Cheshurst Hall.

74

Conversation had been limited as they had made their rapid way along the moonlit roads. Cora had already pacified Kingsley's curiosity by a promise of greater frankness on the return journey, when they would be alone together. Her mind had become occupied with the practical difficulties of maintaining existence with tolerable comfort in an empty isolated house, which it would be difficult to leave in daylight without being observed. Kingsley should have thought of such things before he had rushed them into so wild a plan.

It was true that George had once remained concealed and unsuspected for several weeks in its upper rooms, but that was at a time when she and Kingsley were openly going and coming. They had been able to furnish supplies without difficulty or suspicion. Besides, it had been after Inspector Cleveland had watched the house for weeks and searched it at least once. He had turned inquiry to other directions. As a hiding-place it had had the advantage of a cover that the hounds have already drawn.

All these things would be different now. It was true that the house was fully furnished, whereas it had previously been just emerging from the decorators' hands. Now it had been made ready for Cora to enter it as mistress in three weeks' time.

But—there wouldn't be a bed aired in the house! It wouldn't be possible to switch on a light without the risk of being seen for miles around—even if the accumulators were charged, about which Cora was as vaguely ignorant as women often are. She wasn't even sure whether it would be possible for Delia to get any water, which was pumped by the same plant. As to food—the village would be impossible. Everyone knew everyone there. It meant slipping out at night, and the long walk into Orpington, and staying out somewhere till it would be late enough to return.

It wasn't as though there'd be much help to be got from the garden. It was too early for that. There might be lettuces! There might be better things under the glass, which the gardener had been allowed to use for his own profit while the house had been unoccupied before Kingsley bought it, as he was still doing. That reminded her that the gardener would (or ought to) be about all day. Delia would have to be careful of that. The man had seen a ghost once before.

Cora considered these things in silence, hoping to think of some more cheerful item to improve their total, before she opened her mind to the silent girl who was wedged beside her. She recognized that all this bother was a lesson against shooting obese men in deserted flats, under whatever provocation. And yet, to be fair to

75

Cavendish Taunton, he wasn't making the bother. It was the police, going on in their stupid routine way, that wouldn't leave well alone, or listen to any sense. Men were all alike she thought irritably, in their complacent denseness. Look at Kingsley, dragging them here without a thought in his head of how Delia was to manage when they'd dumped her down!

And they wouldn't have any means of communicating, unless they made a practice of driving over at night. Which would be about as mad as sending letters backwards and forwards—but you couldn't do that, for they wouldn't be delivered to an empty house!

She had spoken at that point: "Kingsley, when we've made a better plan, I'd like to know how Delia's to find out."

"We'll come for her, of course."

Delia heard the note of nervous irritation in Cora's voice, and it was like an echo of the hardly controlled terrors in her own heart. But there was reassurance in Kingsley's confident answer. How different men were!

Cora would have agreed about that, though in a less complimentary way. Now she said impatiently: "Well, if that's the best you can do!" That which had seemed an insurmountable difficulty, became simple as she considered it in the confident spirit aroused by the perception of Kingsley's deficiencies.

"I'll tell you what, Delia. You'll have to go into Orpington now and then. It's the downhill way from the garden gate, and after that to the left, and you'll be on the main road next, where you can't go wrong. You post a letter from there addressed to Mr. Charles Smith, Beach Hotel, to be left till called for. They won't think of interfering with that, and I can get it out of the rack any time. And Kingsley shall send a line to the post office at Little Hempstill saying if any letters come for us before we're back, they can just put them in the letter-box to be ready for when we arrive, and if anything comes addressed to me, you'll know it's really for you."

"And what about if they look inside?" Kingsley inquired.

"It isn't likely they would. If they got that suspicion here, they'd be in the house in about half an hour, so it wouldn't make much difference. Besides, it'll be all right if they do. It's only the words that'll be underlined that'll matter, and Delia'll just puzzle them out. She'll have lots of time."

Perhaps the last remark was unfortunate, however obvious in its truth. It increased Delia's realization of the long solitude which might be before her in the empty house to which she was being taken, to be left till called for. She had had an impulse to ask them to stop the car, and get out, and look after herself in her own way. But a memory of certain matters which she had confided to Cora, and which Cora was half-inclined to pass on to Kingsley on the way back, restrained her. But to be alone so long—in an empty house! *To be alone in the dark.* "What a pity," she thought, "that I'm such a rotten coward." But, in fact, she was showing a fine courage in her own way, when she made no answer except: "Mr. Charles Smith. I had better remember the name."

"Yes," Cora said definitely, "you certainly had. I don't want to have to collar all the letters that are marked 'to be left till called for' at the Beach Hotel."

CHAPTER NINETEEN

IT WASN'T QUITE as bad as it might have been, as, indeed, few things are—or as good either. The electric lights responded to their switches in the usual way, and the inward terror with which Delia had approached the dark shadows of the house by the shrubbery path were at least somewhat comforted by this discovery. And there was a butler's pantry where she could have a light with almost absolute safety, after the gardener would have left, for its window looked on to nothing but the high slope of a rock-garden ten feet away. And there was a large clothes-closet opening from the best bedroom, which had a light within it, and no window at all. And when the tap was turned the water came, though how long it, or the lights, would continue to do so might be better left undiscussed, it being no use to meet trouble half-way. And Cora turned out some other provisions from the car, besides the ham-sandwiches which had been for them to eat on the way, and which they had come so quickly that they hadn't touched. And when Delia said if only there had been something to read! Cora found a whole heap of newspaper that had been used for packing and put aside for the fires, which would be better than nothing, anyway, and of too ancient dates to contain any disconcerting allusions to a murder in Murdoch Mansions. And there was no time for leave-takings, or saying the same thing twice, for they all knew that the sooner the night-porter would be opening the door at the Beach Hotel, the better it would be....

"I shouldn't reckon that girl's got overmuch pluck," Kingsley remarked, as he turned the car into the silent length of Little Hempstill High Street. "She looked scared to death."

"Well, you shouldn't have played her such a rotten trick."

There was no reply to this for a moment. Utter indignation at the outrageous injustice of the accusation paralysed Kingsley's vocal chords. When he recovered, he said: "It's no worse for her than it was for George. It's a lot more comfortable than it was then."

"But George didn't mind."

"Well, it's not our fault if she's got no pluck."

"She's a lot braver than George."

"I thought she was half-dead with fright."

"That's what I said. It isn't brave to do what you don't mind. She's a lot braver than George."

Kingsley knew that any warmth of affection between Cora and his twin sister was an improbable development. Being fond of both, he had the sense to keep silent when they favoured him with their opinions of each other. "Oh," he said, "of course, if you mean it that way," and being mollified by the meekness of this reply, Cora began to consider seriously how much of Delia's confidences he deserved to have.

But she remembered that he had spent a good deal of time with Delia that afternoon—or, rather, yesterday. She expected he'd have found out a bit and guessed more. It was no use telling him what he knew.

"I suppose Delia told you a lot while you were sitting on that tree."

"I didn't sit on the tree."

"Well then, before she sat down."

"She seemed interested in what happens to people who shoot moneylenders by mistake."

"Nothing more than that?"

"I gathered that you had gone up to London to improve her knowledge on that point."

"Did she tell you that she had shot him?"

"It seemed to be more or less understood."

"She didn't tell you about the statement that I took up?"

"No. What was it?" Cora summarized it from memory. Finding that it had reduced her husband to silence, she said, after an interval: "It seemed the best thing to do. If you're thinking anything beastly, you can just as well get it out."

"I'm not thinking at all. I'm asleep. I don't want to say anything that I shall be sorry for when I wake up."

"I think you're absolutely horrid."

But at this point the worm turned. "Look here, Cora, if you could only see how it looks from the outside, you'd know that I'm taking it very well. I don't want to get mixed up in this murder any more than we couldn't help at the first, and I don't want you to either. I don't say I wouldn't have given her a hand if the cops were after her. Any decent guy would. But when it comes to setting them on her track, and then start her running away! It might be good business if you'd found that they'd got the spotlight on her, to get that confession in first, or it might have been best to put her wise, and start her off on the run, but to do both at once—! And when, as far as I can check up, they weren't even looking for her!"

"We didn't mean to do both at first. At least, we weren't sure. It was the way Superintendent Withers looked when he was getting us out of the room..."

"Well, I suppose you can see now what a mess it's likely to be. You needn't have raised the dust, but if you did you'd got to stay where you were, and swallow it the best way you could."

"I don't see it at all. I think it's a lot best as it is, and you'd say the same if you knew a bit more."

"I can't help that, if you won't tell me."

"You haven't taken what I have told you in the right way. It wasn't likely I should go on after that."

The car slackened speed as she spoke, and slid to a quiet stand-still beside the grassy bank at the road's edge.

"What's up now?"

"Only that you've made me so wretched I can't see to drive."

Cora had given way to tears at one crisis of life with which the present narrative is not concerned, but there is no other recorded instance since her hair had been pulled in pre-adolescent years. A truthful chronicler hesitates to say what was occurring now. Even Kingsley could not be sure. Cora may have been over-worried and over-tired. But the moonlight doesn't give a man a fair chance.

When he took the steering-wheel ten minutes later, it was with the assurance that there were undisclosed facts which would demonstrate Cora's wisdom and vindicate her discretion in advice and action, but that these facts were deposited with her in so confidential a manner that, even to him, they could not be disclosed without Delia's explicit authority, and after the reception which he had given to what she *had* told him—

"Well," he said, "I suppose we'd better get back." After that he drove in silence beside a Cora whose eyes were closed, and who may have been too drowsy to notice that he took the wrong turn after going through Horsham, and went so far out of his course that when he approached Worthing at last he was actually on the Portsmouth road, and as he was getting low in oil he naturally stopped at an all-night garage for a fresh supply, and had a short chat with the man in charge, who said that he was the first customer he had had since he came on duty at twelve-fifteen. And Cora kept silence at the right time, and praised him afterwards in the right way.

So, altogether, it was about 4:00 A.M. when the night-porter answered the bell at the Beach Hotel, and a sleepy Cora said as she stood a moment in the hall that she hadn't thought it was anything like that, and it had been a lovely run, and they must go again and see how it looked in the daylight, but it was simply shocking to be so late, and (with a smile at the night-porter) she hoped if anyone asked when they'd got back he wouldn't make it out any *worse* than it was. She had the sense not to tip him about that, though she did about something else during the next day; and Kingsley said she'd managed that rather well when they got upstairs. And it was understood without words that if Kingsley would forget his curiosity, his irritability would be forgotten also, and so (if that were possible) they were even better friends than before.

And when the reception-clerk asked the night-porter casually next morning what time the Starrs had got in, he said: "Well, it *was* a bit after one." And having said that he couldn't very well say anything different two days later when Inspector Cleveland asked him the same question in a different tone.

CHAPTER TWENTY

IT WAS ELEVEN-THIRTY on Sunday morning when Inspector Cleveland called at the Beach Hotel, and asked for Mrs. Starr. He had been in Worthing about an hour before that, but had made a call at the police station, and some preliminary inquiries which (he had hoped) would have saved him from the necessity of asking for Cora's assistance in obtaining an interview with Miss Russell; but these not being immediately fruitful, he had soon decided that the proper course would be to apply to her for the information that she could hardly refuse to give.

In return for the production of Miss Russell's statement on the previous evening, he had obtained from Mr. Wilson some details of her antecedents, occupation and habits. They were not in any way to her detriment, which could scarcely be expected in view of the source from which they came, nor did they include anything bearing directly upon the events of the seventeenth inst., but they might assist him to judge the standard of her veracity, as they armed him with numerous items of information which she could not expect him to have.

Mr. Wilson had not admitted any knowledge either of the murder or of the murdered man, and the obvious anxiety of the inquiries concerning Miss Russell, upon which the Inspector had intruded, might possible be explained as no more than the natural impatience of a lover when the object of his affection disappears for several days without previously disclosing her plans. But his reaction to the written statement had been curious. He had expressed the strongest incredulity, even while admitting that the document appeared to be in Delia's writing. He had seemed no happier (which is scarcely surprising) when the Inspector had agreed with him, in his own way, that the statement did leave a good deal to the imagination: and he had made one half-articulate exclamation of such a nature that the Inspector had wondered for a passing moment whether he were going to say that he had shot Taunton with his own hand....

It appeared that Mr. and Mrs. Starr were at breakfast in their own room. It was rather late for that meal, but it was Sunday morning, and a bridal couple are not expected to observe the routines of the working world. Inspector Cleveland was shown in to them without delay, and was invited cordially to join the meal, from which he excused himself on the ground that he had had breakfast already, though that event might not have been considered a serious obstacle, having occurred in London about five hours before. But the Inspector was a man of routine. Had it been an early lunch— But he did not eat breakfast twice.

"I suppose you think it'll soon be time for going to bed," Cora said cheerfully. "But we were up late last night. We went a lovely moonlight run in the car, and had to knock up the night-porter to let us in."

Inspector Cleveland inquired, with no more than perfunctory politeness, in which direction their exploration had been directed. Cora was not reticent about that, but she was extremely vague. She said that they meant to go over the route again in a better light. If she had kept awake better, she would have seen more.

Feeling no disposition to dispute that, the Inspector came to the point. He had come down to interview Miss Russell upon her statement, and thought that Cora would be able to tell him how he could find her most easily.

"I hope," Cora said, with the familiarity of an old acquaintance which asserted itself more readily in the Beach Hotel than in the atmosphere of Superintendent Withers's room: "I hope you haven't come down in a nasty mood."

The Inspector replied with gravity, but with some measure of reassurance. It was a serious matter, but much would depend upon the full account which Miss Russell would doubtless be prepared to give. He hoped that it might be possible to leave it to the decision of the jury at the adjourned inquest, which she would naturally be expected to attend.

Kingsley said that he had understood that anyone under suspicion was not required to give evidence at such inquiries in England. The Inspector admitted that, but in such a case as the present—if the matter were to be left open until that date— He came back to his point. How could he meet with Miss Russell?

Cora said: "I don't know her address myself. I think I told you that. But she's usually been sitting somewhere on the sands in the afternoon. That's the best place to look."

The Inspector considered the extent of the Worthing sands. In fact, they stretch for about three miles in one direction and about seven in the other. Couldn't Cora be a little more definite?

"Well," Cora admitted, "there's the place where you met us before. That's always been rather a favourite seat."

"But you don't know which way she comes, or about where she is probably lodging?"

"When she went back she used to go up the West Parade, and turn off to the left—the turning before Wellington Street. I don't remember the name, but I'm sure of that."

The Inspector felt this to be a genuine statement, as, in fact, it was. It would have been poor tactics to give him an idea that she was aiming to obstruct his purpose. He rose at once, saying that he would see what he could do.

With the help of the information Cora had given, he demonstrated his undoubted efficiency by discovering Miss Russell's lodging within the next half-hour, but—as we know already—he also discovered that she was not there.

Her ex-landlady is only destined for a single momentary appearance on the present stage, and her name does not concern us. She was a lady of defective sight. That must be her excuse for regarding the Inspector as an eager lover who pursued his dream. She told all she could, and would willingly have told more. But, unfortunately, it was not much.

She had taken in Miss Russell a fortnight ago, come Wednesday. Miss Russell left rather abruptly last evening, but she did not suggest that she also had been taken in. It had been part of the original bargain that Miss Russell could leave at any time. She had offered money in advance, which had been declined, but had paid up before she left. She always knew who to trust. It appeared that Miss Russell was a "sweet thing". (In fact, her sight being bad, she judged mainly by the voices of her intending guests, which may not be a bad way.) Could she say at about what hour Miss Russell had left? Yes. It had been about six. When had she first expressed the intention of going? About an hour earlier. Had she had any letter or telegram at that time? None at all. Indeed, none during the whole period. Had she seemed distressed or worried before she left? It had not been observed.

The Inspector felt that the woman had nothing to hide, and that she would probably not have hidden it if she had.

His next step was to telephone to the Yard, giving instructions that inquiry should be made for Miss Russell at 16 Standish Gardens, to which address he thought it most probable that she had returned. If she were there, she was to be kept under observation till he got back. Being human, he made several errors of deduction, as was his usual experience in such investigations. Yet he would often end up at the right place.

Whatever he might think of the probabilities, he left nothing to chance. Before he returned to London that afternoon, he had instituted a very thorough inquiry as to how Miss Russell had left Worthing on the previous day. He had efficient help from the local police. The booking-clerk at the station remembered such a young lady, who had booked for Brighton. In fact, he remembered two. The second had had to go back home for the money for her ticket, having forgotten her purse. He had gone off duty before she returned. The clerk who had taken his place, being roused from untimely sleep, also remembered the second lady. She had been voluble in explanation of her misfortune when she had come back to book. His description differed materially from that of his colleague. But he could identify her anywhere, if only by the wen on her nose. The Inspector decided that the evidence of the first clerk was worthless. as he knew by many experiences that the majority of such memories are.

Next morning, having returned to London, he talked the matter over with Superintendent Withers again. By that time he had ascertained that Delia had not returned to 16 Standish Gardens nor communicated with that address.

The Superintendent listened to his experiences and did not seem greatly surprised.

"We weren't very popular with that young woman," he remarked, "when she went out of the room." The Inspector observed the implication of this remark, but did not agree. He had considered the possibility of Cora having any complicity in Delia's flight, if such it were, and had rejected it absolutely. In the first place, it wasn't sense. It was silly enough of the young woman herself to make such a confession and then bolt, but that Cora, whom he had known for many years to be an exceptionally sensible girl, should instigate such a course seemed incredible.

"I don't think it was anything to do with her," he said definitely. "For one thing, she had cleared out before Mrs. Starr could have got back."

"There's such a thing as a wire."

"Miss Russell didn't get one on Sunday. I've had that checked."

"Still, you might follow up the idea a bit further. Any theory yourself?"

"I thought I had. Indeed, I made sure I should find she'd come to London before me. I shouldn't have been surprised if she'd called here. It was something I learnt from the young man she's engaged to, that seemed to give the simplest explanation, though it doesn't look quite so likely now.

"She's head assistant at the South Bermondsey Library, and it's been closed for a month to be done up, so that she's been on leave. But it opens again today, and it might soon mean the loss of her job, if she kept away and didn't explain. I thought that might have inclined her to take Mrs. Starr's advice, and own up to what had happened—or what she thought she could get us to swallow—so that she could get back to her job."

"She wasn't under any suspicion if she kept quiet."

"No, but she couldn't know that for sure. We might not have been able to trace her to Worthing, and have been just waiting till she turned up at the Library to run her in.... You see, she didn't put the Worthing address in the statement. She put Standish Gardens. So it couldn't look like running away if she'd gone there. It would have been coming back so that she'd be ready for us to call."

"Any other theory now?"

"I reckon she lost her nerve after she knew Mrs. Starr had come up to town. That's likely enough, especially if she had been a bit over-persuaded to make the statement, and knew that some of it wasn't quite true.... But I'm not certain yet. I shouldn't be altogether surprised if she turns up at South Bermondsey now."

"We'd better make sure about that."

"I've attended to that. The head librarian has promised to ring us up at once when she arrives."

The Superintendent looked at his watch. "Then she isn't there, and it's a good bit after the proper time.... I'll tell you what, Cleveland, you're too soft where Mrs. Starr is concerned, and I'm not going to have you made a fool of a second time. I'm going to run that young woman in."

"You don't mean you're going to have Mrs. Starr arrested? We can't possibly do that on any—"

"No. Delia Russell."

The Inspector made no protest about that. It was very much what his own judgment inclined him to have proposed, but he was content that the suggestion had not come from him. He protested only against the reflection upon Cora which the Superintendent had implied, and which he felt to be somewhat unfair He said: "I don't think you're quite fair to Mrs. Starr. After all, but for her, we should still be barking under the wrong tree. She got us that statement, and whether it's true or not, it's a trump card in the pack.... She put me on the track of Miss Russell's lodging yesterday morning, or I mightn't have found it yet."

Superintendent Withers, playing with a paper knife in an idle way, considered this protest in his usual leisurely manner.

"So you think I'm not quite fair to Mrs. Starr," he said, cheerfully, when he spoke at last. "Well, I don't know that I am. I'm not sure that she would be fair to me." He added, a moment later: "Perhaps we'd better see what Sir Henry thinks," and reached a hand to the telephone, to get through to the Assistant-Commissioner.

Half an hour afterwards, when Mr. Wilson called for the redemption of the Inspector's promise that he should be informed of any development of importance, he was told that Inspector Cleveland was out, but that he had left instructions that Mr. Wilson was to be informed if he called that a warrant had been issued for the arrest of Miss Delia Russell.

CHAPTER TWENTY-ONE

"I RECKON WE ought to have her within two days," Inspector Cleveland remarked confidently. He had spread his nets in London, and was having a final chat over the case before going to Worthing, both to pursue his own investigations, and a number of alleged clues which had been collected by the industry of the local police.

The Superintendent agreed about that. The difficulty of remaining hidden in England, when the whole police force of the country, and a large part of the civil population, are on the search, is very great under any circumstances. At the best, it requires a combination; of money and lawless friends. For the amateur murderer who is without knowledge of the professional criminal world, or experience in the art of going to earth, there is about as much chance as for a rabbit when its hole is stopped and the dogs are round it.

Tomorrow, pictures of Delia Russell, reproduced from a recent photograph, would be circulated to the press, and reproduced in every county of the British Isles. Descriptions of Delia Russell, quite recognizably accurate, and including the damaged finger-nail on her left hand, would be circulated everywhere. The news that she was wanted by the police in connection with the Taunton murder would rouse tens of thousands of people of the baser sort to watch for her in hotels, and boarding-houses and restaurants: even in shops and the open street. Every constable would hope that the opportunity of proving his efficiency would fall, like a promise of promotion, upon the district which he patrolled. No, they didn't anticipate that there would be any difficulty in arresting Delia.

It was after they had made the expected capture that their anxieties would commence: that they would have to prove their skill. For they were too experienced to suppose that the document with which Cora had supplied them would be sufficient to see them home. Suppose that a clever advocate should decline to let her go into the box, or say anything? They had only Cora's word that it was her statement at all. But for her disappearance and the fact that Inspector

Cleveland had obtained some corroboration of the handwriting, Sir Henry would not have allowed the warrant to go out of the office. If they had to depend upon that statement to secure conviction, they must have at least some evidence of motive, some theory of how the crime was committed, some grounds of argument that the event could not have occurred in the way that she had alleged.

They had at present nothing on which to base such an attack except a certain unconvincing vagueness in the statement itself, and the fact that the position of the body when the shot went through it was more consistent with the supposition that a murderer had suddenly entered the room, than an attempt on the part of the victim to prevent anyone leaving it.

There would be the evidence, for what it was worth, of how Cora had discovered her at the flat, and of what might have passed between them then. Cora, if she were so disposed, might be an excellent witness, but that was less than sure.

They would be obliged to call her, and so would be debarred from cross-examination. She might prove a very difficult witness, she might prove a very unsatisfactory one, even if she didn't break down entirely under a hostile cross-examination.

There was the awkward fact, on her own statement, that she had discovered the murder and had failed to report it. She had actually assisted the flight of the woman whom they would now ask a jury to convict on her almost unsupported evidence. What might not a good counsel make of such a position as that?

It might be thought that, with their case in no better form, it was a matter of doubtful wisdom to attempt the arrest, but they knew that many men and some women have been convicted who were first detained on weaker evidence than they already had in this case. What they required was an opportunity of subjecting her to the ordeal of a private examination at which she would be represented by no friendly lawyers, and to which the rules of evidence and cross-examination would not apply.

After that, they might have all the evidence that they would require, or see the way to obtain it, or they might reduce or even abandon the charge against her. Let other inquiries proceed with every possible energy, but the essential necessity was Delia Russell's arrest, which they supposed to be a very simple matter.

"You'd better see Mrs. Starr when you're down there," the Superintendent went on, "and question her a bit more about what happened when she got to the flat that morning. If you make her feel that she isn't so very far from the dock herself, it mayn't do any harm. It's a queer affair altogether, and I needn't say it's not one in which anything can be taken for true till it's well proved.... I suppose you're quite sure that these Starrs aren't in it themselves?"

"Of course," the Inspector answered, "I've thought of that. I've known Cora since she was about three feet high, and I reckon I know fairly well what she might do, or where she'd be sure to jib."

The Superintendent looked unconvinced. "I don't say you're not one of the best here," he said, in his slow, ruminating way, "but you won't make me believe that. No one knows what a woman's likely to do.... If she thought that husband of hers...."

"I don't see that he's in it at all.... Anyway, he wouldn't have been if she'd called the police in at once."

"I wouldn't be too sure of that. ... Now, just suppose—I don't say it did—but suppose it happened like this: Taunton gets that flat in the queer way that we know he did, and it doesn't matter what for— "Being scared of Collins, more like than not."

"Yes. That gets our theory in too. There's no loss in that. We know Collins came out of gaol a few weeks ago, and we know he'd threatened to do him in when he did. We know most of those threats don't mean much, and we may have been a bit too quick thinking of him and letting other things slip past, but it does give an explanation of why Taunton might have got scared, and looked round for a hole where he could be safe.

"Well, suppose that's how it was. He knew that the Major and Mrs. Starr were both being married that morning. He'd got the keys of the flat in his own pocket. He didn't even know that there was a third. Nothing would seem more certain than that they wouldn't disturb him there. The fact that no one had seen him go in or out looks as though he were lying low. It doesn't prove much in itself. It might be the first time he'd entered it, and just chance that no one saw him go up. But that food in the dustbin's rather against that. Anyway, it fits in.

"So there he is, scared at the back of his mind, but feeling quite safe where he is, and Mrs. Starr walks into the flat. Perhaps he just listens, and keeps quiet, hoping whoever it is won't come into his room. But there are those new decorations that she wants to inspect, and she goes into all the rooms and comes to his at the last.... We can't do more than guess what would happen then, but it wouldn't have been very pleasant for her. Even if he did nothing at all, she might have been scared enough to squeal out, and just then Starr comes on the scene, and in ten seconds it's done.

"Taunton was about twice his size, but Starr's the more active man, and we know he's quick with a gun."

Inspector Cleveland listened to this theory with the respect due to the utterance of an official superior, and the Superintendent's reputation, but he looked unconvinced. He asked: "What about Taunton's position when he was shot?"

"Starr might have knocked him back.... Suppose the gun were lying on the dressing-table, as the girl says. It may be the one true thing in the whole yarn, because it fitted in without changing. Starr comes on the scene. Taunton tries to get to his gun. Starr knocks him back on to the bed, snatches the gun, and fires before he can get up."

"Yes. It might have been that way," Inspector Cleveland admitted. He was still less than convinced, but he saw that it was a possible explanation. For one thing it explained the gun. He had thought of the possibility of Kingsley's complicity, and dismissed it on many grounds. For one thing, it wasn't the kind of weapon which Kingsley would be likely to carry. It was extremely improbable, if it had been an unexpected encounter, that he would have been armed at all. Nor, as a fact, was Taunton known to have ever used or possessed a firearm of any kind. But it was the sort of weapon he might have secured from somewhere for his own protection if he were scared by the threats of a wronged and lawless man.... Yes, it was possible. But he was still unconvinced. He said: "On that theory, I don't see where Delia Russell comes in."

"She mayn't be in it at all. Starr shoots the man first, and when he's dead he begins to think. With his record, he doesn't feel it's safe to own up, and his wife agrees about that, so they just walk out of the flat.

"Then Mrs. Starr meets this Russell girl on the sands, and they make friends, if they didn't know each other before, and she tries to be just a little too clever. She gets her to make a fake confession, and tells her she knows us here, and can pull it off so that there'll be no trouble.... And if not, she promises they'll confess at the worst, and get her out of the mess.... But she feels sure she can get you to take it in.... And when she comes here, and is shown into this room, she's a bit scared, but it's too late to draw back.... And when we show her the door, and it hasn't gone quite as she thought it would, she's worse scared than before, and her nerve breaks, and she gives Miss Russell the tip to bolt."

"I don't see how that theory explains the girl who was seen to go up before Mrs. Starr."

"No. It doesn't. It leaves her out. But the girl may explain the theory, though the theory doesn't explain the girl. I've never believed in that girl overmuch myself. We both know what that kind of evidence is most often worth. But suppose, when you questioned Mrs. Starr about that, you put the whole idea into her head?

"We're not looking for her or her husband, who are the real culprits. We're looking for a girl who went up before them. Very well. She provides the girl."

Inspector Cleveland pondered this theory as he went down to Worthing. He saw that it really did clear away a good many difficulties for which he could see no better explanation.

He hoped, for Cora's sake, that it was a bad guess, but he saw that there was a danger that his friendship with her, and more intimately with her brother, might disturb his judgment. Was it possible that, had he been dealing with strangers, he would have been this probability from the first? He remembered the Superintendent's warning that he must not let them make a fool of him for a second time.

He went over this new theory, trying to find some fatal flaw in its logic, some self-destructive inconsistency in its presumptions, and had to admit that it was a possible, if not a probable explanation. He had a moment's sense of having given it a damaging puncture when he recalled that Kingsley had gone to Victoria Station, and had waited to see the train leave. He knew, on Major Cattell-Pratt's own evidence, having elicited it in a casual-seeming conversation that Cora would have arrived at the flat before Kingsley could possibly have called for her. But then he remembered that she had gone to the house agent first. It still left a considerable interval, but it reduced it substantially.

The time when they had been seen to leave the flat, which had seemed to be of no importance, now became a vital factor of the problem. He went carefully over the facts as he knew them, and he reckoned that, after leaving Victoria, Kingsley might have arrived at the flat as much as twenty minutes before he and Cora were seen to leave together. It was true that he might have been later—but it was not the kind of appointment which a man is likely to be slow to keep. If he had been twenty minutes in the flat, it hadn't been a case of Cora meeting him at the door, as she would have had them believe.

He was still far from convinced of the truth of Superintendent Withers's theory, but he was inclined to probe the possibility of either Kingsley or Cora knowing somewhat more about Delia Russell's disappearance than. he had previously supposed. But he saw that all these speculations would be promptly verified or exploded when that young woman had been examined in the right way. If her confession were a fake, as he was half-inclined as he had always been half-inclined—to believe, whatever foolish impulse or persuasion might have induced her to make it, he felt a well-founded confidence that they wouldn't have arrested her many hours before she would be making a statement of a very different kind. That was the vital thing: to get that young woman where she would have some questions to answer. And he didn't anticipate that there would be much difficulty about arresting Delia.

CHAPTER TWENTY-TWO

CORA SAT IN the hotel lounge, with Kingsley beside her. They were talking about Cheshurst Hall, and the advisability of commencing their home life there somewhat earlier than they had first intended to do. They spoke freely, having selected the comfort of the settee with an eye to its position as one from which they could not easily be overheard, a large wall-mirror giving them a good view of anyone who should enter the door at the side, or approach behind them.

"Kingsley," Cora interrupted herself to say, "don't be surprised if I talk rot. There's Inspector Cleveland coming in at the door."

The Inspector observed the occupants of the settee, and (with satisfaction) that the lounge was otherwise empty. This would be an excellent opportunity of asking a few questions before they could consult concerning the answers. If he got one alone, it might be a good way, if he could then question the other before they met, but that might not be possible to arrange. After that, the second one would know just what to say. His experience told him that two people examined together will find it difficult to construct or sustain a convincing lie. The hesitating answer—the hasty interposition—the warning or asking glance—they might not be evidence which could be reproduced, but they would be information to his own mind which would lead at last to the proper end.

He noticed the two occupants of the room, as he approached somewhat beside and somewhat behind them, and (being an observant man) he noticed the mirror also. He could see their faces in it while he was yet unobserved himself. He heard Cora's voice also. He would have attached no importance to that if the name *Aquitania* had not come distinctly in a sentence which he could not otherwise hear. But he heard the following words: "Wouldn't get to New York before...," and then Cora lifted her eyes. They met his in the mirror. She stopped abruptly.... He showed no sign that he heard, nor that he noticed the slight confusion of manner with which she rose to greet him. They were words of no certain significance. She might have been repeating some idle gossip of the hotel—the talk of some-one who was leaving or had just left for the Western Continent.... "It's about time for tea," Cora was saying hospitably. "They'd better bring it in here." She touched the bell as she spoke.

Inspector Cleveland put the *Aquitania* and New York out of his mind for later consideration. He said that he would be glad of a cup.

He seldom turned aside or delayed for food when he was en-gaged in such an investigation, but he usually took it as it came from whatever source. He had eaten with murderers, forgers, thieves, and some of even lower orders of criminality, before he had finally clas-sified them or obtained the information on which he could become active to curtail the practice of their professions. He was not likely to refuse an offer of tea from those who were of an established friendship simply because they had incurred suspicion which he did not entirely share.

"I suppose," Cora said, as soon as she had given the order, and the Inspector had pulled up a comfortable chair, "you haven't found Delia yet, or you wouldn't be down here again?"

"Oh, I don't know that that follows. I expect she's landed by now.... I hope for your sake there won't be any delay about that. I don't want to worry you, but if she isn't found soon you might find yourself in a rather awkward position."

"Me? Why? I don't see that." Cora looked an astonishment which was not entirely simulated.

Kingsley came promptly to his wife's support. "I don't see how you could expect Cora to do more than she did. I'm not sure that she hasn't done a bit too much already. Anyway, before they ask her to do any more, they'd better thank her for that."

"It's how much she has done that we're not sure about yet."

"Meaning Superintendent Withers when you say 'we'?" Kingsley inquired.

"I'm a bit puzzled myself."

"I suppose it's not the first time a girl's found out something you didn't guess?"

The Inspector refused the bait. He asked suddenly: "Mr. Starr, you know one end of a gun from the other yourself. Do you believe that confession?"

"I never saw it," Kingsley answered. "Of course, I've heard more or less what it said."

"Well, judging from that."

"Meaning the trigger'd have a hard pull?"

"Yes. That and other things."

"You want a serious answer to that? Well, I do, and I don't. That is, I'm not sure how far I do."

"I don't see why you should doubt it at all," Cora interrupted indignantly.

Kingsley saw that he had said the wrong thing, though he was not sure how. He had said genuinely what he thought. The confession seemed crazy to him, and, having made it, the flight seemed more foolish still, but he had only received a partial confidence, and was aware that he might go wrong on a blindfold way.

But, in fact, he had done better than he could know. The Inspector, judging his answer and hearing Cora's protest, came to two correct but misleading conclusions. He came to an instant conviction, instinctive rather than logical, that Cavendish Taunton had not been murdered by Kingsley Starr, and he was equally convinced that Cora had received confidences from Delia which Kingsley had not been allowed to share.

It appeared probable that Kingsley might not be in this at all, except so far as a man will support a wife who has occupied that position for rather less than a fortnight, and of whom it is evident that he is very fond. The Inspector decided to make a direct appeal to Cora in her husband's presence and see what might result. He went straight to the core of the matter.

"You see, Cora," he said, "I'm your brother's friend, and I don't mind if you call me yours. I've got my duty to do, and I mean to do it this time. The sort of thing that happened once can't happen again. You ought to have sense to see that." (So she had. It was that perception that had been the larger half of the trouble, and was likely to produce more. But that was something she couldn't say! She listened to the Inspector's wisdom with the friendly innocence of expression about which Superintendent Withers had been so rude last Saturday—but she didn't know that.)

"But, all the same," the Inspector went on, "I want to help you in any way that I can, and I can't help feeling that you're not being quite as frank with us as you might be, and that it might be better for yourself, as well as for us, if you were.

"I don't know whether you quite see that you've started something you can't stop. There's a warrant out for Miss Russell now, and when we get her we shall soon have rather more of the truth than she gave us in that paper that you helped her to write. And the next thing after that you'll find yourself in the witness-box trying to explain why you saw a murdered man in your brother's flat, and walked out without saying a word; and why you got Miss Russell to sign that statement and brought it to us; and, if you gave her the tip to bolt after that—I don't say you did, I only say 'if'—you'll have a hard job to explain that too. And what I want you to see is that it'll be a far harder job if you haven't told us before what the truth is. I don't say we can save you having a rough time in the box. We're not the jury, nor the judge, and if Miss Russell gets a good counsel he won't care much about us or you, if he can get her off at your cost; but still, we can do more than a bit, and if you're helping us, we shall help you."

"Well, of all—" Cora began, and there is no reason to doubt that she would have handled the position with the tactical adroitness which it required, but what she would have said must remain unknown for ever; for Kingsley had made up his mind as the Inspector's argument was elaborated that a movement, not of tactics, but of major strategy, was imperatively needed.

"Shut up, Cora," he said, with a curtness which reduced her to startled silence. "You'd better leave this to me.... Inspector, you're a straight man. What you mean is that when you've arrested Miss Russell there'll be a lot of trouble for us to follow? You can't say no to that? Well, you've asked Cora to talk, and I dare say she'd have talked for an hour, but she won't say a word more unless she's going to quarrel with me. You say she ought to have put you wise when she found that dead guy in her flat, and I don't say you're right or wrong, but she's told you since, and a lot more that she'd no need. So I reckon she's square with you about that. She's talked too much and she's done too much, if you ask me, and she shan't say a word more. If you want her when you've got Miss Russell, as you say you will, well, you must just pull her in, but till then we don't want to hear and we don't mean to say a word more.... But leave that out, and we're good friends still, and you're a man that we're glad to see."

The Inspector had trained himself for many years not to let his feelings appear, unless it were of a clear expediency. He listened impassively to this out-burst, recognizing finality in Kingsley's voice and manner. He turned formally to Cora to inquire: "Am I to understand that you adopt that attitude also?"

"Yes," she said definitely. "I might have said quite a lot, but if Kingsley feels like that, it goes with me too."

She was aware of an inward gratitude for that intervention which she could not express until the Inspector was out of sight. But that was an event that very promptly followed. He shook hands with some reserve, but without apparent resentment or further protest.

After all, he wasn't sure that it wasn't the best way.

When he had gone Cora expressed her feelings with a display of affection which was something less than habitual. "Kingsley," she said, "you're the right sort. I'm almost glad we got married."

CHAPTER TWENTY-THREE

IT WAS FRIDAY afternoon when Inspector Cleveland returned to Scotland Yard, and went at once to the office of Superintendent Withers, who was expecting to see him.

The Superintendent had been engaged for the past two hours with the Assistant-Commissioner and two of his own colleagues, in discussion of the Taunton case, which was in an increasingly unsatisfactory condition. Delia Russell had not been arrested. She had disappeared absolutely from the moment when she walked out of her Worthing lodgings, apart from one doubtful glimpse upon the Horsham Road. He had a file of reports and correspondence before him, including some lengthy wireless messages from the Commander of the *Aquitania*, of the substance of which the Inspector had been, more or less, acquainted already by the medium of the long-distance telephone; and he had one document which would be a surprise and which he determined to keep back until they had exhausted the discussion of earlier incidents.

The Inspector had not been idle. He had, indeed, conducted inquiries in the Worthing district with the efficient energy for which he had a securely established reputation, and it would have given him an unexpected gratification had he heard the tone in which these efforts had been recognized at the discussion which had just concluded.

"The *Aquitania*," the Superintendent informed him, "isn't likely to dock before tomorrow morning, if then. She's lying somewhere off Ambrose Point, with a thick fog in the harbour. But Sir Henry says we can't do anything more, and I think he's right. We can't have a man detained that we've got nothing against, with no better reason than that we want a woman of the same name."

"There's a bit more in it than that."

"Yes. Perhaps there is. But not much."

"I've got a feeling that if we got that man back we should unwind the whole skein, though I'll own that I can't see how.... If it's coincidence, it's one of the queerest I ever met."

"Well, some of them are queer. Anyway, that's the decision."

"It's about what I expected."

"Of course, we'll have him watched after he lands."

"Yes. I suppose that's all you can do."

It was disappointing, for, two days ago, Inspector Cleveland had thought that he had located Delia, and added another, and a particularly spectacular item, to the long list of his past successes. And even now—he was not satisfied that the mistake had been his. After he had been politely shown the door of the hotel lounge, he had telephoned to Scotland Yard, and received instructions to leave the Starrs alone for the present, beyond having their movements and correspondence watched, and to concentrate upon inquiry as to how Delia had left the town, and in particular upon whether the Starrs had been concerned in that disappearance.

He knew, in view of his acquaintance with Cora, and of incidents which had occurred previously, that if there had been such complicity, and he should fail to discover it, it would be peculiarly detrimental to his reputation, and might even be misconstrued into a deliberate negligence, if the information should. be obtained in other ways.

Within the first twenty-four hours he had obtained a copy of Cora's telegram, considerable approximately accurate information as to Kingsley's movements before her return, and the fact of the moonlight run, though there was some discrepancy of evidence as to the time when the Starrs had returned to the hotel. He had the report of an exceptionally intelligent young constable, who had been on night duty, and had seen Kingsley's car (he actually gave three of the four numbers and the letters correctly) driving north at a high speed upon the Horsham road. It had been braked rather abruptly at a cross-road where he had been standing, at the sound of a warning horn from another direction, and he had seen the face of the driver distinctly. It had been driven by a woman, and he thought that it had two other occupants. But he said frankly that he was not certain about that. There" might possibly have been only one. Being instructed to watch those who entered or left the Beach Hotel, he identified Cora as the woman who had been driving.

The evidence of the man on duty at the garage from which oil had been purchased on the Portsmouth Road had also been obtained. He was engaged in a business in which it is of particular importance to be on good terms with the police. He had had a little recent trouble with them which he was anxious to obliterate from the official mind. Such considerations, supported by a rather liberal bribe, induced him to stand for some hours at the corner of the Beach Parade, until he identified Kingsley and Cora among the passers-by. It was a convincing method of identification.

Inspector Cleveland decided that this man's evidence was equally reliable as to the time at which the oil had been obtained. The hotel porter must have a bad memory or a lying tongue.

Getting half-way to the truth, he became convinced that the Starrs had taken Delia out of Worthing, and were responsible for her disappearance. He concluded that the start upon the Horsham Road had been a deception of a transparent kind, followed by a leftward swerve which had headed in the direction of Southampton. A telephone conversation with the police station at that port produced the information that the *Aquitania* had sailed with the tide at 3 A.M. on Sunday morning, and had taken on passengers till midnight.

Adding these facts to the words which he had overheard in the hotel lounge, it was not difficult to conclude that Delia was on the Atlantic, and would remain there until the end of the week, having adopted the almost routine method by which murderers in flight simplify pursuit and ensure capture. It remained only to identify her upon the passenger list, and arrange for her arrest, neither of which processes seemed likely to present any serious difficulty.

The Inspector. proceeded to Southampton, considering on the way that the Starrs' part in this business must be more serious than he had been willing to believe, or than, in fact, it was.

For there was the passport difficulty. No sudden impulse of flight, born of Cora's dissatisfaction with her Saturday morning interview, could have placed Miss Russell on board the *Aquitania* on the midnight of the same day unless she had a passport already in order, and with the *visa* of an official of the United States. Kingsley's money might have done much. It might have paid her passage at the last moment. But it could not have done that.

Still confusing his hardly-discovered facts with surmise and error, as must always be the slow and patient process by which the truth in such investigations may be gained at last, he reflected that, when Cora travelled to London with that statement, which might be no more than a clumsy lie, it must have been planned already that its author should, or at the least might, be secretly sent abroad on the same night.

Having shown his credentials at the shipping office, and explained the object of his search, he was enabled to scrutinize the passenger list and to interview such members of the staff as had been on duty on Saturday in that department.

It is customary for those who go on an ocean voyage to book their passages at least a day or two before sailing, but there are usually a few whose decision is taken at the last moment, and who have the documents which were once the assurance of a nation's protection of its wandering members, and have now become a species of ticket-of-leave by which the individual is transferred from one national gaol to another, sufficiently in order and up-to-date to permit them to do so.

On the present occasion, there had been three only who had booked last-minute passages, and two undesirables who had unsuccessfully attempted to get on board. It should be a very simple matter to discover Miss Russell among so few, or to decide that she had been already booked, and her flight a settled thing on an earlier day.

The two undesirables were men known to the police of three continents; communists of disputable nationality, but Italian origin. They could be eliminated, as could two of the passengers—the wife of an American banker and her half-grown son. The name of the fifth was William Trevor Russell.

Inspector Cleveland started at the name, and then considered it with a puzzled frown. He felt he was nearly home, but if she had disguised herself as a man, why did she still use her own name? Probably the passport difficulty would explain that—doubtless he would find that she had a brother or cousin whose passport was to see her through. But what fools women were to think that they could escape by devices so transparent, which were only sufficient to make their capture certain, and to add an admission of culpability, or why should such tricks be tried?

He examined the details of the passenger list, and found very much what he expected to see. He questioned the clerk who had issued the ticket, and learnt very much what he had expected to hear.

Mr. W. T. Russell (the clerk felt sure, and persisted in the belief that he was a man) had arrived at a late hour, and in a scarcely controlled anxiety to learn that he was not too late to be able to join the boat. He explained the hour of his arrival by saying that he had motored from London, and had a breakdown on the way. He gave an address in Bayswater. He described himself as an engineer, unmarried, aged twenty-five. He booked through to Montreal, including the rail journey from New York to that city. His passport, which the clerk had inspected with care, for (as he said) they usually got the queerest fish at the last moment, bore the United States *visa*, for transit through that country only.

Inspector Cleveland reflected on the shrewdness of this method of procedure. Such a *visa* may be obtained much more readily than for a visit to the United States. Few countries ask fewer questions than Canada regarding people of British birth who approach her shores.

Mr. Russell had booked tourist single. He had paid in one-pound notes. He was dark, rather slight, well and inconspicuously dressed. His luggage had consisted of one suitcase only, of moderate size. It was all much as might be expected.

The Inspector did not doubt that his quarry had run herself into a hole from which there was no escape. He was sorry for Cora. He hoped that it might be possible to conclude that she had acted under her husband's influence. It was always the same. Once a criminal, always a criminal. He had little doubt now that it was Kingsley's hand that had pulled the fatal trigger in the Knightsbridge flat. What a pity he had been cajoled oh a previous occasion into the bargain that had let him free to do further mischief, and entangle a previously innocent girl in its degrading meshes. What on earth would Ted say when he knew?

After that discovery, it was rather from methodical habit than with any expectation of further profit that he had gone carefully and systematically through the passenger list, and noted those who could, by the remotest possibility, be Delia Russell in disguise.

Having reported his discovery by telephone to the Yard, where the resources of wireless telegraphy should be adequate to the apprehension of Mr. (or Miss) Russell without concerning him further, he had been instructed to remain on the ground, and endeavour to obtain confirmation of the movements of Mr. Starr's car, and of who had been its occupants between Southampton and Worthing. It was recognized by his superiors at headquarters that he had shown himself to be a particularly capable officer, as he had done so often before.

He felt sorry for Cora. But the whole incident showed the folly of those who seek to defy the law.... Later in the week, he became less certain of several things.

There had been reports from the Commander of the *Aquitania*. He said that Mr. W. T. Russell was a man: there was no doubt about that. Then had Delia Russell been a man in disguise? Scotland Yard considered that problem seriously. But her landlady and the head

103

librarian where she had been employed denied it with emphasis. There was no doubt about her femininity. It was an absurd question to raise. Other witnesses, hastily sought and questioned, confirmed this judgment.

Then had Mr. Russell's name, and his late and agitated arrival, been a mere exasperating coincidence? If that were so, might not, or must not, Delia Russell have been one of the hundreds of passengers who had gone up the *Aquitania's* gangways that Saturday evening without apparent haste, and with tickets previously obtained and papers in order? Wireless messages flashed again in a continual stream of question and reply. The number of passengers who were politely invited to an interview in the Commander's cabin may have been a record for the trans-Atlantic service.

The fact was that Scotland Yard had decided that Delia Russell was on that boat, and it was determined to have her. Not that she was now pursued as a probable murderess, nor as one who, as she said, had committed an unintended and perhaps excusable homicide. Rather, she was regarded as having been used by the actual murderer to divert suspicions from himself. To obtain her tale, to put her in the witness-box, against him, would be the surest, perhaps the only, way to bring him to the justice that he deserved.

Besides, it felt that a position had developed in which its prestige was at stake. The degree of confidence, necessary or expedient, which it had given to the Press when the aid of its publicity had been sought for the apprehension of Delia Russell, had been supplemented by the activities of many enterprising reporters, and sufficient of the truth had been discovered, hinted, or guessed, for an impression to be created that the police had blundered badly. It was an imputation from which they could not defend themselves without disclosure of the actual facts, and even that might be doubtful in its results. Much would depend upon the final solution of the nature of the crime, and the identification of the criminal. These were ends to which there had appeared to be only one path—the arrest of Delia Russell, in which they could not afford to fail.

The position was not improved by some guarded references, in the less reputable section of the daily press, to the previous incident of the Bulfwin murder. Skirting the perils of the law of libel with practised skill, they made discreet allusions to the curious coincidence of Mr. Kingsley Starr's late partner having been found shot dead in his office, after an interview with him, and of Mr. Taunton's body having been found in Mrs. Starr's flat after she and her husband had visited it. It was done with an adroit obliquity, stating no more than was admittedly true, so that for Kingsley Starr to have shown resentment would have been to accuse himself; but the inference was not difficult to make that he might have been concerned in both murders (and the police, though not the public, knew that this was true of the first) and that the police were impotent to convict him of either. That, so far as the police were concerned, was no more than the truth. They were impotent regarding the first (if murder it could be called by a pledge which could not now be broken: they were impotent regarding the second, if it had actually been Kingsley's work, for lack of evidence, unless they could obtain it through Delia Russell's arrest. It is not surprising that, believing her to be on the *Aquitania*, they were determined that she should not escape.

As the ship lay in the outer harbour of New York, and the fog bells tolled, excitement was increased among the stewards and in the pursers' offices by the news that a reward of £100 had been offered by Scotland Yard for information leading to Delia Russell's identification upon the boat. A rumour that there was a notorious criminal on board, variously described as a German poisoner of wholesale methods, an anarchist of Portuguese origin who specialized in the bombing of Atlantic liners, or an English drowner of many brides, spread among the passengers, and about twenty persons who had "left their country for their country's good" were reduced to a state of nervous prostration in consequence. Several people of various degrees and impeccable characters became the objects of unjust suspicions among their fellow-passengers, and a lecturer on entomology sat in the smoke-room in a disconsolate solitude, being no longer acceptable to make a fourth at bridge.

When the bugle sounded for dinner it was the signal for the stewards to commence searching like rats in a hundred vacated cabins, and a passenger who left the dining-room to fetch a poem which he had composed the night before, and was anxious to read to his dinner companions, collided with an unexpected occupant of his cabin in such a manner as to leave him with facial injuries which must be attributed to a loss of footing on a lurching deck.... But they did not find Delia Russell, because (as we already know) she was not there.

Such was the position when Inspector Cleveland heard from the Superintendent, with less surprise than regret, that the Home Office had decided that it could do no more. As the Superintendent had said, very reasonably, you cannot arrest a man against whom you have no charge merely because he bears the surname of a woman you are anxious to find, and, apart from the arrest of William Trevor Russell, it was difficult to suggest any further action, unless the whole vessel were to be turned round at the Ambrose Lighthouse, without landing its passengers, and bring them back to England in bulk, for Inspector Cleveland to look them through.

"Well," he said doubtfully, "if we're not going to fetch her off the *Aquitania*, I suppose we've got to look somewhere else."

It was a position with which they were both familiar. It arose frequently and exasperatingly when their own judgment and experience led them to a conclusion which was legally or officially rejected. Perhaps they would arrest a man for some particularly brutal murder, of whose guilt they had abundant assurance, in evidence of the kind that cannot enter the witness-box. He would be well defended and acquitted by a doubtful jury. But from the moment that that acquittal was spoken they must agree that the man was innocent. It was an official duty to accept the verdict of the law. They must recommence their search for a murderer whom (the law decided) they had not yet found.

"Yes," the Superintendent agreed, "and it's beginning to look as though she really wasn't on board, in which case the sooner you start looking in the right place, the better it's likely to be.... But before you go, I've got a little surprise here.... What about reading the confession of the man who shot Isaac Marks?"

"You mean someone else has confessed?"

"Yes. That's one of the little matters that we've had to consider this afternoon."

"One of those silly fakes that we're always getting?"

"No. I wouldn't say that.... Anyway, we've had it since yesterday, and we haven't proved it to be untrue. It stood the first test we applied."

"Who is it this time?"

"A gentleman you unearthed for us. Edward Burdett Wilson. I've got his detailed confession here."

"Then it really wasn't anything to do with the Starrs?"

"So it appears."

"And it seems genuine?"

"We've got a certain amount of confirmation. Mr. Wilson is secretary of the Bloomfield Archaeological Society. He is very regular in his attendances. On the day of the murder he didn't get to his office till after lunch, and appeared agitated."

"Well, that gives a motive for Delia Russell's confession. She must have done it to shield him."

"Yes, unless he's doing it to shield her."

"That's rather less probable. I've always thought it looked like a man's work."

"Perhaps so. But we've got to remember that he's got more motive for faking such a confession than she had, because when she made it he wasn't under arrest or suspicion."

"She mightn't have known that."

"No. But she might have waited till she did."

"But if he knows she accused herself, and he did it, it gives him a strong motive for confession."

"Yes. That's true. He looks the more likely of the two.... And besides that, it explains her flight."

"Meaning?"

"Meaning just that. If she accused herself to save him, and got the tip from Mrs. Starr that she wasn't likely to be believed, she'd know that she'd make a bad break, and couldn't stand being questioned here.... You've got to remember she confessed after hearing you say that no one but a girl had been seen to enter or leave the flat. After that, she might think that if she gave an account of how it happened, no one would be in a position to doubt her word, and no one else would ever be suspected at all.... But if we didn't believe her, and got questioning her here, she might have a job to avoid telling the wrong lie, and perhaps getting him into the soup whom she'd been trying to screen."

"I expect you're right. How does he say it happened?"

"Very much how we guessed, except that it was Miss Russell and he who were concerned, and not Mr. and Mrs. Starr. We were even correct about knocking him back on to the bed, and shooting before he could get up."

The Inspector recognized the generosity of the repeated plural, for his part in the matter had been no more than to assent politely to the theory which had been put before him. He said: "It was you who had that idea. What are you going to do now?"

"That's the real difficulty. We can't put them both in the dock, and let the jury decide, though that might be the most sensible thing to do. We've got to choose one or the other, and go all out for a conviction, when we've done that.... We can't afford to hesitate and we can't afford to be wrong.... Of course, if we could set up that they were jointly responsible, it would be simpler in a number of ways. But Sir Henry won't hear of that. Nevinson tried to argue that it might be that way, but there's no proof, and not much probability. Of course, if they'd been breaking into the flat, or been there for an unlawful purpose, it might make it different as regards him. But even then, she's just where she was."

"Still, how do we know they weren't?"

"We don't exactly. But we don't know that they were. And that's where character tells. It isn't likely that two people with their records would be housebreaking or planning murder beforehand. They've both got excellent characters. We've got to pick the one who did it, and probably be content with a manslaughter charge.... We can't do much with any certainty till we've arrested that girl, and put a few questions to her. It ought to be clear enough after that."

"What are you going to do about Wilson?"

"I've invited him here for seven-thirty. You'd better be present, and have Johnson to take down."

CHAPTER TWENTY-FOUR

IT WAS A few minutes before seven-thirty when Inspector Cleveland entered the Superintendent's room, bringing back Mr. Wilson's confession which he had been studying since his previous interview.

"It seems likely enough," he remarked as he laid it down, "and it fits in with Delia Russell having gone up alone. The only point where it goes wrong is in calling it the room on the left. It was the one on the right. If it's a faked tale, he'll have a bit of a job to explain that."

"Yes, I noticed that."

"Has he turned up?"

"He's been here about five minutes, but there's no harm in that. It never does them any harm to sit waiting a bit before we begin."

"I'm not sure that he's that sort."

"No? I should say everyone is, more or less. But we'll have him up now."

"Just a moment. There's something here you may like to see first."

He passed a slip of flimsy typescript across the table. The Superintendent read:

> This afternoon Mrs. Starr took two letters from the hotel rack. One was addressed to herself, Paris postmark. The other, not foreign, was addressed to Mr. Charles Smith. She read the Paris one in the lounge and went upstairs with the other still in her bag.

The Superintendent read the telephone message, and remained silent for a few moments. He was of a quiet thoroughness in his processes of thought, as in his more active procedures. He had mentally reviewed and rejected several possibilities before he said: "This seems rather like the right brand. Nothing more so far, I suppose?"

"I've had Burroughs on the wire since he sent that through.... I've told him to get that letter by whatever method, except that he mustn't risk alarming her by an unsuccessful effort. If he can, he's to take a copy of it and put it back.... If any more come through addressed in the same way they'll hold them up at the post office till they get instructions from us."

"It's a pity it wasn't looked at before she got it."

"Well, I didn't think we ought to hold up all the hotel correspondence. It seemed going a bit too far, and, besides, it meant delaying every delivery, and the post office would have had complaints, and there'd soon have been an outcry in the hotel that would have put the Starrs on the alert."

"Yes, it may have been best, and it seems likely to turn out well enough. They seem to have a rather loose system regarding letters at that hotel."

"Well, it's rather unusual for a place of the size, but the manager told me that he finds his guests like it better than having them pigeon-holed, and having to apply at the counter every time they want to know whether there's anything for them. He started it once, and had to keep a woman for a week for nothing because they didn't give her a letter that was pigeon-holed wrongly, and she made a tale of what she'd lost or got-muddled by the delay.... Of course, it's a residential place: it's not like a big commercial."

The Superintendent may have lost interest in this explanation before it ceased. He said: "We'll have Mr. Wilson up now."

The Inspector took a seat at his right hand. On the other side of the broad table there was a vacant chair for Mr. Wilson's reception. At the far end, Sergeant Johnson sat ready to take record of the examination.

Mr. Wilson entered the room.

"Take a seat, Mr. Wilson." The tone was coldly official. There was no formality of greeting, or shaking of hands. But if it held an official distance, it was not one of hostility. The Superintendent, who had not met his visitor previously, looked at him in a pause of considering silence. He was very much what he had expected to see. It happens so often in these crimes of provoked violence that the slayer is by every standard the better man. In most cases there is no likelihood that he would be tempted twice, even if he would react again, in the same way. His destruction by legal process can only be defended, if at all, by appeal to the moral influence of that sequel upon the future conduct of other members of the community.

But in this instance there was not even the certainty that he was a criminal at all—unless a false confession, made under such circumstances, can be accounted crime.

Now he sat silent, looking straightly at Superintendent Withers, waiting for him to begin. The Superintendent judged him to be a young man of strong will and passionate moods, who was now in a condition of restrained excitement, having resolved that he would face whatever might be coming without loss of his self-control.

"Mr. Wilson, you won't need to be told why we asked you to call here tonight. We've had the statement you sent us, and, if it's true, Miss Russell must have tried to mislead us with a false confession, and the death of Isaac Marks is a matter for you to explain to a jury as best you can. We've got two confessions now, and they can't both be true. There's this difference, that you're facing the music, and Miss Russell sent us the confession and disappeared. We've got to make what we can out of that.... You know Mr. Charles Smith?"

Mr. Wilson was not startled by this inconsequent question. He looked blankly puzzled.

"No," he said, "I can't say I do. Not to remember. It's rather a common name."

"Well, it doesn't matter. That was by the way. I just thought you might.... What I was saying was that we've got to decide whether to believe your confession or not.... Of course, when we suspect a man in a murder case, we ask him here, and listen to whatever he's got to say, but when he tells us he didn't do it, we don't take overmuch notice of that. We know we shall hear that at first, though we may be hearing something different before he's through. We think a lot more about whether he could have had a motive, and what it was. And when we get such a document as you've sent us now, we ask ourselves the same question first: 'What's the motive for sending this confession to us'?"

"I should have thought that was plain enough."

"Will you tell us in your own words?"

"Because you've got a warrant out against an innocent girl."

"Do you know where Miss Russell is now?"

"No. I wish I did."

"So do we. But it's looking as though we shall before long.... We did wonder whether she'd sailed on the *Aquitania*."

"It doesn't sound likely. I don't believe she'd have left England without letting me know."

"You may be right.... You call her an innocent girl. Then why did she accuse herself?"

"She was afraid I might get charged."

"You think that's a probable motive for such a confession?"

Mr. Wilson commenced to speak and checked his reply. He saw the pit towards which he was being led and answered cautiously: "It's the sort of thing a girl like Delia might do. There aren't many who would."

"Or a man who cared enough for her?"

"That's absurd. You must see for yourself which tale is the more probable. Delia never shot as much as a sparrow."

"That's her own tale. But she might have shot Marks all the same.... Are you used to shooting?"

"I've shot more rabbits than you could count. I was in the Territorials for two years."

"You feel sure Miss Russell hasn't left England?"

"I don't think she'd go off like that. Not without letting me know. Besides, she wouldn't have had any money with her. Probably not more than a pound or two at the most."

"You mustn't build anything on that. Kingsley Starr's got plenty. She's getting money from somewhere, or we should have had her before now. Have you thought that Starr may have shot the man when he found him in his wife's flat? I'm not going to give away any official secrets, but we happen to know that he can be rather quick with a gun."

There were three men who watched Edward Wilson's face with keen experienced eyes as this possibility was suggested. If he had not thought of it previously, if he should hesitate over the idea, however briefly, it would be strong evidence both that he had not committed the act himself, nor been present when the shot was fired.

But he showed nothing beyond momentary surprise, which was consistent with any theory of innocence or culpability, before he answered:

"I couldn't think that when I've told you that I did it myself."

"You're sure you and Miss Russell didn't go into the flat together?"

"No. I didn't catch her up. She'd been there some time when I arrived."

"What time was that?"

"I don't know exactly. I wasn't thinking about that."

"How did you get in?"

Was there a moment's hesitation, a moment's confusion, at this question? If so, it was too short, too controlled to leave anything beyond a faint doubt in the minds of these experienced judges.

"The door wasn't fastened. I just walked in."

"And you heard cries from the bedroom at the end of the passage on the left, and went straight there?"

"Yes."

"You're sure the room was at the end of the passage?"

"That's how I remember it to have been."

"On the right or the left?"

"On the left."

"The body of Isaac Marks was on the bed in the right-hand room."

"Then, of course, it was the one on the right. It shows how easy it is to make mistakes.... I may have opened the door of the one room before I went into the other. I didn't waste any time thinking. I just ran along the passage and rushed in."

"Yes, I see.... And when you'd shot him, you rushed out again, and left Miss Russell there?"

"I know that's how it looks, but I've explained that.... I thought she'd gone out before me. She must have gone into the other room, but I didn't guess that."

"And you didn't go back to look?"

"I haven't said that."

"Did you?"

"I didn't go straight back. I went later, and it was locked up.... I never thought anyone would accuse her of a thing like that."

The Superintendent's questions ceased. He sat silently turning his paper knife in a trick he had, and then said, in his deliberate way:

"Mr. Wilson, I'm going to be quite frank with you. We've got your statement, and we've got Miss Russell's. They can't both be true, and on several points yours is the more likely tale. It's true you're a bit mixed as to which room it was in, but I don't know that that mayn't be natural enough. We more often get that kind of muddle when anyone's trying to tell the truth than in a tale that's been made up to deceive us.... But I'm going to tell you why I'm not sure that we've got all the truth even now.... You say there's enough motive for Miss Russell's confession, and we ought to be able to see that, but I can't say that I do. That is, I can't see sufficient motive, if she's an innocent woman. It would have been different if we'd arrested you.... It seems a lot more reasonable that she should have made such a confession if she were guilty, and going to bolt, and didn't want you to be falsely accused after she'd gone.... She knew that she was the only one who'd been seen going up, and she might think that if she confessed nobody'd think of looking elsewhere. But

113

I don't say that that's very clear either.... That's our difficulty. We can't see why she confessed at all, and if we say she didn't do it, it becomes more difficult still.... There's something we don't know and perhaps we shan't till we've heard her tell her tale rather differently from how she wrote it with Mrs. Starr's help.... And we can't quite place the Starrs either. I wouldn't have betted much this time yesterday that Kingsley Starr hadn't pulled that trigger himself, but, of course, if what you've told us is true, it lets him out.... But they're in it somehow, and rather deep. We shall soon know a bit more about that.

"But our position is that we've got a warrant out for Miss Russell's arrest, and we can't blow hot and cold, and we're not going to withdraw that. Not yet, anyhow.... You've got a passport?"

"Yes."

"You must let us have that.... And you must give us your word that you won't leave London without our permission. I don't mind telling you that you mightn't find it easy to do."

"You mean you don't believe what I've told you?"

"Not at all. It's the most likely tale we've heard yet, but we haven't quite made up our minds.... We might be able to give you the choice of being charged on your own confession, or telling it to a coroner's jury, and leave it to them to settle. You'd better be prepared to attend the adjourned inquest on Tuesday. But I don't say you'll be called. It's more likely to be adjourned again. We may seem a bit slow to you, but we usually end up at the right address."

Edward Wilson rose, and stood rather uncertainly. He had come prepared for what seemed to him the natural consequence of the confession he had signed. He had expected to be detained, with what degree of discomfort or indignity he could only vaguely imagine. He seemed confused by this inconclusive termination. It was as though he had come for martyrdom and there were no lions. Or it may only have been that he was a little uncertain of the etiquette of leave-taking under such circumstances.

If that were so, Superintendent Withers cut the knot. He held out his hand. It was no more than an official, unemotional handshake, but it was no less a gesture of significance. After him, Inspector Cleveland shook hands in a slightly more personal manner. Mr. Wilson went.

The Superintendent looked thoughtfully in the direction of the closing door.

"Speaking among ourselves, if he did shoot Marks, I shouldn't say he did any particular harm, and I don't know that he's got over-

114

much to fear either. But I'm not sure that he did. It might just as well be the girl.... And whichever it is, they won't find a jury overhard, or a judge either. The way they're backing each other up.... But that's, of course, if one of them's told the truth, or enough of it to stand its ground.... We shall probably be able to judge a bit better when we know who writes to Mr. Charles Smith."

"Yes," Inspector Cleveland agreed. "I wish I hadn't come up now. I should have had that letter."

"You don't think Burroughs is quite up to his work?"

"No. I think he's done well to watch what was in the rack, and to notice what had gone. He couldn't have done more. But I should have had that letter, knowing the handwriting."

"You think it was from Delia Russell?"

"It seems a safe guess."

"Then we can give up the idea that she's on the *Aquitania*?"

"I suppose we can. But it doesn't make much difference now what we think about that. If she's on the boat, she'll be a clever woman if she gets off with that reward on her head, and if she doesn't we shall know in a few hours. Anyway, there's nothing more to do about that. I think it's Worthing again for me. I'm just wondering whether there was any postmark on the letter. Burroughs wouldn't be the man to miss that."

CHAPTER TWENTY-FIVE

KINGSLEY TOOK UP the receiver and asked to be put through to the police station. When he had made the connection, he said:

"This is Kingsley Starr. Speaking from the Beach Hotel. You might tell that cop to have his bike ready at four-thirty. We're running over to Brighton as soon as we've had some tea.... Don't know what I mean? Well, tell someone who does." He added, as he put the receiver back on its hook: "That ought to choke them off, if anything will."

"I expect he'll come along as usual, or else there'll be someone else."

"Well, we'll separate. He can't follow both. If I put you down to do some shopping he'll most likely hang on to the car."

"I ought to get a few minutes that way that he can't check."

The trouble was that they could not walk out without a suspicion that they were under continual supervision, and if they took the car there was no doubt of the objective of the motorcycle which pursued their tracks. Now it was Cora's difficulty that she wanted to go to the post. She had three letters to despatch, any of which would be sufficient to bring disaster if it were intercepted; but that seemed an improbable trouble if only they could be posted unobserved.

One was short, truthful, and misleading, with the absence of ceremony which an only brother must expect to experience:

Dear Ted,

I'm in the most ghastly muddle over that man you let the flat to shooting himself or getting shot as he did, it doesn't matter which as far as I am concerned, but your pal Cleveland would get me shot if he could, but he can't quite see how.

I can't explain in a letter which anyone might read, but if you write a word to Inspector Cleveland about this you'll be sorry as long as you live, and a good bit more if we both go to the same place when we're dead, as it's quite likely we shall. Anyway, you never know, and it's best to be on the safe side.

I want you to *fly* back when you get this, and ring up Kingsley's office, without mentioning who you are till you hear my voice in reply. You're the *only* one who can get us out of this mess—Kingsley is in it as well as I—and think what George will say about that if you're not on time, and find our corpses all over the place. That reminds me, speaking about George, I want you to bring her passport. That's *particularly important*. Don't jump to any idea that I'm going to use it instead of her. I am not quite such a fool as that. But it's just as important as though I were. Ted, please, you mustn't fail about this. There's a note enclosed for George. I don't know how private it is; it isn't from me. But when she reads it she'll let you come.

Till then,

Your loving sister,

Coraline

"I think," Cora had said, as she read this note over to Kingsley before folding it, "that'll about do the trick. It's quite true what I say about not being such a fool, because I'm not a bit like. And at the same time, if you see what I mean, it sort of puts the idea into his head by putting it out."

Kingsley said that he saw that. He made certain of the Major's appearance, and that of his sister's passport, by the note which was enclosed for her reading.

Dear G.,

Hope you are not dull. We're having a swell time here. We've got Cleveland dancing round the hotel. Something about that guy who got himself crocked in Ted's flat. I don't know what he thinks he's doing, and I'm not sure that he does himself, but he's got one of his cops in every cupboard in the hotel, and a few more in the street. Cora's written to Ted what he's to do, and if he does just that, and doesn't ask why, we've got a straight flush. I want you to see it goes. You mustn't mind it being from her it's from me too.

K.

(Hope you've got a Joker in Ted. Cora's that all the way, so you've got to quit feeling the way you did.)

Having written this note, Kingsley was able to dismiss from his mind any fear of his brother-in-law failing in the blind obedience which he was required to exhibit. He was confident that George had sufficient influence to insure that, even if Cora's would have been separately insufficient, and that George would fail him did not even enter his mind. That is one of the advantages of having a twin—advantages which are so numerous that no one would consent to be born otherwise, if they were more generally understood.

Cora's second letter was addressed to herself at Cheshurst Hall:

The Parade, Brighton

Dearest Cora,

It was jolly of you to come over and see us this afternoon. I'd been hoping you would ever since I heard you were staying so near.

I think *Kingsley* (I may call him that, mayn't I?) is just too sweet. Mary and I are coming (or should it be I am? I are sounds so queer, somehow) to Orping-ton some time next Monday, and I forgot to ask whether you'll be home by then, and be ready for callers. How ripping it must be to be able to talk of having a home like that.

Yours to the last drop,

Flossie

It had taken Cora a very short time to draft this letter, though she had spent a much longer period in writing it in a variation of her own hand which she considered sufficiently different and sufficiently natural in appearance to endure even a hostile scrutiny. She was rather pleased with it herself, and amazed that Kingsley looked dubious. Being pressed, he avoided the reference to himself, for which few men would be warmly grateful, to object that the last drop was hardly a well-chosen expression to put in a letter which was intended to be studied by one who had confessed to homicide, and now fled from the outraged law.

But Cora said she had known a girl named Flossie at school who wrote just like that. They didn't want it to be how she'd write to Delia. The fact that Kingsley didn't like it just showed how good it was. Cora's third envelope contained a note from Miss Russell addressed to the Bloomfield Archaeological Society, which Delia had asked her to post, as it should not bear the Orpington postmark. It might be unlikely to matter in view of its contents, for suspicion and discovery would walk hand in hand if it once came under the notice of the police, but it was Delia's idea of abysmal cunning, and Cora, not without hesitation, decided to risk posting it, as she was requested to do, and without knowledge of its contents, for it was sealed when it reached her hands.

As it would be inexcusable to keep a reader in avoidable suspense, it may be said at once that Delia achieved her object, though with unexpected consequences, which is a frequent human experience. Would she have sent it if she had known that it would result in her being locked up with Inspector Cleveland before a week was over? It is hard (and needless) to say.

In hesitating whether it would be better to detain Mr. Wilson, Superintendent Withers had been influenced by what he considered to be the first and necessary step toward a satisfactory solution of the problem which confronted him—the capture of Delia Russell.

Would she come forward in voluntary surrender, if she should hear that her lover had confessed the crime? Would she sooner or later attempt communication with him, if she regarded him as remaining in a freedom to which no suspicion attached? Neither question admitted of a certain answer, but by delaying his arrest or detention it would be possible to test them both, which could not be done in the reverse order.

There was now a very close watch upon any attempt to communicate with him, and a letter addressed to him privately, or personally at the Society's office, would have been certainly examined before (if ever) it should reach his hands. But the police had not gone to the length of requesting the post office to hold up all the Society's correspondence. Delia knew that, in the ordinary course, Edward opened those letters himself, but she had provided against the possibility of her communication coming into other hands by the simple expedient of an inner envelope addressed to Edward Burdett Wilson, Esq., and marked "strictly private" in a very conspicuous way....

Kingsley's call to the police station did not succeed in reducing the petrol consumption of their attendant cyclist, but the plan of separation on arrival at Brighton, needlessly supplemented by the simple device of walking in at one door of a shop and out at another, enabled Cora to post without observation, and, being thorough in her methods, she provided support for the contents of Flossie's letter, should it come under the observation of the Orpington Police, by walking into one of the larger Brighton residential hotels and sitting in the writing-room for twenty minutes, unregarded by any. In the perhaps improbable event of the letter to Cheshurst Hall being examined at that end before delivery, and in the still greater improbability of its authenticity being checked, who could say that in that time she had not been talking to Flossie of the vague address?

Such manoeuvres may seem to be of a needless elaboration, while the sending of any letter to Delia was an imprudence. Why not go on Monday unannounced? Delia would be likely to be at home and not unwilling to see them, nor to leave the solitude of the empty house. But the explanation lies in the substance of the letter to Mr. Charles Smith which still lay unpurloined and unexamined in the security of Cora's bag:

My dear Charles,

I am enclosing a letter for the Bloomfield Archaeological Society, which I shall be glad if you will forward to them as I am short of stamps.

I have had many adventures since we parted so long ago, and you returned to the comforts of civilization, leaving me to the dark caves and the surrounding wilderness.

Shortness of food, sometimes quieted with the raw eggs of unfamiliar birds, sometimes relieved by perilous expeditions which the darkness hid, or by bartering with savages of uncertain amity in the distant village of the vale below, was the least of the evils which I endured.

In the inner cave which you saw me enter before we parted, have I not cowered for hours without food or water or any light, trusting that its hanging festoons would hide me, after hearing sounds which may have been no other than a night-bird's cry, but roused the terror of invading foes? Have I not gone again and again around my poor defences, strengthening them at a score of points, and then heard in the darkness the approaching sound which waked the fear that they had eluded all my precautions, and turned my torch-light upon the bright eyes of a startled rat? Have I not been tempted a hundred times to abandon the hardships of secret vigil in the wilds to return to the centre of civilization which I left so lightly?

Enough of that. I will tell you all, dear Charles, when we meet, and may it be, I pray an indifferent Heaven, at no distant date. Then will I tell you of the hours when courage faltered and I was tempted to forget all resolutions, all plans, all pledges, that I might arise and flee from the desolation which I had been persuaded to observe so long.

When, oh when, dear Charles, can we meet again? Let it not be long is the constant prayer of your devoted disciple,

Elisha Topweight

The letter bore neither date nor address (which was a tactical error) and the name in which it was signed (taken, in fact, by random selection from an old newspaper) had an unnatural sound, but otherwise it showed some adroitness in conveying information in a form which might disclose little to one who had no previous clue to its meaning.

That Delia had ventured to do some vital shopping in Orpington, that she had resisted with difficulty an overmastering inclination to return to London, that she had hidden in the clothes closet when frightened by noises in or around the house, crouching or standing behind the hanging garments which Cora had already taken there in anticipation of her own advent, these things were plain enough. If she conveyed the impression that she had been robbing hedge-row nests of eggs of a dubious freshness, whereas the "unfamiliar birds" were Buff Leghorns to whom she had not been previously introduced, in a neighbouring hen-house, it was not a material difference, and was certainly, under the circumstances in which it was undertaken, the more perilous enterprise.

There was one other fact which emerged plainly. Delia was using bolts and bars and keys and shutters for the full value of their intended purposes. To make a quiet call upon her at 2:30 A.M., and have her promptly collected and running full speed on the London road, might not be a simple operation unless they should be expected callers, and the necessity for creating Flossie became apparent. Though, in fact, it was to be no more than a wasted labour, for the course of events was now to be controlled by more urgent currents, which Flossie would have no power to deflect, and before which the plan which her letter indicated would be swept away.

CHAPTER TWENTY-SIX

IT WAS WHEN she was lunching with Kingsley in the hotel dining-room next day that Cora reached down for her bag, which she had put to lean against the chair-leg on the floor beside her, to take from it a handkerchief which was not there. Failing to find it in the outer pockets, she opened the inner fastness, and disclosed to Kingsley's observant glance the letter to Mr. Charles Smith. It was still in its original cover, for Cora suffered from the inexplicable feminine habit of putting letters back into their violated envelopes, and Kingsley, recognizing the post-marked corner which protruded, remarked that it would have been safer to destroy it.

"I know that," Cora replied, "and it's what I'm going to do at the first chance, but it's not so easy as you might think, with no fires I've been able to find, and central heating all over the hotel. I suppose it would have been safe enough to put it into the wastepaper basket, but you never know, and I thought it was better not to."

Kingsley agreed, but still thought there were plenty of ways in which it might have been destroyed or scattered beyond recovery. At the worst, there were the street drains. Even Inspector Cleveland's energy might be insufficient to lead him into the depths of a city sewer to recapture scraps of paper of no certain value, simply because Mrs. Starr had been observed to have torn them up.

"Let me have it," he answered. "I'll find a way of getting over that difficulty."

"All right," Cora replied, "but not with all this crowd looking on. I'll give it you when we get upstairs." By this time she had recognized fact, and ceased the attempt to persuade herself that a handkerchief could be where it certainly wasn't before, because she had looked elsewhere for five intervening seconds. She had put the bag back on the floor, as fifty thousand other women in five thousand other restaurants were doing in this pocketless period, but she was not careless of the bag, which her foot touched in a frequent mechanical way, and the absence of her handkerchief leaving her mind troubled with the consciousness of a defect of powder which she could not remedy, she cut the meal short, declining coffee, and they went up in the lift together.

Entrenched in the privacy of their own apartment, Cora opened her bag again and handed Kingsley the envelope.

She had scarcely assumed a woman's natural position, when the mirror showed her that Kingsley had drawn out the contents of the envelope and was looking at it with some bewilderment.

"I suppose," he said, "that this was in case Cleveland got rather too close?"

"What was?"

"This." He held out a blank sheet of paper.

"I don't know what you mean." She turned round; half-bewildered, half-incredulous. "Was that in the envelope?"

"It's all that was."

"Then I must have given you the wrong one."

"No, you haven't."

"No, that's the one.... Kingsley, nobody *could*.... I've never let it go for a moment. I never do."

By this time she had taken up her bag again, and was emptying its contents on to the bed. It is an operation which usually only takes place once every eighteen months, more or less, when someone gives you a new one.

Seventeen letters and post cards, a notebook, various bills, some tradesmen's cards, two small sets of keys and several odd ones, rouge, mirror, lip-stick, an empty card-case, a glove-buttoner (heaven only knows why, for when did Cora wear buttoned gloves?) fragments of silver or coloured paper from which the chocolates had departed, parts of a manicure set, a small brush such as is used in the cleaning of typewriters, a circular rubber, a cutting from the *Morning Post* announcing her betrothal to Kingsley Starr, and two handkerchiefs each about the area of her own palm, which had been too deeply buried to be retrieved by any less drastic process, were among the articles which met Kingsley's astonished gaze.

"It's like an inside," he remarked. "I expect you'll have the same trouble putting it back."

"I don't know what you mean," she said, rather irritably, as she separated the letters and papers from the rest of the heap, and commenced a useless scrutiny.

Kingsley replied that he had read somewhere that the contents of the human body are packed so closely that if they are taken out it is impossible to put them back in the same space, and he feared that any attempt to re-pack her bag would be confronted by a similar difficulty. But Cora brushed this proposition aside with a woman's practical and contemptuous mind.

"What a horrid idea! Besides, how could anybody have found out? Fancy trying to put back the blood. Besides, nobody'd want to. There's not much here I shall put back. When I empty my bag I always make a fresh start. I expect it's about the same with— No, it couldn't be that. What silly things men do say.... It feels ever so light at first and then it gets back gradually to the old weight. It's a kind of fattening process.... *Kingsley, it's not here.*"

"I haven't lost any time thinking it was. Cleveland's given you the once-over right enough. It's one up to him at this hole."

"One up," she said, rising to the gaiety of his own tone, "and two to play, if we're quick. It's no use waiting till Monday. We've got to be there tonight."

"And give ourselves away by hurrying back?"

"I don't see that. It's no crime to go to our own home. It said in the *Times* this morning that this weather wouldn't last much longer. It's far better to go back with happy memories than to shiver and soak before we've got the sense to pack."

"That means going back openly?"

"Isn't it the best way, if we're quick?"

"Perhaps it is. I should say that depends on how long they've had the letter."

"Kingsley, they *can't* have had it long. Let me look at that piece of paper again.... I'm *certain* the letter was there when you saw the envelope half an hour ago."

"Sure...? *Quite* sure? Bet the whole stakes on that?"

"Yes. I'm quite sure I saw a bit of the letter "

"Then there ought to be time before they puzzle it out, and get busy. There's one thing that's lucky for us. That's the postmark. I don't see how they could learn much from that."

Not for the first time, they looked at it together. About a third of the obliterating stamp had come down beyond the edge of the envelope. "Ington" was to be clearly read, curving above the date. Knowing what to look for, they could detect a shade of darkness upon the edge of the envelope which was the outmost curve of the upper part of the "P". No one could tell much from that, unless it were by a shrewd guess. The number of post offices in Great Britain, the names of which end in "ington" has to be suffered from to be believed.

"Besides," Cora said, "they don't seem to have troubled about the envelope."

"Well, I wouldn't say that. But they thought it best to use it the way they did. They didn't want to put us wise to the fact that they'd got the letter till they'd had time to think it over and get to work.... And we mustn't let them guess now."

"I wonder what made them suspicious about that letter."

"Same here. But it's no good trying to guess that. They may have meant to scoop it themselves, and you got it first."

"It looks as though someone saw me take it out of the rack."

"Or saw it wasn't there after you'd been."

"That means they were on the watch all the time."

"Well, it's no use guessing. I reckon Cleveland doesn't mean us to beat him twice, and we've got to sit up.... I'm going down to tell Withers to give the car a good clean."

CHAPTER TWENTY-SEVEN

HALF AN HOUR after Kingsley strolled down to the garage, Inspector Cleveland sat in the Worthing Police Station receiving the report of a little man about five feet high whose sharp clean-shaven face was now illuminated with an irrepressible grin of impish triumph.

"I suppose you really are Burroughs," the Inspector said in a voice which was not yet free from doubt. "I didn't feel sure till you spoke, even though I knew what to expect."

Burroughs grinned happily at the compliment. Yet he had done nothing to disguise himself except shave off a very luxuriant and outstanding moustache by which he was universally known at the Yard, and to use scissors and razor upon his eyebrows in a way which transformed the previous expression of his twinkling light-grey eyes. When this case should be over, he would retire to some remote solitude with sufficient leave to allow time for his face to assume its normal aspect.

He was a natural artist at pocket-picking and all kindred methods of thievery. Yet he was not of a criminal, nor even of an abnormally acquisitive temper. He was employed, after a past, and under circumstances which may be told at another time, as a door-keeper at the police headquarters, with occasional interludes for special service such as that on which he was now occupied, for which he was required to disguise himself beyond recognition lest he should be captured in the course of some infra-lawful enterprise to the confusion of those he served. But Burroughs had never failed.

"No, sir," he was saying now, "I'm sure they noticed nothing at all. It was just pushed under the table, and I; Florrie fielded it at the far side, just as Mullins upset his soup at the other end. No one gave her a look, and it wasn't likely they would. It was just as though she'd been busy with her own bag. And inside a minute I had it back at the lady's foot."

"And you're sure this was all it showed?"

Mr. Burroughs had provided a little sketch of the postmark, accurately representing it as we already know it to have been.

"Yes, sir. That's just how it was."

The Inspector did not doubt that, but he cursed it in his heart. Another letter would have been so much more!

"Well, tell them to bring me a meal in here. It doesn't much matter what, if it's sharp. I want to get back to London, and I don't want anyone to know that I'm down here. Tell Reynolds to keep in touch with the Starrs whenever they go out, and of course you'll go on doing it, with Florrie's help, when they're inside. The local police will give any assistance you ask for. You'd better have a word with Reynolds while I'm here, and let me know if the Starrs seem concerned about anything."

Burroughs went out to execute his orders, and the Inspector settled down to study the letter to Mr. Charles Smith.

He did not understand it all at a first reading, but he felt that victory was near, for of one thing at least he was already sure. It was in the handwriting of Delia Russell.

It showed that she was still in England, and incidentally that she had not sailed on the *Aquitania*. Had that been a most cunning trick to mislead him, or was it just a blind coincidence—just the bad luck of the game? He was not fully satisfied with either explanation. Well, perhaps the end would show.

And it was clear now that, wherever she had gone, it was with the Starrs' knowledge. What was their part in the matter? Why should they first bring her confession (whether true or false), and then be active to hide her? Why should they be so concerned in her fate that they should be corresponding with her in this elaborately deceptive way? He considered again, and again rejected the theory that Kingsley was the assassin, and Delia no more than a decoy to divert suspicion from him. It was not so much the fact that Wilson's confession complicated the probability of this solution, as that his instinct rejected it. He admitted Kingsley's reputation, the manner of life of his youthful years, his admitted homicide. All these things were against him. That he had entered the flat to find his wife assaulted by a man who had no business there, and that a dispute had followed, in the course of which he had shot him with his own gun (for he recognized that Kingsley would never have carried that heavy and clumsy weapon)—that was possible enough, and fitted in with everything, apart from the doubtful evidence of the girl seen going up the stairs. He recognized that as a matter of abstract logical deduction; but, in fact, he was sure that the explanation was of a different kind. His judgment, defying analysis, told him that had this been so, both Kingsley and Cora would have appeared, spoken, acted, somewhat differently from how they had. But he felt that he would soon know the truth now—he would know it when he had arrested Delia. He resumed the study of her letter to Mr. Charles Smith, of which he had already made a copy, and would take a final look at the original before returning it.

He was interrupted by the return of Burroughs, who had done his errands, and reported that the Starrs were sitting in the lounge, seemingly at leisure, and with minds at ease. He did not think that they were going out again, for Mr. Starr had been in the garage and had given instructions for his car to be thoroughly cleaned and over-hauled.

"Which," commented the Inspector, "might allow plenty of time for them to go out afterwards."

"Yes, sir; if they said when it was to be done, but they haven't. Mr. Starr said that any time before tomorrow would do."

Well, that certainly looked as though they were quietly settled here. It seemed to give him at least a few hours of uninterrupted inquiry, which might be indefinitely extended if the letter could be returned to Cora's bag without rousing her suspicions, as he felt certain that Burroughs would be able to do.

So he said. But the man did not make the expected response. "It's too late for that, sir."

"You mean she's found out it's gone?"

"No, sir, I don't think so. The lady's been at the writing-table. She was turning out her bag, and tore up quite a lot of papers. She threw this in the paper-basket."

He drew out from his pocket some torn fragments of envelope. The blank sheet which it had contained had been torn up with it, apparently without observing that it was not the original letter.

"This is just how it was thrown away?"

"Yes, sir."

"Did she destroy other letters besides this?"

"Yes, sir. Quite a number."

"Without looking at any of them?"

"She just glanced at the envelopes and ripped them up."

"Nothing else of importance to us?"

"No, sir. Nothing at all."

"How did you get this, if they are still in the lounge?"

"The porter always straightens up the lounge and clears the basket during the afternoon. It was just the usual routine."

The Inspector recognized that the whole thing sounded natural enough. Yet he had learnt some respect for the Starrs, and the need for caution where they were concerned. He was less than sure. His mind was constantly on the time when Cora had manoeuvred him once before into a bargain which had left an act of homicide, if not of murder, outside the judgment of the law. And, in this case, there had been the baffling, provoking episode of the *Aquitania*, in which he felt that they must have had some part, though it was hard to say what.

Still, it was a doubt that led nowhere. He must take what the gods gave. Separating the fragments of envelope from the blank paper which they contained, he examined the truncated postmark again. Of course, he would find out. At the worst, an examination of the cancellation stamps at all possible post offices would provide a certain means of identification. But how long would that take?

What a pity that it was the first portion, instead of the end, of the name that was missing! Had it been reversed, he could have found all the possible names grouped together in the Post Office Guide. As it was, he must wade through the entire list. He tried to think of names ending in "ington", and Bridlington would not leave his mind, obstructing all others. He did not know why that was so. He had never been there—was not even clear as to where it was. But he felt sure that it was not the place which he wished to find. He would go back to London, taking the torn fragments of envelope, and the letter with him. If necessary, he must obtain the assistance of others to resolve the problem in an exhaustive way. But he hoped that inspiration might come to him before that.

He read the letter again and felt that the inquiry should not be either long or difficult. He had no doubt that the Starrs had taken Delia to some place of hiding in their car on the night of her disappearance. So far, he had groped forward another step toward the discovery of the truth. But he did not forget that they had returned by the Southampton road. He thought they had taken her to some solitary hiding-place of which Cora must have known previously (for Kingsley could hardly have done so), probably a cave or ruin, which she had found it difficult to endure. By the time they had been absent it was possible—even probable—that the place might have been forty or fifty miles away. It might be in Hampshire—perhaps even as far as, perhaps in the actual neighbourhood of, Southampton.

Then, when they had found him investigating, they had realized that he might learn, by inquiry at the garage where they had called, that they had returned by the Southampton road, and so Cora had made that remark about the *Aquitania*, to mislead him if he should be on the trail. And the man named Russell had been no more than one of those provoking coincidences which confuse such inquiries continually.

So he concluded; patiently adding to his facts, however adulterated with error. If that were so, he had nothing to do but to consider those places ending with "ington" in the neighbourhood of Southampton. It would not take many hours to call on them all, and compare their cancellation stamps with the postmark which he held. After that, it should not be a difficult matter to capture a young woman already half-starved and sick of the solitude in which she hid. The letter told him that she was on high ground. She came to "ington" sometimes, and it was in "the vale" below her.

He decided not to go back to London. He would take up this pursuit immediately. It would be pleasant to make a single-handed capture. He summoned Burroughs again, and asked for a good map of the surrounding country.

CHAPTER TWENTY-EIGHT

THE INSPECTOR STUDIED maps, and meanwhile Kingsley and Cora, having first engaged the assistance of the reception-clerk in obtaining seats for an evening performance at a variety show, were having tea in the lounge and discussing plans.

It appeared that Kingsley had made arrangements in the garage that went beyond cleaning the car.

"No one round?" he asked Cora, who was better placed than himself both to survey the room, and to make use of the opposite mirror.

"Not unless they're under the seat."

"Then they're not more than four inches thick. We needn't worry about that."

"Have you fixed anything up?"

"Yes. I've fixed a getaway for one-thirty tonight."

"Do you think we can do it without being seen?"

"I shouldn't think they'd watch all night, with a car ready to follow."

"You mean it won't really matter what they see, if we once get clear?"

"More or less. But we're a lot better off if they don't know.... We're not going out the front way."

"I didn't know there was any other—not for the car."

"Tonks didn't either. Not till I showed him."

"Who's Tonks?"

"The man who has charge of the cars."

"He won't give us away?"

"Not he. I've squared him."

"I expect you've given him about ten times too much."

"I haven't given it yet."

"Well, how much is it to be?"

"He's not English. Born somewhere in Maryland, and wants to get home.... I've told him I'll pay his passage back if he does what I want tonight."

"It seems a lot to pay."

"You can call it that. But when I start anywhere I like to arrive. Besides, I'd have done it for him, whether or not."

"I don't see why."

"I'm sorry for any guy who wants to get out of here."

Cora looked up startled. It seemed ominous of future trouble if Kingsley were tiring of his adopted country before they had even commenced the new life in the home to which they would be returning under such unusual circumstances tonight. She saw suddenly that she might soon have more immediate troubles than those of Delia Russell. Well, she must deal with them when they came. If it meant no more than a visit to Western lands, she was not sure that she would mind. And wherever she might be, it would never be dull with Kingsley. Even in this matter of Delia Russell, it would all have been different if he hadn't asked her to join them at Hammersmith. Probably they needn't have been in it at all. And yet, as Kingsley put it, it had seemed the best thing to do at the time.

Kingsley broke the silence with: "Said the wrong thing, I suppose?"

"I didn't know you thought England such a bad place."

"Nor I don't. England's swell. But every man likes his home best."

"Well, you can go back, if you like."

"So I would, if you'd come along."

"Or without?"

"Not a yard. You know that."

"Well," she said, with a sudden change of mood, "I don't see why we shouldn't wander across.... But we've got to get clear of this mess first.... How's he going to get us out?"

"There's a passage at the back. It's never used for cars. It's about twenty yards long, and only about three inches to spare all the way down, but I measured it yesterday, and we can get through.... I don't suppose there's any real need. It isn't likely they keep watching all night in case we come out, but it's the safest way all the same."

"We might come in again that way before morning, and they'd never know we'd been out at all."

Kingsley didn't look hopeful about that. "I guess too many cops know the number of that car," he said doubtfully. Cora saw she had said a rather stupid thing. They might get out unobserved and un-chased, but there could be little doubt that all the police in the sur-rounding district would have been warned to look out for their car. To expect to be able to leave Worthing and return during the night without being observed, was to ignore the probabilities of the situation. Still—they might. More possibly they might get clear of Wor-thing without a close pursuit, and might succeed in reaching Cheshurst Hall before others would be there, and get Delia away. That was the obvious and first necessity. If the meaning of that letter and the place from which it came were still unguessed—

"Cleveland's down here," Kingsley added. "His bike's been here. He had it put right at the back where it wouldn't be seen. Tonks gave me the tip."

"It'll mean that man being sacked if they know our car's been out, and can't find out how."

"He's reckoning on that. That's why the price isn't any too high."

"I don't see how we're going to put Delia anywhere, and get back before morning."

"We've got to, somehow. We've got to clean up the house too, so that, if anyone has a look round after, they won't know anyone's been there.... We'll have to put her on rail somewhere, and she'll have to do a bit on her own."

"Why shouldn't she go to the flat?"

"To the flat?"

"Yes. Why not? Nobody'd look there now."

"There'd be the going in and out— Still, it's an idea."

There was something humorously possible in the suggestion. If it were known or suspected that she had been hidden at Cheshurst Hall, and the place should be searched too late to catch her, that they should then attempt to hide her at the flat might seem an audacity too improbable for serious consideration.

The natural buoyancy of their dispositions responding to the humorous quality of this idea, they went out very happily to get a stroll on the beach before the show would commence. Mr. Burroughs, observing the aspect of their departure, went back confi-dently to the Inspector to report his conviction that the theft of the letter had not been discovered.

CHAPTER TWENTY-NINE

INSPECTOR CLEVELAND STUDIED the map, and was not pleased.

Within ten miles to the north of Worthing there were three possible places—Ashington, Washington, and Sterrington—assuming only that there were post offices at these villages. But these were dismissed as improbable. It was unlikely that either Cora or Kingsley would be familiar with the places, unlikely that they would supply the topographical requirements of the position as the Inspector conceived it to be, and most unlikely that the car would have been away so long in the night had it only gone so short a distance.

But looking further westward, he observed a large assortment of "tons" without the prefix of the essential "ing". For many, many miles the map gave him no encouragement, and when at length he encountered Rustington and Catherington, the length of the second name caused him to consult the postmark anew. He decided that, if the obliterating stamp had been symmetrically designed, the missing letters could not be more than three. Northington and Harnington, still further to west and north, were alike too lengthy.

Of course, if they had gone direct north—but, if so, why return on the Southampton Road? Suppose it had been no more than a blind, and the call at the garage a deliberate trap? Further north or east— The Inspector, gazing at the map, assumed the expression of a man hypnotized. His eyes were fixed as though fascinated by what he saw.... He pulled out the letter and read it again. He looked again at that mutilated postmark. Then he said, with an emphasis of expression that he rarely used: "What a damned fool I've been!"

And after what happened before at the same place!

Well, there was only one thing to be done now—to fetch Delia Russell out of her hiding-place.

He could best redeem his reputation for having more intelligence than a ten-year-old child by bringing her in himself, which it should be easy to do. If he remembered the young woman accurately, she was the sort that would come quietly enough.

Of course, a search-warrant ought to be obtained first, but it meant some formalities, possibly some delays, and a different manner of approach. Were his idea wrong—or were he to prove again too late (but there wasn't much fear of that)—he didn't want to take half Scotland Yard into his confidence. There might be an element of irregularity in invading Cheshurst Hall in its owner's absence. But it was the kind of risk which he and his colleagues must often feel obliged to take—a technical illegality which must be justified by its results. And there was one thing of which he had a reassuring certainty—neither Kingsley nor his wife would be active to put the law in motion against him, even if he should burgle their home in earnest. He had done too much for them in the past.

It might be true that he was not acting the part of a friend now, yet he was not an enemy either. They had intruded—Cora, in particular, had intruded—into a matter which did not directly concern them. At least, he hoped, and more or less confidently believed that it did not. Anyway, he was doing no more than his duty. If they used their home for the shelter of criminals whom the law pursued, what must they expect?

There were aspects of the matter about which he was not very happy. He was half-glad that the Major was away, and that there were no awkward reticences where there had always in the past been a confident friendship: and he was half-sorry also, for the Major might have influenced Cora even against her newly-taken husband to a frank disclosure, which might even yet be in time to save her from the consequences of her almost certain folly.

Yet, on this last point, he owned to a double doubt. He was not sure that Cora would yield much to her brother's influence, nor that she was now acting under that of her husband. The last twelve months had seen her develop an amazing capacity for going her own way.

He walked restlessly up and down the room as these thoughts disturbed him. He saw Kingsley and Cora going out in the street below. They laughed in a carefree way. He wished he knew what the truth might be. He hoped he was not striking an unsuspected blow which would turn that laughter to tragedy. But, above all, he was resolved that this occasion should vindicate his own character and ability, both to his colleagues and his own conscience. He meant that there should be no mistake this time about Delia Russell's arrest.

He knew Cheshurst Hall. He knew how it could be entered most easily. To make the attempt in the night-time, when its lurking occupant would be unprepared for flight, and when observation and interference from others would be least likely, was an obvious decision. He would not start till a later hour.

When Kingsley and Cora descended the fire-escape stairs in the rear quarters of the hotel, about 1:00 A.M., and took their silent way to the garage, they found that Tonks had the car in readiness. They thought little of it when he told them that the Inspector had been seen to leave Worthing about two hours earlier. The car moved slowly down the narrow passage, taking no more injury than a bumped mudguard. It came out into the street at the back of the hotel, which showed no sign of life, and slipped away unhindered and unregarded. Let the Inspector go to London, and discuss the pilfered letter with whom he would! Let him guess its meaning as soon as he liked! He would be a day too late.

But Inspector Cleveland, telling his intention to none, had gone already to Cheshurst Hall.

CHAPTER THIRTY

DETECTIVE SISKIN, DETAILED to the shadowing of Mr. Wilson, and with instructions to warn, and if necessary, to arrest him should he attempt to leave London, had a hard day.

He had kept him under the usual unobtrusive observation as he left his lodging in Fishwick Gardens, and proceeded to the offices of the Archaeological Society by way of the Central London Railway, and had settled down to a somewhat perfunctory watching of the entrance of the building which contains them. In fact, he had just come back from the purchase of the drink which he found to be so refreshing at about 10.30 A.M., when he was startled into activity by the sight of Mr. Wilson, who had already left the building and was crossing the street in reckless disregard of the surrounding traffic. Mr. Siskin had a beatific vision of some disabling accident which would result in it becoming his duty to watch for weeks beside the bedside of an injured man. To have under arrest a man with a few broken bones in a hospital ward is about the easiest method of earning a living which enters a detective's dreams, and its opportunities for obtaining light refreshment either on the premises or round the corner have little practical limit.

But the lorry's brakes were jammed on, and Mr. Wilson, sufficiently athletic when he became aware of his danger, took a flying leap to the pavement, and shouldered an impatient way along the crowded street. Detective Siskin followed, feeling annoyed.

He did not think that Mr. Wilson was attempting escape or evasion. He was of too long an experience in the movements of men. In fact, he was an exceptionally intelligent officer, only held back from the higher branches of his profession by the love of liquid refreshment which had nearly been his undoing on this occasion. It was no attempt at flight which he must now rather pantingly follow. But it was annoying, for he was not fond of prolonged pedestrian exercise at such a pace, and he had been informed (and his own short experience had confirmed it), that Mr. Wilson *never* left the office from when he entered it at ten, until he went out to lunch at twelve-forty-five. So what on earth was he doing now?

The question became more difficult as the rapid walk proceeded. A man may have many reasons for approaching Charing Cross, but he does not usually do so from Essex Street by way of Kingsway and Shaftesbury Avenue: being at Charing Cross, he may desire to visit the neighbourhood of the Zoological Gardens, but he is unlikely to select a route that includes Piccadilly and Park Lane, with Pall Mall as an eccentric link of connection between them.

Would the man never pause? Did he never eat? Had even liquid refreshment no charms?

It was mid-afternoon when Detective Siskin realized sadly that his legs had been tired in vain. Mr. Wilson, having made no call, no pause, returned at last to the office from which he had started.

At 4:30 P.M., being relieved by Detective Howson, Detective Siskin got on a bus and was very glad to sit down. On his arrival at Headquarters, he reported the exercise of the day to Superintendent Withers, who, not having the correct clue to Mr. Wilson's lively conduct, decided that his nerve was beginning to break, and that he might soon be in a mood to give a fuller and more genuine confession than he thought his first one to be.

At a later hour a telephone report was received from Detective Howson. Mr. Wilson, showing no further sign of mental instability, had left his office at the usual time, proceeded to his lodgings in the accustomed manner, and remained there during the evening. At 10:30 P.M. the usual light had appeared in his bedroom window, and at 10:50 P.M. it had been put out. After a day of unusually violent exercise, it might be supposed that he would sleep well.

But Mr. Wilson did not sleep. He had not even got into bed. The opening of that private inner envelope addressed to Edward Burdett Wilson, Esq., which had been among his morning post, had been followed by an acute mental disturbance which had only subsided as his resolution was taken to risk the adventure to which it called.

In the privacy of his back second-floor sitting-room, where it was certain that he could not be overlooked when the blind was down, and with the additional precaution of a bolted door (though there were few things more certain than that Mrs. Corbett would not come up again till he should ring for her to clear away), he had taken out a letter which he knew by heart already, and given it a last perusal before it must be pushed down into the central blaze of his evening fire. For he saw that if he were arrested before morning (as was likely enough) it must not be found upon him, and if his room were searched in his absence, which was an even greater probability, it must not be there. This is what he read:

My dearest,

I know it isn't a very wise thing to do, but I simply must write, and I think I know a way by which this letter will reach you safely, or it won't matter if it doesn't, because there's another that I must send, and I'm putting it inside that, and if that one gets found out, there won't be much more to be learned from this.

Anyway, I'm at Cheshurst Hall, Little Hempstill, which is a village near Orpington, and I'm alone in the house. I've been here years already, or it seems a lot more than that, and I just can't go on any longer without letting you know.

It's Mr. Kingsley Starr's house and he's let me come. They've been very kind, and brought me here in the night, but it's dreadful being alone, and the water stopped yesterday, though the lights haven't yet, but I'm afraid to find they have every time I touch a switch.

I don't know why they've done all they have except that they didn't want any fuss at the time when they found me in the flat, and Mrs. Starr says that he got into the same sort of trouble through shooting a man that needed it even more than Mr. Marks. That was what she said. I don't know anything about it myself. Mrs. Starr says it was in all the papers, but you know I never care to read that kind of news.

This is a lovely house in its own grounds. There's a lane at the back where hardly anyone ever comes, and an iron gate with a wall one side, and a hedge the other. The gate's locked and chained, but that doesn't matter because you can squeeze between the hedge and the pillar of the gate. At least, I can quite easily and I'm sure you could manage somehow. But you must come at night, because the house is supposed to be empty. I shall expect you as soon as you can get this. I simply *must* see you and have a talk. There's a little window in the butler's pantry at

140

the back, opposite a rock-garden, after you pass an old pump which doesn't work now (I wish it did), and I'll leave the bolt off. You'd better not switch the lights on, but bring your electric torch, and come up the front stairs and turn to the right, and knock on the second door on the left. Knock three double knocks and then call out. I shan't answer till I hear your voice, because I shall be terrified in case anyone else has got this letter and tries to come in the same way.

Edward, you must come, even if you have to get back before morning, as I expect you will, if it's to be at all safe, but I've had a wretched time, most of all because I haven't let you know anything, and I knew how dreadfully worried you'd be about the way I'd disappeared. I've got into a state that I can't sleep but just lie listening to the owls, and worse noises than theirs. I don't really mind them. They seem company, in a way, and I hope they're catching the rats, though I suppose it's rather cruel to wish that, but I do hate their eyes when they come round the corner suddenly and stare at you for a second before they run back. I expect you think I'm an awful coward, and worrying about the things that don't matter, instead of those that do, as you always say.

But we really must meet somehow and talk things over, and have some plans. I can't stay here for ever, and I suppose I've lost my job now. And there'll be no more money coming from Mr. Marks, at least suppose there won't. I don't see how it could reach me while I'm hiding away, even if there's any due, and I don't know that there is.

Oh, Edward, I could cry when I think of the—

The letter didn't end here. It may rather have said to have begun. Nor did it contain any revelations which an adroit narrator would conceal for subsequent climax. It went on for six further pages of such a character that their publication could only be justified by a plea of necessity, which does not arise. Mr. Wilson read it again, and reluctantly placed it upon the resolving flames.

CHAPTER THIRTY-ONE

THE OCCASIONS ON which a woman has intimated that she would unlock her door in the night must be very numerous in the history of a sinful world. Those when a man has received a note to indicate such a willingness must be numerous also. They must have been received with many varying feelings, of which pleasure and excitement, (it is polite to suppose) may have been the most frequent, but fear, hesitation, reluctance, and even more decided antipathies, must have had their places.

Mr. Edward Burdett Wilson, on receiving perhaps the most innocent and excusable of such letters which was ever penned, experienced most of these emotions in a confusion of mind which, had it had leisure or mood for introspection, would have found it difficult to decide which predominated among them.

The joy of hearing from Delia after a fortnight's silence, during which he had not known where, or in what extremity of trouble she might be, the further satisfaction of knowing that she was as yet free from the clutches of the searching law, the delight of the thought that he might hold her in his arms again in so few (or should we say so many?) hours ahead, all these were complicated by the remembrance that he must not leave London, under penalty of immediate arrest if he were discovered to be attempting to do so, and the fear that he might be followed and betray her hiding-place if he should attempt to see her.

He had already had leisure to speculate as to whether he were not being left in freedom by the police so that he might attract to their net their more immediate quarry, and he had resolved that even if Delia should communicate with him he would have strength of mind to resist the temptation to put her in such a peril. Better far that she should think a letter to him had miscarried, better even that she should misjudge him as a faithless or faint-hearted lover, than that he should be the decoy that would betray her to her watchful foes.

That had been his resolution when it was no more than an abstract proposition which he considered. It became a different matter with her appeal before him. Go? Of course he must. It was too much to ask that he should wait till the darkness fell. And yet— Was that not precisely what he had resolved beforehand that he would not do? Let the police watch him in vain, while Delia would think that her letter had failed to reach him, and these Starrs, who had shown themselves already to be sufficient to out-wit the detective force, should contrive to place her in a more permanent safety. And when the police realized at last that she was beyond their reach, they would end the suspense by arresting him on his own confession, and he must suffer such penalty as the law would inflict.

So his mind debated in the first few minutes after he had read the letter—or rather, while he read it again and again, pacing the carpet in a restless impatience at his own uncertainty.

He was not long in realizing that he could do no work in the excitement that disturbed his mind—nothing, certainly, till he had resolved whether he would take the risk of visiting that lonely house. He would take a quiet walk, and think it over. Detective Siskin had not called it a quiet walk, but it is fair to recognize that his legs were shorter.

When he returned to his office he had decided (perhaps there had never been any real doubt about it) that the risk must be taken. Rather, he had resolved that (for Delia, at least) there need be no risk to take. He would so contrive that the police, even if they were upon his trail, should be shaken off before he should leave London. If he should fail in that, it might lead to his own arrest—and that thought showed him that he could not afford to fail. Should he do so, he would not hold the girl who loved him in his arms that night. Perhaps not again until who could say how long? Perhaps *never*. With such a stake at issue, could any mortal fail? In an active mind, he had made plans.

So in the evening, having burnt the letter, he read Browning for the eternity of an hour, and then went to his bedroom at the usual time. After a sufficient interval, he put out the light, having equipped himself with such things as he felt that his expedition required, and walked downstairs to Mrs. Corbett's kitchen. He was going to take a walk in the garden, as the terms of his tenancy gave him a right to do.

He told a somewhat startled lady that he was restless, and thought that a stroll outside would do him good.... No, she needn't wait up. He'd lock the door himself when he came in.

Being in the garden, he lost no time. He scaled the wall on the left, as he had resolved beforehand that he would do. He scaled a higher wall at the foot of that garden. He descended into the garden of a house in the Feltham Road. He made rapid way through three hedges of little strength, and over palings that were not four feet in height. He gained a passage between two semi-detached houses that led into Feltham Road. In the darkness of the alley he paused a moment to give his clothes the benefit of a brush he had brought for that purpose. He looked out from the shadows on to a road that was quiet and bare. He crossed it rapidly, but without haste, and turned into Ashchurch Avenue.

Reaching the main road he boarded a passing tram, and transferred himself at the next halt to one going in the opposite direction. Leaving it in a few minutes he entered an Underground station, and took a number of short journeys, leaving each train at the last moment at stations where another could be entered at once from the opposite side of the same platform. He felt that if he were being followed he had acted in such a manner that his arrest would be a natural consequence—unless it were considered more important to keep him within sight and discover his object or destination.

The doubt made it the more necessary to be certain that he was unpursued, or that he had succeeded in evading the chase.

He left the railway at last at North Lambeth, and walked crookedly through streets that were dark and crowded, till he came to the Elephant and Castle station, and took the railway again.

Then, altering his manner of procedure, he went directly and without hesitation to Charing Cross, and took a ticket for Tonbridge. He felt confident that, if he had been trailed at all, he had shaken off the pursuit, but he could not tell what watchfulness for such as he there might be at the great terminal stations. He supposed, rightly enough, that his description had been widely circulated, and that the police would have instructions either to arrest or trail him if he should appear to be leaving London. Charing Cross station appeared to him to be his greatest remaining danger. But he knew that it is the man who loiters or hesitates who attracts the attention of others. The number of those who leave Charing Cross every evening for suburban destinations is very large. The available detective force cannot be sufficient to inspect them all.

He got out at Orpington station and walked straight into a waiting-room. Were he to be noticed or questioned, he had decided to say that he had left the train because he felt unwell, and was proposing to proceed by the next. There could be no cause for suspicion in that. Twenty minutes later he walked out of the empty station un-challenged and unobserved. If he had been stopped, he would have had ready that same tale of illness, with some necessary modification. His ticket was sufficient justification. It is no crime to leave a train before it reaches the station to which you have booked.

As it was, he did not give up his Tonbridge ticket at all, nor had one been issued to Orpington. He walked in a quiet way through the lighted roads until he was clear of the town, and assured that he was not followed, when his pace quickened to the anticipation of the expected meeting.

Delia, who had previously showed no lack of contrivance when she was not too frightened to think, had enclosed a rough sketch of the whole way from Orpington station to the back of Cheshurst Hall, and though Edward had been sufficiently prudent not to risk such an evidence being found upon him, he had memorized it in a mind trained by his profession to accuracy of detail, and supplemented that memory with pencilled hieroglyph in his pocket-book which could mean nothing to any except himself. Confident in his ability to find the way to his destination without delay or inquiry, and with the joy of the expected meeting only shadowed by uncertainty as to what would follow, Edward Wilson went rapidly along the darkness of the up-hill road.

CHAPTER THIRTY-TWO

IT WAS A dark, still night. Inspector Cleveland would have preferred a moon. He would have preferred a wind. Even rain would not have been unwelcome, for he cared much less for his own comfort than for the success of his enterprise.

With more than a burglar's caution, after pushing his motorcycle through a field-gate, and leaving it behind a hedge at the lane side, he approached the dark rear of the silent house.

It showed no light, but he had not expected that. Even had it been legitimately occupied, it might have been in darkness at that hour. He had the advantage of some previous acquaintance with the premises, and only the caution of silence, and the desire to keep in the darker shadows, delayed his approach to the window of the butler's pantry, which he had in mind as the most vulnerable point of attack.

He did not move with the burglar's dread of rousing those who might prove to be of an active hostility. He had no fear of an alarm being given which would put the forces of law upon his track. But he was in pursuit of one whom he was determined to capture, who might be alert, and ready for flight at any threatening sound, and might be very difficult to follow in the darkness.

He showed his lantern for the first time as he left the grass edging along which he had approached, and crossed the gravel path on noiseless, rubber soled feet, to reach the narrow flower-bed beneath the pantry window.

He had brought a small bag of tools such as any burglar might envy, and expected little difficulty in shooting back the window bolt, after it had been oiled to silence, or in taking out a pane of glass if it should be necessary for him to insert a hand for the purpose; but, to his surprise, the bolt was unfastened, and the window was even slightly open—not more than half an inch, but yet sufficiently to make it easy to insert his fingers beneath it and push it noiselessly upward.

He was inside in a moment, and his light, flashing swiftly round, sought for evidences of human occupation, and found nothing until he went on to a housemaid's pantry, the window of which was opaque in its lower panes, so that it would yield nothing to the casual glance of a passing gardener. Here, beside the sink, he observed, with a smile of satisfaction, the evidences of a recent meal.

He looked at it with some attention. One cup and saucer and plate. Crumbs of cheese and bread, and fragments of lettuce too fresh to have been shop-bought. Tea-leaves in the cup. A tea-pot also, showing, when he lifted the lid, that three or four spoons full of tea had been used. The china was of good quality, probably chosen from the best that the house held. Almost certainly a woman's meal. Inspector Cleveland felt that he was very near to success. Silently, he left the pantry, and commenced a systematic inspection of the lower rooms.

He had hesitated as to whether he should not secure the window through which he had entered, or the door of the pantry, to frustrate any attempt to leave the house by that way, but he had to consider the possibility that Delia might have left already, on some expedition that the darkness covered. She might be absent now. To close her entrance might be to warn her of the danger within. Even now, if she were out, she might have seen the moving flicker of the lantern, and be already in panic flight down the lane. That was a small chance, but with success so near he could not be content that there should be risk of failure, however small.

He went swiftly and silently from room to room, his light searching every corner where a bed might be, or a figure crouch. He moved as noiselessly as a burglar, though with an opposite motive. He wished to avoid rousing the sleeper, to ensure her capture, not his own escape. He did not expect that she would be on the ground floor. A bedroom was more probable. It was not only that the comfort of the beds would be on the upper floor. He was aware of the primitive instinct which is in many men and most women, causing them to prefer to sleep upstairs, as in the security of a high tree. It is almost as general and as strong as is that primeval instinct of later growth which causes them to put a bed at a wall's side, as though they would sleep with a guarded back in a cave's recess. A woman may arrange the furniture of her bedroom a dozen ways, and be discontent with all, but it will never cross her mind that the bed might stand in the centre of the room. Without understanding the source of her own feeling, she will regard it as an impossible thing.

He had little doubt that he would find Delia on the upper floor, for such instincts would be abnormally active in one isolated as she now was, and hunted as she knew herself to be, but he would leave nothing to chance. To go upstairs while she might possibly be standing somewhere in the darkness below him, waiting to slip from the house, was a risk that he would not take.

If she were not below, he had little doubt that he would find her above: if she were not there, he would close his lantern-and remain alert and silent until she should return to the house and walk into his arms. His mind reverting to the possibility that she might be out, he considered that, in that event, the sooner his lantern should be closed, the safer it would be. But, apart from that contingency, he was not conscious of any need for haste. He supposed that the Starrs were sleeping peacefully in Worthing, and Mr. E. B. Wilson in Mrs. Corbett's apartments.... Having exhausted the possibilities of the lower rooms, he went upstairs.

CHAPTER THIRTY-THREE

HAVING GAINED THE landing, Inspector Cleveland commenced a systematic examination of the bedrooms. Their doors were all closed, and must be opened with silent caution, but, being entered, he found them to be empty, one after another, till he came to the fourth, which was locked.

Up to this point he had been able to move quietly, but not in absolute silence. Cora's comfort-loving disposition had covered the floors with carpets of unusual thickness, and his rubber soles gave no sound. But the house was old. Hinges had whined once or twice and floorboards creaked. But they had aroused no sign of life.

The locked door might mean no more than that the Starrs had secured some of their more valuable possessions within the room to which it gave entrance; but it was more probable that he would find that his search had ended here.

He knocked sharply.

Was there a slight stir in the room? He could not be sure.

Anyway, there was no answer. He knocked again. "Open the door!" he called. "Open in the name of the law…. Miss Russell, you must open the door."

There was no reply. He could hear no further sound. Deliberately, with the skill and knowledge acquired in a life-time spent in the study of criminal devices, he commenced to pick the lock.

He opened it in a few minutes and stepped inside. He switched on the light, and gazed round an empty room.

With a sense of baffled exasperation, he noticed that the bed was neatly made. No one could have done that unheard while he had been working upon the lock. He stepped to it, and turned the bed-clothes back. The sheets were cold and smooth. He saw that it was enormously improbable that Delia should have occupied the room till that hour and that the bed should be still unused. And he had made noise enough by this time to alarm her if she were in any other part of the house. This might be the one room which she had not been allowed to enter: the one room where she could not possibly be. And while he stood within it, she might be slipping along the landing escaping down the stairs. There were still several rooms unexamined. He stepped uncertainly toward the door, and had he regained the landing he would have had a surprise; but even as he moved he noticed evidences of female occupation which convinced him that the room had not been closed up. No, he was at the right place. Besides, when he picked the lock, *the key had been on the inside of the door*. There could be only one explanation of that. He looked in an unlocked wardrobe, large enough to have sheltered half a dozen Delias. He looked under the bed. Finally, he looked in the clothes-closet. It had an electric bulb within it, which glowed as the door opened. Clothes hung from its ceiling. He entered it, pushing them aside. He saw, beneath the hanging of a fur coat, a small pair of bedroom slippers which contained feet. Even as he did so, he heard a click behind him, and the light went out.

He turned quickly in the darkness, thrusting at the door. "Who the devil?" he exclaimed, with an unusual loss of his self-control. The door would not yield to his hand. Feeling along the wall beside it, his hand came to a switch, and the light shone again.

"Miss Russell," he said, in the tone of a man who had his temper under doubtful control, "will you be good enough to tell me how to open this door?"

Miss Russell emerged from the cover of the fur coat. She looked frightened, as she had reason to be, but showed more self-possession than might have been expected. She was fully dressed, for since there had been a possibility that Edward might come to her in the night, she had sacrificed on the altar of a late-remembered propriety by sleeping in the daytime. Her room was prepared for a different visitor than he who had so rudely invaded it. Hence the coldness of the bed which had nearly misled him into withdrawal. She said, in a voice controlled to such firmness as she could command: "Perhaps you will tell me who you are?" But she remembered him as she spoke. The conversation on the sands: the lunch at the Imperial.

"I am Inspector Cleveland, of Scotland Yard. I have a warrant for your arrest for the murder of Isaac Marks. I have to warn you that anything you say may be used in evidence against you.... Will you kindly tell me how to open this door?"

"You turn the handle."

"It appears to require something beyond that."

"It's always quite easy."

She came forward, trying it herself. It would not move in the least. It was a solid, close-fitting door. As she turned the handle and pressed it, she had a well-founded conviction that it was locked. She said: "Someone must have turned the key."

"Was there a key?" It was a natural question, for there was no key-hole on the inside.

"Yes, there was a key in the lock."

Delia had no doubt about that. She had examined that door on the first night that she had been in the house, and if there had been any means of securing it, it would have been used on that occasion—and probably on this also. But was it likely there would be any provision for locking, such a door on the inside?

"I suppose you know who's done this," the Inspector said, angrily. "You're doing no good for yourself. You'd better call to them to let us out."

"I don't know in the least. It must be someone who came in with you."

"No one came in with me. They'd better open it, or there'll be trouble for them before long."

Delia made no answer to this remark. The threat could hardly be meant for her. Besides, though she had spoken with sincerity when she said that she did not know in the least who had turned that key, the words had been followed by a half-fearful half-delightful doubt. Suppose the explanation were that Edward had had her letter? *Suppose Edward were here.*

Getting no reply, the Inspector turned his attention to the door. It did not appear that it would be easy to force. The neat little bag of burglar's tools which he had brought with him might have been useful here, but, unfortunately, he had left them on the dressing-table on the other side of the door.

On the other hand, it did not appear to be so difficult a position that any anxiety need be felt concerning it. The door was certainly stout. It might not be easy to burst it open. It might be true that no one knew that they were in that empty house—except the owner of the hand that had locked them in—and, of course, the Starrs at Worthing knew that Delia might be there.... They could expect no rescue.

Yet the Inspector did not anticipate starvation. He did not doubt that, with sufficient effort, even without his tools, he could break a way out either through door or wall.

But if a little patience, or a sufficient protest, would result in someone unlocking the door, it was a simpler and more dignified method of exit.

There was, of course, the possibility that the one who had locked the door had gone to fetch aid which would be used to rescue Delia from his hands, but he did not think that to be a likely solution. With a well-practised ear, he had recognized the sincerity in her voice when she had disclaimed knowledge of whoever had been there.

Yet that it should have been the act of one who had been her companion in the locked bedroom, and whom his search had overlooked, was obviously the most probable explanation. If the bed had been occupied at all—still more, if it had shown signs of a double use— Or if she had faltered in her denial of any knowledge of whom it was— He hammered hard on the door, shouting to be released. There was no reply. He listened, and could hear no sound. Well, he had the consolation that he had arrested Delia. For the moment, he had no fear that she could escape his hands. He said: "If the fool doesn't come back soon, we shall have to find a way to break out. It'll be an expensive joke for him, if I get my hands on him."

Delia wondered whether he would be more likely to return to let them out if he were aware of the reward which the Inspector's words foreshadowed. She was curiously serene of mind now that the crisis had come. Perhaps she had had so much of solitude that even the company of Inspector Cleveland, on whatever errand, was better than its continuation. Besides, that key turning so opportunely gave her a sense of support: of invisibly surrounding friends. Friends who must have some plan. It would be absurd to lock her up with the Inspector unless they had some further scheme for her rescue. She was one of those girls in whom it is natural to rely on others, and on men more than women. Even a police-officer who was arresting her on a murder charge might be better company than none.

But when she wondered by what friendly hand, and with what object, the key had been turned, a doubt came.

"Mr. Cleveland," she said sweetly, "oh, Cleveland, is it? I think that's a much nicer name—did you fasten the door after you when you came in?"

The Inspector, not usually a slow-witted man, stared for one uncomprehending moment. It sounded mockery of a most inopportune kind. She added: "I don't mean this door, of course. I mean the front one when you came in."

"I didn't come in by the front door. I came by the pantry window."

"Well, did you leave that open?"

The Inspector saw the idea. Where he came in a burglar might have followed. He might have locked them in while he proceeded at leisure to ransack the house. If that were so, how would he appear in the public eye? Rather a fool, at the best. The thought caused him to examine the door again, and the conclusion was not satisfactory. It would be a work of time to break out with the help of the clasp-knife, which was the only tool that he had.

What would be his measure of responsibility for such a burglary? The question reminded him that he had not forced the window. It had been open before. So he said.

Delia, with a doubtful logic, had been considering this last item of information in a happy mind. If whoever had followed the Inspector had come in by the pantry window, it seemed to make it more probable that it was Edward, as she had told him to come by that way. But the Inspector must not think that she had left it open for such a purpose. She answered with a delusive frankness.

"Yes, that's the way I usually go in and out."

The Inspector banged the door and shouted again. There was no sound in reply

He began to think that he might use the time to better advantage if he should engage his prisoner in conversation. If he had got to force his way out in the end, there would be no hurry for half an hour. If the door should be opened, he might have cause to regret that he had made no better use of the interval that had been his. Even if Delia should be rescued by force, something might have been gained, if he should obtain vital information from her in the meantime.

"It's lucky," he said, "that we've got a light. Isn't there anywhere for you to sit down?"

"There's only this hat-box," she said doubtfully, "and it's not very strong.... I think I prefer the floor."

She sat down as she spoke, tucking under her the small feet that had attracted the Inspector's first attention when he had opened the closet door. It occurred to him that anything less like a murderess he had seldom seen. Still, you never know.

With some hesitation, he sat down beside her. There was an informality, almost an intimacy about this position, which he would not willingly have adopted.... There was one Inspector at the Yard who had made a great reputation by an opposite code of conduct. He was renowned for his "fatherly manner", which had gained the confidence of at least two murderers until it cajoled them into confession which had cost their lives at the last. Inspector Cleveland recognized his ability, but there were few men whom he disliked more.

Still, he hadn't got himself locked up here, as Inspector Hitchman might have done. It was not his fault that there was no broad table between himself and his prisoner, as he said:

"Miss Russell, you needn't answer unless you like, but I can't help wondering why you sent us that confession."

"Isn't it the right thing to do when you've shot anybody?"

"It was the motive, not the propriety of the action about which I was less than clear."

"I don't see that I'd done anything wrong.... Cora—Mrs. Starr—thought it was the right thing to do."

"Do you mean Mrs. Starr thought it was right to shoot Marks, or to make the confession?"

"To make the confession, if that's what you call it. She called it the explanation. I expect she'd have meant both."

"I dare say she would, but the law may think differently, and that's what matters to you.... And now do you mind answering the question?"

"I'm not sure what it is."

"Why did you send us that confession?"

"Because I thought you'd better know how I shot him."

"But you were not under suspicion."

Delia was silenced for a moment. Then she said: "I don't see what that's got to do with it."

"No? Most people would. Do you mind telling me what really happened?"

"What I wrote, of course."

"But you might have written rather more. In what way was Marks rude to you?"

There was a second pause at this query.

"He wouldn't let me go."

"Was that all?"

"I didn't say so."

"No. You might have said a good deal more than you did." He added, as Miss Russell made no further response: "Or than you do now.... Miss Russell, I'll tell you frankly that there's one thing in your statement that we don't understand. If Marks was lying on the bed when he was shot—and I'll tell you plainly that he seems to have been, not only from how he was found but from the direction which the bullet took—I'm not trying to trap you, I'm only trying to get the truth, which is often best in the end—if he was lying like that, and you were standing nearer the door, we don't see why you need have shot him at all. We don't see why you shouldn't have walked out, especially when you'd got hold of the gun."

Miss Russell considered this proposition with thoughtful eyes. "You don't think he could have caught me up?"

"I don't know. But if that's how it was, I think you ought to have tried before using the gun."

"Perhaps I should," she answered, with a smile which reduced the rudeness of the actual words, "if I'd had time to ring you up and get some advice."

"You'll need a better answer than that, Miss Russell, if you want a jury to accept your tale. If Marks were lying back on the bed—"

"I didn't say that he was."

"I suppose you'll tell me next that you pushed him back first, and shot him afterwards." It was the suggestion of how the tragedy had occurred which Inspector Withers had first imagined, and Mr. Wilson had separately asserted to be the actual course of events. Looking at Delia's slender form, and remembering the gross bulk of the murdered man, it became an absurdity if it had been her hand which had fired the shot.

She did not answer directly. She said: "I've told you I didn't know that it would go off."

"And that is the one point where you are right."

"Right about what?"

"That it wouldn't go off."

"Wouldn't go off? But it did."

"Not by mistake."

"You mean you're going to say that I shot him on purpose when there was no need that I should?"

For the first time there was fear in the girl's voice—unmistakable fear.

"I'm not saying anything. You've made a statement which can't be true, and I'm showing you where you stand."

"You must see it couldn't have been like that. I shouldn't have had any reason to do it, even if I knew how."

"That doesn't follow. You might have had any of a dozen, though not the one that you say.... How did you know that his name was Marks?"

She opened her lips to speak, hesitated, and stopped. After a pause: "It's no use saying anything, if you don't believe what I say."

"I should be more likely to believe you if you told me the truth."

Miss Russell did not dispute this, but the assurance did not rouse her to any further confession. She said: "I wonder how long we're going to sit here before somebody comes."

But, for the moment, the Inspector had lost interest in that speculation. He had gained little beyond a conviction that the key to the enigma was in the brain of the girl beside him. He had always thought that. Now, however cleverly she might fence, he felt that he was not wasting his time. He tried the effect of surprise.

"You see, Miss Russell, we happen to know that your tale cannot be true because the real murderer has confessed."

He watched her keenly as he said this, for she could scarcely be other than surprised and incredulous if it were really her own work; or alarmed if it had been that of a lover whom she had tried to shield. If, however, it were the work of she knew not whom, and the two confessions (as he was half-inclined to believe) were no more than the efforts of two more or less innocent persons, who were conscious that they had come under suspicion, to protect each other, her reactions would be of a different kind. There was no doubt of the effect of this statement.

She might control her eyes, as she did, but she could not control her blood. She went white to the lips. "I don't believe it," she said at last, "you're just making it up."

"Oh, no, Miss Russell," he said confidently. "You believe me quite well, and that's why you're so upset."

He saw that her hardly controlled emotion made it probable—indeed, almost certain—that Edward Wilson's confession was substantially true. After all, it was the most likely thing, though there might be a good deal more to come out.

"I'm not upset," she said stubbornly, "I'm only startled that someone should say they've done something that I know I've done myself."

"That's what we've got to find out. At present I'm inclined to think that Mr. Wilson's confess—"

"*Mr. Wilson's!* Why, what nonsense! He wasn't there."

"But he has admitted that he was. He says he heard you cry out and rushed in, and that's how the trouble began... Miss Russell, if that's really what happened, you might find it better to tell the truth—better for him as well as for yourself."

"But it isn't true, I tell you! It isn't true! Edward never came there at all.... He's just saying it to get me out of a mess. You ought to have guessed that from the first."

The Inspector listened and half-believed. I here was sincerity in her voice, or she was an even better actress at such extremity than most women are. Yet, if her lover were as innocent as she said—if he had never been there at all—why had she gone so white when she had been told that the murderer had confessed.

"Miss Russell," he said, "if Mr. Wilson is really innocent, there's one way of getting him off, and that is to tell the truth, which you must excuse me saying that I'm quite sure that you haven't done yet."

She made no answer to that, getting up from the ground as though in an uncontrollable agitation of uncertainty, and then sitting again, as she realized that there was no space there in which physical exercise could relieve her mind. "I wish I knew," she muttered restlessly to herself. "I do wish I knew!"

Then it seemed that a thought struck her, for she turned to the Inspector with the abrupt question: "Didn't you say you were arresting me for the murder of Mr. Marks?"

The Inspector admitted that he had that duty to perform.

"Then you can't be arresting Edward, unless you're going to say he's been murdered twice."

The Inspector was reduced to silence for a few seconds by the invincible quality of this example of feminine logic; then he said weakly: "It isn't quite as simple as that. There might be cases where—"

Miss Russell interrupted him unceremoniously.

"Listen! I believe they're coming to get us out."

CHAPTER THIRTY-FOUR

SOMEWHAT LATER, AND more slowly than the Inspector, for no map can give instructions to equal the advantage of a previous acquaintance with premises so invaded, Edward Wilson located the gate at the back of the grounds of Cheshurst Hall, and found his way through the gardens and along the dark rear of the house till he came to the further side, and the rising wall of the rock garden was on his right, and the window of the butler's pantry on his left hand.

He had no doubt that he had found the right entrance, nor that he was an expected visitor, for it was not merely unbolted, it had been pushed up. He had nothing to do but to get a leg over the sill, and squeeze through the opening as best he could. It was not exactly easy, for he was a larger man than the Inspector, and the window was both narrow and low. There was one uncomfortable moment when he felt that he was stuck fast, being neither out nor in, but a final struggle landed him on the right side, with a sound of tearing cloth which he did not pause to investigate.

It gave him a queer feeling, entering thus by night to a house where he certainly had no right to be. He had no fear of any who might be within it, but he saw that if he should attract the attention of a patrolling constable, he would be unable to give a satisfactory account of his presence, and the fact of his being arrested there would betray Delia's hiding-place. Probably it would lead to an examination of the premises and her immediate discovery. But he felt confident that he had entered without being observed. He had met no one in all the length of the up-hill winding lane. Now that he was in the house he might feel almost secure. He made his way through passage and hall, with an occasional flash of his torchlight, to the foot of the softly carpeted stairs. He had no occasion for extreme silence now, when he knew himself to be an expected and welcome visitor, but an instinct of caution caused him to move noiselessly through the dark house which he had entered by a robber's way; and as he went up the stairs his heart beat uncontrollably at the thought of the meeting which he supposed to be so closely before him.... Then he heard a sound on the landing in the direction in which he had been told to turn. It was not exactly a furtive sound, but it did not occur to him that it was one which Delia would be likely to be making at that hour of the night. It was, in fact, the sound of Inspector Cleveland picking the lock of her bedroom door.

Very cautiously, blessing in his heart the soft thickness of Cora's carpets, he turned the corner at the stair-head, and observed the crouching form of the Inspector. He had set his lantern on the floor so that its light fell upon the lock which he was manipulating. He turned his head somewhat as he selected a tool from his bag, and Edward recognized the officer who had invited him to his first interview at Scotland Yard. It was not difficult to guess what he was doing at that door.

Inspector Cleveland would never know how near he was at that moment to feeling two hands on his coat collar, and being flung down the stairs by the sudden onslaught of a stronger man. But Edward thought again, and he stood still where he was.

Had he been the owner of the house, he might have justified himself for assuming that he saw a burglar in that crouching form. But his own position was too ambiguous for such an assertion. He had to consider whether any demonstration on Delia's behalf, even any revelation of his presence, might not do her more harm than good.

If her presence here were known, and her arrest inevitable, he might do her the best service in his power by remaining unseen and returning to London without it being known that he had left his lodgings.

Thinking first—indeed, only—of her, he restrained the impetuosity of his desire to effect her immediate rescue. Yet he did not—he could not have easily brought himself to withdraw. He recognized something peculiar in the Inspector's method. Why had he not come openly, with any assistance that might seem desirable, to surround the house and effect a daylight arrest? If he were alone, might there not even yet be an opportunity to remove Delia from him, either by force or guile? And yet what would it avail? Could the matter be fought on such lines? Still hesitating, he watched. When the door opened and the Inspector entered, he drew more closely to it. He expected to hear Delia's voice raised in alarm or protest. That he could have overcome the temptation to go to her rescue in such an event may be unlikely enough, but he was not tested in that way. The Inspector entered the room, and silence followed. Edward came closely to the half-open door. He saw the Inspector turn down a bed which had not been occupied since it was made. He saw the annoyance of disappointment upon his face. Evidently he had drawn a blank. Delia must have had warning and fled. She might be far away now or she might be lurking in some other part of the empty house.

He saw the Inspector look under the bed. He heard him search vainly in a wardrobe he could not see. He saw him go to the closet which was in the wall at the right. As the Inspector opened the door toward his unsuspected observer, Edward saw the key in the lock. It was about three yards from his hand. The temptation was irresistible. He stepped forward, closed the door on the Inspector's back and turned the key. He went out of the room, confident that he had placed him out of action at least long enough to enable him to seek Delia in other parts of the house, or to escape if she were not there.

CHAPTER THIRTY-FIVE

KINGSLEY SAID: "WE'D better not leave the car in the lane." Cora agreed about that. They did not aim only at removing Delia, who would presumably have to be roused from sleep. They intended to remove all evidences that she had ever been in the house. If they could do that, and it should subsequently be searched, they argued that the theft of her letter would be an actual advantage to their plans, for the police, having been foiled in applying the right interpretation to it, would mislead themselves in fresh ingenuities of solution, and while they investigated their own imaginations, Delia might be conveyed to the safe seclusion of a Paris *pension*, leaving no trace of her flight.

The theory was sound enough, if its premises were of an equal solidity, which they soon had reason to doubt. Kingsley got out, and opened a field gate in the lane. Cora, with her lights full on, steered through a gap that gave few inches of clearance into a rough field.

"Reckon you'd better turn her now," Kingsley said, reasonably. "We don't know how much time we shall have to spare when we go."

The lights moved over the field as the car came round. They moved along the hedge at the gate side. They paused a moment, as though fascinated, upon the spectacle of a motorcycle beside the hedge. They moved on, and returned.

"Kingsley, look at that.... Isn't it rather like Inspector Cleveland's bike?"

"It isn't like it, it's his."

Cora had left the car by this time, and they were inspecting it together.

"Considering that he was in Worthing this afternoon—"

"Yes, it does look rather that way."

"He may be only suspicious, and having a look round."

"He'd hardly try to break in during the night."

"I wouldn't bet much on that. Anyway, we can't call this a healthy place for leaving the car."

"It'll be all right if we back it a bit up the field."

"The question is whether we ought to stay at all."

"If he's seen the lights, he may be on his way here now."

"Then the sooner they're out, the better."

Cora agreed about that. She switched them out, and as their eyes got used to the darkness, she got into the car and backed it some distance up the field, into an oak-tree's shadow.

"It ought to be all right there. He isn't likely to search the field to see whether it contains a stray car."

"Not unless he sees the marks of the tyres."

"It wouldn't be likely, even then. There'd be more risk that we'd meet him on the road."

"We may do that if we're on foot."

"But we can make ourselves small rather more easily, if we hear him coming along."

"The real question is what we mean to do now."

"We've got to go on trying," Cora said obstinately. "We've got to get her out, if we can. If he doesn't find her, it doesn't matter so much if he sees us."

"Nor if he does," Kingsley observed, with an equal logic. "If he finds her there, he'll know who gave her the address, whether we're about or not."

"So it's still the only chance to be first," Cora said cheerfully. "We'd better get a move on, instead of standing here, waiting for him to come back."

That being too obvious for argument, Kingsley made no reply. They walked briskly, listening for the sound of approaching feet. But the lane was silent and vacant, as they came to the back entrance of Cheshurst Hall.

"Got a key for this gate, or only for the house?" Cora queried.

"I've got a key, but I'd rather we'd gone in at the front door, as the owners should."

"We can't do that except through the gardens, unless we go about half-a-mile round the road."

Kingsley admitted that by the act of unlocking the gate. But he could not bring himself to walk through his own grounds with a trespasser's furtive caution. He went boldly round to the front door, which he unlocked and entered. As he did so he thought—he was almost certain—that a man's form disappeared through the open dining-room door. He did not doubt that it was Inspector Cleveland,

162

but whoever it might be, it was too late to draw back. As he had said before, they had a right to enter their own house when they would. Inspector Cleveland's right to be there could only be justified, if at all, by Delia's arrest; and whatever the position might be, they would not improve it by allowing him to see them in flight down their own drive.

Kingsley's knowledge of English law was not extensive, but it had become somewhat detailed in connection with certain situations which are liable to arise between the police and the criminals they pursue. Now he said, with a confidence partly born of that knowledge, and partly of his own disposition: "If that's the Inspector, we'd better give him a chance to say what he's doing here, before he gets out through the window."

Cora, responding to his mood, switched on the hall lights. They approached the dining-room, the door of which stood half-open, together. Kingsley pushed it wider. He called out: "Whoever's skulking in there, he'd better come out."

There was no answer. Cora's hand on the switch flooded the room with light. It did not (as we know) reveal the form of Inspector Cleveland, who was safely locked away on the floor above, but that of a man about half as large again, who stood beside the central table, looking as though he was not sure what he had better do next. After a moment of mutual silence, he said: "I wonder whether you are Mr. and Mrs. Starr?"

"And I'm quite sure you are Mr. Wilson," Cora responded with cordiality. "Kingsley, you'd better close the front door; and if Inspector Cleveland calls we can let him ring twice."

"He won't do that. He's upstairs."

"*Upstairs?* Then where's Delia?"

"That's what I was trying to find out. I've searched the house rather thoroughly, but I think she's gone. I've locked the Inspector in a bedroom cupboard."

"Then there's no hurry about him," Cora said cheerfully. "You'd better tell us the tale."

Mr. Wilson did so; but, in fact, apart from the location of the Inspector and the absence of Delia, he had not much to tell.

When he had finished, Cora took control of the situation.

"We can't leave the Inspector there," she said with decision, "whatever trouble he was trying to make. We've got to be sure first that Delia isn't about, and clear away any signs that she ever was, and Mr. Wilson's got to clear too, and then we've got to face letting him out."

CHAPTER THIRTY-SIX

"I DON'T SEE that we need explain anything," Cora contended. "We're quite sure Delia isn't anywhere about, and Inspector Cleveland can't have found her, or he wouldn't have been searching an empty room.... We've told him before that we won't discuss that murder again, and it's for him to tell us what he was doing among my clothes. We'll just go into the room, and if he kicks up a noise, as he's sure to do when he hears us, we'll let him out and see what he's got to say.... We'd better give Mr. Wilson a few minutes to get off and then go upstairs."

This was about twenty minutes after Edward had been discovered by the side of the dining-room table. They had made a thorough examination of the lower parts of the house, the bedrooms of which he had explored before they arrived. It seemed certain that Delia had taken alarm, or become intolerably weary of her monotonous solitude, and left the house. Most probably (they decided) she had gone to London, seeking Edward there while he sought her here. The possibility reconciled him to returning, which he might otherwise have been more reluctant to do. If he went back at all, it was evidently desirable to do so before his absence should be discovered. Thinking it imperative to avoid Orpington station, in view of the probability of inquiries there following the Inspector's release, he proposed to walk toward London until he should be overtaken by some vehicle which would give him a lift in that direction, either for money, or good-will.

"Can you ride a bike?" Kingsley inquired.

Edward said that he thought he could. A motor-bike? Yes, any kind.

"Then, you'd better go out the back way—the way you came—and turn in at the first field gate on the left as you go down the lane, and look under the hedge.

Edward looked pleased at the opportunity which these directions indicated, and then doubtful. "I don't want to take anything that you might be needing—and I don't quite see how I'm to return it to you.... Not in a safe way. The less I appear to be in touch with this place, the better it might be."

"It isn't exactly a bicycle that you need to return to us," Cora interposed. "It's just one that happens to have been left in a field where we put our car. If you left it somewhere where you could get an early morning tram, or perhaps a train, I'm not sure that it wouldn't be the best way.... And it might be best to go a few miles the wrong way first, as though you weren't going to wherever you are."

Mr. Wilson could take a hint. His life, up to this night (apart from his own confession of homicide) had been singularly free from crime, but he felt that the position was not one which should be dominated by the scruples of an unenterprising conventionality. A few moments later the offensive noises by which a motorcycle commonly declares its presence could be heard in the lane, receding rapidly in the direction of the London road.

Having disposed of Mr. Wilson's presence, and of various evidences of recent occupation which they felt that it would be inexpedient for the Inspector to see, Kingsley and Cora went upstairs together to their own room, as a bride and bridegroom on entering their home at a late hour may reasonably be expected to do. For a few moments there came no sound from the closet, within which the Inspector waited in a natural anticipation that those whom he could hear to be entering the room were the same who had previously locked him in, and that the purpose of their return must be to release him now. But he heard them moving about the room and the key did not turn. He recognized Cora's voice with no more surprise than was naturally occasioned by the fact that he had believed her to have been in bed at the Beach Hotel about fifty miles away. She was, in fact, somewhat embarrassed by the Inspector's silence. Had Mr. Wilson made a mistake? It seemed incredible that the Inspector had settled down in that closet without protest for the night. Or had Mr. Wilson been guilty of under-statement? Had he left them with another murdered man on their hands, and had they once again assisted the criminal to escape to their own undoing? Cora had prepared her mind for the moment when the Inspector should walk out. She had thought of several things which it would be appropriate to say. But she had not rehearsed a preceding interval, embarrassed by the fact that it could not be discussed without the probability of being overheard. It was evident that they must not walk to the closet and open it, as though expecting to find anyone there. With a duplicity which it is easier to record than defend, she talked to Kingsley about hot-water bottles which the bathroom might be expected to supply.

We ought," she said in a clear voice, "to have let 'Kate know we were coming, so that she could have been in, and had the room ready." She considered the advisability of asking Kingsley to see if her dressing-gown were in the clothes closet.

Kingsley, with such freshness of excitement in his voice as he could contrive, exclaimed at the evidences that the door had been forced, concerning which they had failed to demonstrate properly as they had entered the room. Cora called out sharply: Kingsley, what-ever's this?" as she discovered the neat little case of burgling in-struments which the Inspector had left on the dressing-table.

When the Inspector decided that it had become time to bang on the door, and shout for it to be opened, Cora felt a pleasant relief in the knowledge that he was alive, and an entire adequacy to deal with the situation. She said: "Yes, Kingsley, it's Inspector Cleveland. I know his voice. You'd better open the door," with a cheerful antici-pation that she was about to give him an uncomfortable ten minutes, which might be followed by another when he went to look for his bicycle. But she became aware of the inappropriateness of her men-tal preparations when, showing no sign of embarrassment, he walked out of the closet, and Delia Russell emerged behind him.

CHAPTER THIRTY-SEVEN

THE UNEXPECTED APPARITION having reduced Cora to an unusual silence, Kingsley was the first to open the conversation.

"Perhaps you won't mind telling us," he inquired, "what you were doing in there?"

Delia said: "Somebody locked us in."

"I should say you're the best one to answer that question," the Inspector added, without cordiality. But he felt no very active resentment. The time in the closet had not been wasted, and he was on the right side of the door once again. Besides, he had won the game. The victor can afford to be generous.

Cora had had time to recover her breath. "We didn't lock you in," she said, "if you mean that. We should have too much sense. Besides, we've only just come. All we've done is to let you out. We're always helping you one way or another, and getting no thanks at all."

"You mean you've just come together?" the Inspector queried.

"Yes. We haven't been upstairs till five minutes ago. How long have you been shut up in there?"

It cannot be said that Cora had always pursued the path of an absolute candour through the difficult circumstances that had surrounded her since her first meeting with Mr. Kingsley Starr, but the fact remained that she had been a naturally truthful girl, and the Inspector recognized the note of sincerity in her voice. He did not feel any confidence that she always told him the truth, but there were times when he felt sure, as he did now. But if it were not the Starrs who had locked him in, who could it be?

He asked: "How did you get in?"

"Through the front door, of course," Kingsley answered, with an inward satisfaction that he had selected that method of approach. "I suppose Miss Russell let you in the same way?"

"No. I came in through the pantry window."

There was no reason to conceal the fact now that his entry had been justified by the arrest he had made.

"And left it open behind you, more likely than not?"

The Inspector could not deny that. His official caution warned him that there was a possibility of trouble here, if he had been the means of giving entrance to those of less honest intentions. Still, all the facts being as they were—

Kingsley said: "It seems to be a case for counting the spoons."

"Never mind the spoons," Cora interrupted, with a sound instinct that the burglar theme had served a better purpose than would result if they should develop it further. "The question is what you're going to do now."

"There is no question about that," the Inspector answered. "Miss Russell must come with me."

"Without any breakfast?"

"It's scarcely time for—"

"No, we all ought to be in bed."

"But as none of us is—"

"I was just seeing about the hot-water bottles. You couldn't expect us to settle off with that noise the other side of the door."

The Inspector had sufficient wisdom not to continue the argument. He said: "I don't think you need trouble about them. I expect Miss Russell's kept the bed aired." And then to Delia: "You'd better get your things together, and come with me."

Cora exclaimed: "You're not going to walk through the rain!" Three of them became aware for the first time that the wind was rising and rain beat on the window.

Inspector Cleveland did not reply. He turned to Delia: "Miss Russell, I'm sure you don't wish to give any needless trouble. Are you willing to ride pillion? It need only be into Orpington. We can take the train from there. We can wait till this shower's over, if you like, if it isn't too long."

"Kingsley," Cora said, as Delia, who had never ridden pillion on a motorcycle before, and did not much like the idea, hesitated in her reply, "you saw where Inspector Cleveland had left his bike. You'd better go and see that he doesn't take our car by mistake."

"If you could lend me the car—" the Inspector began.

"I'm afraid we couldn't. Not if it's to take Delia out on a night like this. It's not a right thing to do. You forget it's an open car."

The Inspector was annoyed into the retort that they seemed to have forgotten it themselves when they left it in an open field.

Cora was unperturbed by the inconsistency of this proceeding with the bold approach through the front door. She said, perhaps if he hadn't put his bike there— It was like the first sheep. She added, returning to her own point, that they should want the car for themselves. If he was going to take Delia to London, they'd need to come too, to see that things didn't happen a silly way.

"I think, Mrs. Starr," the Inspector answered, with a rather formal seriousness, "I can't give you better advice than to keep out of this matter, if we are still able to let you. You've done Miss Russell no good by hiding her here, and you've placed yourself in a more perilous position than you appear able to realize.... You won't help Miss Russell by any further interference, and you might do her a great deal of harm. If your brother were here, I'm sure...."

"Of course, if Ted were here, things would be altogether different. You don't need to tell me that," she added, audaciously throwing an item of most misleading truth into the discussion. "I've written to him to come back just as soon as he can."

Once again the Inspector had the wisdom to leave her with the last word. He hesitated a moment, and then, with the soundness of judgment which had brought him to his present position and reputation, he decided that there would be no need to take Delia out in the rain, with a wrist manacled to his own, while he fetched his bicycle.

"Miss Russell," he said, "if you will give me your word not to leave the house while I am away—you perhaps hardly realize how foolish a thing it would be to attempt to do, now that I know where you are—if you will give me your word, I will leave you here while I bring the bike to the front door, and we can get off by the main road.... That is, I will do it in that way if Mr. Starr has left the gate unlocked or will give me the key."

Kingsley said that the gate had been left unlocked.

Cora said that of course Delia wouldn't do anything silly. She'd be having a meal.

The Inspector said that if she didn't think him rude, he would prefer to have Miss Russell's word rather than hers.

Delia said definitely that she would await his return. She would help Cora get some breakfast while he was away, though she was afraid there wasn't much in the house. The idea was not unwelcome to the Inspector. In fact, they were all feeling the need of food which becomes urgent when the hours of sleep are replaced by a prolonged and unnatural activity. Only Delia, who had occupied the bed during the daylight hours, was unconscious of such fatigue.

"You needn't worry if there's not much in the house," Cora said, "as long as you've got some tea. There's lots of food in the car. Perhaps" (to Inspector Cleveland) "you won't mind bringing it up."

The Inspector was quite willing to do that. He went out in the confident expectation that he would find his bicycle where he had left it behind the hedge. The simple straightforwardness of this narrative has prepared the reader's mind for the fact that it was not there.

CHAPTER THIRTY-EIGHT

INSPECTOR CLEVELAND'S LIGHT shone upon the mark of a bicycle tyre which had been going out of the gate, and turning down the lane towards Orpington. It was quite fresh. The Inspector was an expert in the reading of such evidences. He was sure that the rain had commenced to fall before it had come through that gate.

Considering the circumstances, he had little doubt that the hand which had stolen his bicycle was the same that had locked him in, making the theft safe. He had an inspiration. "It's Wilson, more like than not." He must have come down to see Delia, been lurking in the lane, seen him hide the bicycle, followed him into the house, and stolen the opportunity of locking him in without knowing that Delia was there. So he guessed, being nearly right. But of the extent of the Starrs' complicity he could not be sure. Had Wilson decided that Delia was not in the house, and left him there to starve if he should be unable to break out? His opinion of the character of Edward Burdett Wilson descended sharply. That he was the murderer of Isaac Marks appeared much more probable than it had done previously.

Well, there would be time to catch him before he could get back to his rooms. The Inspector walked rapidly through the rain to the Police Station at Little Hempstill.

He roused a sleepy officer there, and learnt that he was unable to get about owing to an attack of rheumatism. The other half of the establishment was patrolling the lanes, and would be back at 6.45 a.m. But the telephone was available, and a suitable communication to Orpington Station, gave the Inspector a comforting conviction that it would be difficult for that bicycle to gain the vicinity of Mr. Wilson's lodgings, even if it could enter London at all, without coming under the notice of the efficient police service of the Metropolis.

As to that, it may be said at once that Mr. Wilson got safely home. The bicycle was found abandoned in the neighbourhood of Croydon, and his immunity from capture may be attributed to the fact that he neither took the direct road to London, nor ventured to

171

approach his home on the borrowed bicycle. We may also observe that the interval between the time when the Inspector telephoned to Orpington, and that at which the bicycle was deposited in a Croydon alley, was quite short.

Mr. Wilson returned home by the garden route which he had used when he left. The risk of observation was greater in the early morning hours, but audacity won, as it often will. The officer who had been hurriedly sent to watch the only legitimate approach to his lodgings, when the news of his suspected absence had reached the Yard, reported that no one entered or left, until Mr. Wilson emerged at his usual hour. He would doubtless have gone on his usual routine to the offices of the Bloomfield Archaeological Society, had he not been met, at the end of his own road, by another officer, who requested him to get into a taxi with him, and instructed the driver to convey them to New Scotland Yard.

Having done what he could to secure the apprehension of the author of that impudent borrowing, Inspector Cleveland's thoughts returned to the prisoner whom he had left in a temporary liberty, regarding which his mind was not entirely at ease. He had a vision of Mr. Wilson riding up to the front door of Cheshurst Hall on a borrowed bike, while he searched the rain-beaten field, and going off triumphantly with Delia on the seat behind him. He had a sound opinion that she would find it more possible to ride if that position if she were clinging to Edward Wilson's waist. But he remembered also that he had promised to bring some parcels from the Starr's car. He was a man of his word, and one who was not easily flurried. If he had made a mistake in trusting Delia, it was too late to regret it, and he was not going back with a tale that he had forgotten his promise.

He went back to the car and collected three rain-soaked parcels. He returned through the garden gate, being the nearest way from the field, but he would probably have gone round to the front door had not the wet parcels developed a disconcerting tendency to burst apart, and a tin of pineapple escaped to bounce beyond recovery down the darkness of the sloping path. In this difficulty he made for the nearest entrance, being the pantry window.

In his absence a meal had been laid—or rather the preparations for it—on the dining-room table. There was everything there except the food, of which Delia had only been able to produce a piece of rather stale bread, a small quantity of butter, and half a cucumber. But the tea had been made.

A fire had also been lighted, for it was chilly in the unaired room. The three sat round it, wondering how long it would be before the Inspector would ring the front door-bell; and as they sat they talked.

The dining-room door stood partly open, and the Inspector, approaching with loaded arms, made no sound with his rubber soles on the thickly carpeted hall. He stopped, hearing Delia's voice.

"Of course, Edward only said he did it because he thought it was the only way to get me out of the mess. It couldn't have been him, because—"

"It couldn't have been him, because it was you," Kingsley's voice interrupted, in a tone which was not free from a suggestion of sarcasm. He appeared to share the Inspector's feeling that Delia was handing out the truth in very limited quantities.

"It isn't only because of that," Delia answered. "He never came there at all. He didn't even know the address. I couldn't have told him, if I'd wanted to do such a silly thing, which I shouldn't, because I should have known there'd be a row if Edward ever met Mr. Marks, even without the trouble there was. He hated to hear his name. But I couldn't have told him the address. I didn't know it myself."

"Delia," Cora interrupted, "don't you think we'd better tell Kingsley what really happened?"

"I don't mind, if you think it's safe, so long as the police don't get any idea."

"You needn't worry about them," Cora said confidently. "They haven't got the foggiest yet, and I don't suppose they ever will. They'll keep on worrying their heads as to whether it was Edward or you, and when they've made up their minds about that, and most likely wrong, I don't see that they can do you much harm. They won't get any jury to say you went there to shoot him with no reason at all, and it being with his own gun. They'll say you had to, and quite right and a good thing too."

The Inspector listened to this disparaging opinion of the force of which he was a well-reputed unit, and could afford to smile.

"Well, you can tell Mr. Starr if you like." Delia's voice had none of Cora's cheerful assurance. It sounded rather that of one who had resigned herself to the expectation of trouble. She may not have felt entire confidence in Cora's optimistic prophecy as to the jury's verdict upon the experiment in homicide of which she was self-accused....

"It's rather a long tale," Cora began. "You see, Delia and her brother—" A tin of pressed beef burst from its sodden wrapping, and fell heavily on the mat. The Inspector felt that there was nothing to be done but to walk in.

CHAPTER THIRTY-NINE

THE INSPECTOR ATE a good meal. There had been an occasion when Cora had visited that house for the first time, and had passed too many hours without food for her own liking. It had been one of the consequences of linking her fate to a man who had been brought up on three meals a day, and was not over-particular about them: a man who thought tea to be the name of a beverage rather than a meal.... But she had made up her mind that that incident should not occur twice. On the way home from the show last night she had bought food, not guessing that a substantial portion of it would be for Inspector Cleveland's nourishment.

It was a silent meal, for his presence did not encourage the other three to any fluency of conversation, and during its later portion the taxi which he had ordered from Orpington waited ominously at the door. His own mind was sufficiently occupied with consideration of the words which he had overheard. Curse that bursting parcel, and his own blundering grip! In another moment he would have heard the truth—or, at least (and it might be an important distinction) what Delia had thought best to represent to Cora under that guise, or what Cora thought would be most suitable for her husband's consumption.

But, if Cora were to be believed, he had learnt two things—that he was not yet on the right track: that however much or little truth there might be in either Wilson's or Delia's confessions, he had not yet got a correct idea—"not the foggiest"—of what had occurred on the morning when a bullet had taken about the longest possible route through the body of Isaac Marks; and that Delia had a brother, or had had one at the point at which Cora's narrative had been about to begin.

He was puzzled about that brother. The inquiries about Delia Russell had been almost exhaustive and had not disclosed the existence of such a relative. He thought at once (not being a fool) of that William Trevor Russell who had been a last-moment passenger aboard the *Aquitania*. After all, had he been the actual murderer, and had they let him escape? He congratulated himself upon the thoroughness which had arranged to keep the man under observation. That had been due to Superintendent Withers. He had not only requested the United States police to watch the man through their country, and the Canadian police to continue the observation when he should arrive in Montreal: he had instructed a private inquiry agency to do so also. If Mr. Trevor Russell could evade them both, he would be an exceptionally clever man.

They could not have done more than that, for what evidence had they? Even now they had none. No evidence or motive. None that he was ever on the scene of the murder. Delia had (or had had) a brother. Or (to be exact) Mrs. Starr had said in Delia's presence that she had (or had had) a brother, which Delia had not denied. But even that was going too far, for Delia had had no time for denial before the beef-tin fell.... And a man named Russell had sailed on the *Aquitania*. You couldn't make much of that. Yet the Inspector felt that the game was won, Evidence could always be found, with sufficient patience, when you were once on the right track. The first thing would be to follow up the antecedents of William Trevor Russell more thoroughly than there had yet been time to do. (He did not know that (Superintendent Withers had already done this, with interesting results.) There were the guarantors of his passport, who had given answers that were satisfactory but somewhat vague, when they had been questioned last week.

But first it would be interesting to learn some particulars from Delia herself about this shadowy brother of whom no one knew. He might not have heard much but perhaps he had heard enough....

Cora drew Kingsley out of the room as the meal ended. They had a word apart. Then she came back to Inspector Cleveland:

"Do you mind if you give us a lift in your taxi? I expect our car's about soaked through, leaving it out like that."

Her tone seemed to convey a vague accusation that the Inspector was in some way responsible for the car having been left unsheltered, and that he was under a consequent obligation to give them the accommodation for which they asked.

His common sense rejected this subtlety of implication, but he did not therefore refuse the request. He had been troubled by a doubt as to whether it had not become his duty to detain Cora, if not her husband, in view of what he had overheard, and of the use which had been made of Cheshurst Hall for the hiding of Delia. He found it difficult to decide how far his mind might be deflected by previous friendship. It was in every way convenient that they should themselves elect to accompany him. He decided that they should have the experience of interviewing Superintendent Withers when they got out of the vehicle. He said he should be pleased for them to come.

Cora had no settled plan of campaign when she made this suggestion. She felt a serene confidence that Ted would be waiting in London with George's passport in his pocket; and that she could prevail upon him to take Delia on a visit to Paris, from which she would not return, but she saw substantial difficulties in carrying out this programme while she remained in the custody of the law. Was there a chance that when Superintendent Withers had heard the truth in its naked simplicity (that is, as it had been outlined in Delia's confession) he would recognize the folly of attempting to secure the conviction of one so innocent (and so attractive), and let her go? Was there otherwise a chance that they could obtain bail in such a case? Bail of such moderate amount that Kingsley would consent to lose it in so good a cause? Would they be likely to accept him as surety after his too obvious complicity in her previous retreat? Better than any of these somewhat slender hopes, might not some opportunity arise by taking swift advantage of which Delia might yet regain her freedom, and avoid a trial of the precarious clemencies of the law? It was clear, at least, that to take advantage of such opportunity, they must remain together long as ingenuity could contrive it. That they should go back to London in a single vehicle was a plan at which they were all pleased.

Even for the condition of the open rain-soaked car in the field at the other side of the lane, Cora had no regret. Using the fallacious arguments familiar to a hundred thousand English women of her period, she had already half-persuaded Kingsley that there would be economy, amounting to the actual saving of money, in the purchase of a new car. Should not this incident, if handled with her usual efficiency, give the scale its final pressure in the right direction?

CHAPTER FORTY

INSPECTOR CLEVELAND ENTERED the office of Superintendent Withers feeling that he had done well. He said:

"I've brought the Starrs along, as well as Miss Russell. I'm not sure what course you'll think that we ought to take, but I overheard enough to know that Mrs. Starr can put us on the right track if she likes. I thought you ought to know this if Miss Russell proves difficult, as I think she may."

The Superintendent said he had done quite right. Beyond that, he said he had done well. It had been a clever capture. Another one to add to the long list of successes on which the Inspector's reputation was so securely founded. But he said it in a preoccupied way, as one who had other things on his mind. Conscious of this attitude, and a little rebuffed, the Inspector said: "Shall we have Delia Russell in now? I expect you'll like to question her first?"

"No. We'll have them all in together." The Superintendent smiled at his own thoughts. "But there's no hurry about that. I sent for Mr. Wilson. I thought there'd be no harm in having a word with him first."

"You think we shall get them to tell us the truth better if we get them contradicting each other first?"

"Oh, I don't know. I dare say we should. But I'm not going to ask them to tell us anything. Not at the first. I'm going to tell them for a change. There shouldn't be much difficulty after that.... Cleveland," he added, with a change of voice and expression, "what mugs we've been...! You don't see what I mean? No, I didn't suppose you would, but you soon will.... Just have a look at this."

He held out a snapshot photograph. It looked to be an amateur production taken on a ship's deck. It showed the form and profile of a young man who was slim and dark, and of a rather sinister aspect. It was not precisely a criminal expression, but rather that of one who was accustomed to the hostility of circumstance, and his fellows: who gave no friendship to an unfriendly world. It was an expression with which they were too familiar upon the faces of the photographs with which they dealt.

The Inspector examined it closely, but without recognition. He had a well-trained memory for faces, and he was sure that it was one which he had never seen before. Of course, it must be that of William Trevor Russell. Thinking this, he thought also that he could trace a resemblance to Delia.

"Meaning it's her brother, I suppose," he said. "That rather fits in with what I heard Mrs. Starr say. But it's hardly enough to fix it on him unless we've got a bit more to go on."

"Yes, he's her brother. You'll know more about that in a few hours, even if she doesn't tell us herself, as I think she may. But it isn't there that we've come unstuck. Have a look at this next."

He picked up another photograph from his desk. "I suppose you don't know this either...? No, you wouldn't. You weren't in the case.... That's William Collins, who got sentenced for blackmail, and came out of gaol about a month back."

"That makes it a sure thing?"

"Yes. There's only the work of fixing it on him now, and we're half-way through with that. One or two of our men had been digging up a few useful bits of evidence before this arrived, and it all fits in.... We got this from one of the stewards on the ship. He passed it over to a friend of his on the *Île de France* while they lay in New York harbour last week, and it's got here almost as soon as they've tied up at that end."

"Then the two confessions we've got must be about equally faked?"

"Yes. It seems simple enough. The girl makes it up to give her brother time to get away, and the man does it to clear her."

"Doesn't it fit in almost a bit too well?"

"No. I wouldn't say that. It's all likely enough. But it's no use going over the same tale twice. You'll hear it all when we have them in.... What's that, Simmons? Mr. Wilson arrived? Then show him in here. I'll have a few words with him first, and then you can bring in Delia Russell and Mr. and Mrs. Starr. And you'd better stay to take down. We'll hear what they've all got to say, but they'll listen to me for a bit first.... You'd better seat Wilson over on that side, and put Delia Russell as far apart as you can."

Mr. Wilson entered the room. Not knowing of Delia's arrest, and supposing she had escaped from Cheshurst Hall before the commencement of the Inspector s search, which he had been able to interrupt with the argument of a locked door, he could form no certain anticipation as to the reason of the invitation he had received, or the nature of the interview that was before him. But a man who is self-accused of a violent homicide is scarcely in a position to refuse such a request, and he had, in fact, no desire to do so. His mind was not on his own peril. It was tortured with anxiety for the welfare of the girl he loved. It was insistent in its hunger for information concerning her. To what refuge had she fled? Were the police on her trail? Had they succeeded in arresting her? There was one hope of information, whether bad or good: one place where it might be obtained. Edward Wilson felt no reluctance to keep the appointment which had been thrust upon him. He walked to it with quick steps when he left Victoria station, and arrived before his time.

"Mr. Wilson," the Superintendent began, before the others had been shown into the room, "I have asked you here because Miss Russell was arrested a few hours ago, and because certain information from other sources has come into our hands, which, incidentally, may be held to justify our decision not to act upon the confession which you lodged here a few days ago: a confession to which, I may tell you frankly, I never attached any great importance; and which I am now satisfied is definitely and entirely untrue. I assume with confidence that that confession was put forward in a foolish effort to discredit the one from Delia Russell which we had previously received, and which had been shown to you.

"If you still have Miss Russell's interests at heart, it is possible that you may have an opportunity of doing her a very real service by advising her to tell us the truth, which I am as confident as in your own case that she has not yet done.

"She is at present under arrest on a charge of wilful murder on her own confession. She has given an explanation of her alleged act which is inconsistent with the position in which the body was found, and which might be very difficult to persuade a jury to believe. The seriousness of her position, in view of these circumstances, cannot easily be exaggerated. She will be brought before the magistrate this morning, and the course which we may be prepared to take will depend almost entirely upon whether she is prepared to supply us with a more credible narrative."

"I have always told you she didn't do it," Edward replied, "but you can't expect me to go beyond that unless you tell me the nature of the information you have received."

"That," the Superintendent answered, "is exactly what I intend to do.... Simmons, have the Starrs and Miss Russell brought in."

CHAPTER FORTY-ONE

DELIA ENTERED, ACCOMPANYING the policewoman to whose care and custody she had been transferred on arrival at New Scotland Yard. She made an impulsive forward movement, and an exclamation in which pleasure and apprehension mingled, when she saw that Edward Wilson was at the further side of the room.

The woman's official instinct to restrain her was checked by a word from the Superintendent. "Never mind, Mrs. Murphy. Miss Russell isn't going to jump out of the window." But she had no need for a second step, for Edward was already at her side.

"Oh, Edward, why did you do it? You know you never—"

"I ought to ask you that question first. But we'd better not talk here. I expect there'll be a better chance before long."

"They haven't arrested you too?"

"Not as far as I know. But Superintendent Withers has got something he wants to say. How long have you been here?"

"If you'll be good enough to sit down, Mr. Wilson," the Superintendent interjected. "The Court opens in an hour's time.... Over there, if you please. Mr. and Mrs. Starr are waiting for those seats.... Now, Miss Russell," he went on, when the audience he had collected was settled before him. "I am going to ask you some questions that might have saved a good deal of trouble if you'd answered them last week instead of bolting off as you did, and if you're a wise young woman you'll know the right way to take them.... You're under arrest now, and you're not obliged to answer anything, and it may be used in evidence against you, if you do. You've got to understand that. But if you've made a statement that isn't true, you've got the best opportunity to put it right that you're ever likely to have.

"I've got some questions to ask you, but before I begin them I'm going to do a little talking myself. I'm going to tell you a few things we've found out, and when you've heard them you'll see better where you stand, and how useless it is to try to fob us off with a lying tale.

"Rather more than two years ago we arrested a man named Isaac Marks whom we were particularly glad to get. We had known him for a long while as one of the worst blackmailers in London, but we had been unable to stop his activities. Either his victims declined to prosecute, or he was too cunning to enable us to obtain the legal evidence we required. But on this occasion we felt that we had got him at last. You will observe, Miss Russell, that the police are not always right. Unfortunately, we cannot assist the jury with the record of a man we catch under such circumstances. That can only be disclosed after a conviction has been obtained.

"The man went into the box, and told a plausible tale, and a timid jury gave him the benefit of a doubt which no intelligent man ought to have had. They found him not guilty on the major counts of the indictment.

"Still, we had done something. He was sentenced to a short term of imprisonment, and he had received such a fright that he discontinued the practices by which he had accumulated a substantial fortune, and registered himself as a moneylender in another name.

"But that was not all. Along with him we had arrested a young man who had not been under our observation previously. He had been known in the case as William Collins, and this name he gave, and refused any address, or further evidence of identity. We now know that his proper name was William Trevor Russell, but at that time we failed to discover this. You may observe that the police do not always find out all that they would like to know. But they find out a good deal.

"We had regarded this young man as the tool of Marks, if he were guilty at all, and his arrest was of importance only to complete the case, and with a hope that he would talk when he found himself in our hands. Had he been franker with us, he would probably have ended in the witness-box rather than the dock. Though we are sometimes credited with different motives, I can assure you that it is never our desire to procure the conviction of an innocent man—or woman.

"But this man declined to give us any information. He declined to say anything in his own defence. He declined to go into the witness-box. If, as we were afterwards inclined to think, he had been the unsuspecting tool of the older man, he must by that time have realized how he had been used, and known also that he could not give evidence in his own defence without damning the man who was in the dock beside him; and that, from whatever motive, he declined to do.

182

"But Isaac Marks had no such scruples. If there were any truth in that plausible tale which he told in the witness-box, there could be no doubt that William Collins was guilty. So the jury decided.

"Isaac Marks received a sentence of three months' imprisonment, but as he left the dock, William Collins, still standing there to receive his heavier sentence, uttered a threat in a low voice which was yet audible to everyone in the silent court.

"We knew, and the judge knew, that the principal criminal had not been adequately punished, but there could be nothing said about that.

"The judge, so we subsequently learnt, was not entirely satisfied with the jury's verdict against the younger prisoner. But such a verdict cannot be ignored. He was a man who had refused his address. He had declined to give evidence. He had been convicted of blackmail. He was sentenced to two years' imprisonment.

"The conduct of William Collins while in prison was such that he received the usual remission from the full term of his sentence. He was released about a month ago. He disappeared from our observation immediately. We thought of him at once when we learnt that Isaac Marks had been murdered, but our ignorance of his antecedents, even of his real name, rendered it particularly difficult to trace him. Still, we have managed that, though not quite so quickly as we should have liked to do.

"We now know, Miss Russell, that the young man who had used the name of William Collins at the instigation of Isaac Marks, and in what he may have supposed to be no more than an innocent mystification, was William Trevor Russell, and that he was a brother with whom you had quarrelled some years earlier, and with whom you had ceased to live.

"We also know—I am sorry to have to allude to circumstances which must be painful to you, but it is necessary to do so, however briefly—we know that your father shot himself ten years ago, about a fortnight after your mother's death, the act being attributed to his grief at that loss, Which, I am sorry to have to say, was not the whole truth.

"Since the death of your parents, you have been supported by Isaac Marks—entirely so, until you obtained your present position; and you were receiving an allowance from him up to a month ago.

"Your brother, also, received an income from him, on which he had elected to live, without seeking any regular occupation. The fact that he was financially dependent, and the belief that he was a distant relative (which I understand to have been the explanation which

Marks gave of his apparent generosity towards your brother and yourself, and which was untrue), may have—"

"I always told you the bounder wasn't—" Edward Wilson burst out, looking across at Delia.

"If you please, Mr. Wilson," the Superintendent interrupted, with a sharper tone than he often used, "I must ask you to be quiet until I have finished what I have to say. Afterwards, I shall be willing to listen."

Delia did not appear to notice the interruption. Her face was colourless, and her eyes continued to be fixed on the Superintendent, who, having secured silence, went on with his narrative.

"The reason I have stated may have inclined your brother to a mistaken loyalty toward a man whom he believed to be a relative, and whom he regarded as a benefactor. He may even have believed him innocent until the moment when he heard the lying tale in the witness-box, by which he was sacrificed to procure the escape of the actual criminal. Then it is not surprising if his feelings abruptly and entirely changed.

"Why—the question inevitably arises—did Isaac Marks support you and your brother with a liberality so alien from his natural character, if you were not related to him?

"The answer to this, I am sorry to have to explain, is bound up with the circumstances of your father's death.

"When your mother died, her illness was of so sudden and severe a character that she had no opportunity to go over her private papers, or put her affairs in order. She had—or was supposed to have—a fortune of £15,000, which, by a will made at about the time of your birth, had been left to your brother and yourself. Her death disclosed the fact that that fortune was almost entirely gone. Your father's investigations revealed that the money had been paid to Isaac Marks by successive instalments of increasing amount. Correspondence which she had left disclosed the most frequent explanation of such payments. Isaac Marks was in possession of letters which your mother had been resolved, at whatever cost, to keep from your father's knowledge.

"Had your father consulted us, and placed these evidences in our hands, a blackmailer's career might have terminated a good many years earlier than it did. But he may have felt it impossible to adopt a course which would have revealed to the public gaze matters which your mother had hidden at so great a cost. Matters which, to an outside view, it is right to say, were of a far less serious character than, to her, they may have appeared to be.

184

"Yet he dealt with the position, before taking his own life, in a way which he considered would be to his children's good, but which, in its final issue, has brought you here today.

"He placed the evidences of Isaac Marks's black-mailing persecution of your mother in a sealed packet in his bankers' hands, with instructions that it should be forwarded to us if, at any time, Isaac Marks should fail to make adequate provision for your, and your brother's, support. The conditions of the withholding of that packet from our hands were such that your financial welfare would be secured, even in the event of the death of Marks, under provisions that it would be tedious to detail now.

"Isaac Marks found himself in the position of one of his own victims. And it was a case beyond argument, for your father was dead. He had either to satisfy the bank that he had made the financial arrangements which were required, or it would have become a matter of mere business routine that the evidences of his guilt should be forwarded here.

"Being so placed, he showed no hesitation in complying with the conditions which had been imposed upon him. Indeed, he continued to do so even when it was known to the bank that your brother was suffering imprisonment as a convicted blackmailer; and when he was released he found that a sum of several hundred pounds had accumulated to the credit of his account. It was by drawing upon this money that your brother was able to obtain funds for his requirements after his release, and to book his passage to Canada, though we have reason to suppose that, when he left England, he had a much larger sum in his possession.

"Your father's forethought had secured your financial welfare. He could not foresee that Isaac Marks would seek to use your dependence upon him to bring you both under his influence, so that he might use you for his own criminal purposes. In your case, we know that he failed, and that, in spite of his enigmatic financial generosity, you had repulsed any approach to a personal intimacy; and, if we are correctly informed, you had obtained your position at the South Bermondsey Library with the object of becoming independent of his support. But with your brother he was at least partially successful.... So much we know.

"When the date of your brother's release approached, it appears that Marks was in a condition of genuine and well-founded terror. He knew enough of his character to anticipate that his life was in danger.

"Under the influence of his fear he took two precautions. He rented Mrs. Starr's flat with an elaborate anonymity which must have been very expensive to arrange, but was similar, we have ascertained, to a method which he had employed previously when he had required a flat for the blackmailing of a wealthy foreigner, from which he could disappear, leaving no trace of his identity when it had served its purpose. On these premises he felt that he would be able to sleep securely, while his assistants were to negotiate with your brother for a peaceful settlement, which was to be effected by a large cash payment.

"He also provided himself with banknotes for £15,000, with which he hoped to buy your brother off, if he should succeed in tracing his hiding-place. He is believed to have had these notes in his pocket-book when he was shot, since which time they have disappeared. We have known of these notes from a time within twenty-four hours of the commission of the crime, though we have not allowed the knowledge to reach the Press, and their disappearance has been one of the reasons why we have never been able to regard the confessions put forward either by Mr. Wilson or yourself as entirely genuine documents.

"Now, Miss Russell, I come to the morning of the crime, and the question of your own complicity.

"We have reliable information that your brother had an interview with you on the previous evening, and it is evident, from the course of subsequent events, that he had traced Isaac Marks to the flat which he had only just taken, and that he must have told you of his intention of visiting him on the following day. "On that morning he left his lodgings at 8:30 A.M., and, at about 9:20, a man corresponding to his description was seen by two witnesses of good character, whose evidence we only obtained last Saturday, to go up to Mrs. Starr's flat.

"The banknotes of a total value of £15,000, which Marks is known to have had in his possession, were in that of your brother when his effects received a somewhat thorough examination at our request from the Customs Officers at New York.

"Your own time of reaching the flat cannot have been less than half an hour later than that at which your brother arrived, and whether he had then left is a point on which, I will tell you frankly, we are not yet sure.

"If, as I am disposed to believe, your object in going there was to prevent a crime, which you were too late, or otherwise unable to do, and if you are now prepared to give us such assistance as we

186

have a right to expect, the fact that you have endeavoured to mislead us with a false confession, and given us a good deal of subsequent trouble, need not, even now, entail any very serious consequences.

"Your brother, with whatever purpose, did not go straight through to Canada, as he had declared his intention of doing. He delayed in New York, where he may have supposed that he had eluded official observation, on which point he will find that he had been mistaken.

"We are now expecting to hear at any moment that he is detained by the New York police, and will be returned here to be tried on a charge of the wilful murder of Isaac Marks. Whatever provocation he may have considered that he had received, the law does not allow that it can justify such a crime, though it may be taken into account when the question of penalty arises.

"If your confession was made, as I suppose, with the intention of drawing suspicion away from the real culprit, and giving him time to escape, you will see that it can serve no useful purpose to persist in it either for yourself or him.

"If you are prepared to give us a full and frank account of your connection with the matter up to the time when Mrs. Starr discovered you in the flat, it is possible that we may withdraw the prosecution, so far as you are concerned, and ask the magistrate to discharge you this morning."

Superintendent Withers stopped at last. He looked at the girl whose eyes had been fixed upon him during the length of his narration as though hypnotized by what she heard. For a time she made neither movement nor answer. She sat silent among those who had become equally silent, waiting for her reply.

The telephone bell rang sharply on the Superintendent's table in the quiet room.

He frowned slightly at the interruption, not wishing anything to divert his attention from the reply for which he was waiting.

"Take it, Simmons," he said, "and tell them I'm not to be disturbed, unless it's Sir Henry himself."

Simmons moved to the instrument, and as he listened to the message which was coming through, Delia spoke at last.

"I can't say anything more than I've said already. It wasn't Edward at all. I shot Mr. Marks myself."

Superintendent Withers made an impatient ejaculation. Then he controlled himself to ask: "Who do you mean by Edward? It was your brother of whom I was talking."

"I mean neither, of course. Mr. Wilson had nothing to do with it. He wasn't even there. I don't believe he knew the address."

"Miss Russell, if you persist in asserting that your brother was innocent, in the face of the facts which you know already, and those which you have just heard— Well, what is it, Simmons? Tell them to wait for a few minutes."

"I thought you might like to know: a cable from the New York police."

Superintendent Withers reached out a receiver.

CHAPTER FORTY-TWO

WILLIAM TREVOR RUSSELL sat in a popular restaurant in West 42nd Street. He could have afforded a more palatial resort, but he had no desire to render himself conspicuous in any way. He wished to be lost in the crowd. Yet he was in no great anxiety, though somewhat bewildered, after two years of seclusion, by the rush of the city life, and in frequent danger from a whirl of traffic which moved in an opposite direction from that to which he expected to face it.

Yet he felt that the game was won. It was true that he was lingering in New York, which he had no right to do, but, even if he were apprehended for that offence, what worse could happen than perhaps a fine, and to be passed on to the destination to which he had booked? And it was an unlikely thing that anyone would concern themselves about so short a pause, for which he had business reason enough, though it might not be one which he would be over-ready to put forward in explanation of his delay.

There had been moments when he felt much less comfortable then he did now. He had had a worried time on the boat. There had been nerve-shaking interviews in the purser's office, and afterwards in the commander's cabin. But the last of these had been of a most satisfactory kind. It had been apology and explanation that he had not been the one they sought. A case of mistaken identity. They must all blame the police.

There had been the final ordeal of a most rigorous examination at the Customs, extending even to the contents of his pockets, and the disclosure of the banknotes he carried. He was too inexperienced to know how far it exceeded the routine procedure, but he had been worried by the fact that the numbers of those notes had been taken. They might not immediately identify William Trevor Russell with the convict Collins, but if it were known that they had been in the recent possession of Isaac Marks, they would go a long way on that road. He did not forget that his finger-prints were recorded at Scotland Yard. They were a means of identification beyond denial. Suppose he should be detained while they were forwarded to London for comparison? (They were, in fact, already on the way there, having been taken before he left the boat, by a simple process which left him without suspicion.) He knew that the United States has no hospitality to offer to the output of English gaols. If his identity were proved, there might be no necessity to formulate new charges against him, no process of extradition; he might be shipped back at once to the care of the English police.... Reflecting on these things, he had decided that he would be more comfortable when those banknotes had left his hands.

There is one easy way to dispose of paper money of doubtful history or dangerous associations. It is the way that the gambler takes. But even so, English banknotes in units of £1,000 could not be staked without drawing dangerous inquiry, and risks of loss on a scale which he was not willing to face.

To take them boldly to the money-changers might seem to offer no added peril, in view of the fact that he had been already officially identified with them. But when he thought of that, the fear came that he might be questioned before notes of such magnitude would be negotiated. He might be asked to show his papers. They would reveal that his only right in the United States was to travel through it via Buffalo to Montreal. Suppose they rang up the police?

He made one adventure into a subterranean Broadway gambling hell, near Thirty-Ninth Street. He exchanged one note for counters at the rate of something less than three dollars to the £, and he was glad to slip out half an hour afterwards at a time when attention was concentrated upon a row at the other end of the room, with about seven hundred dollars in his possession. It was an experiment too dear to repeat.

Now he sat opposite to Mr. Silas Flickwin who was receiving twenty dollars a week from Mackenzie's Information Bureau to keep him under observation, and report his movements. Naturally, he did not know that. He knew Mr. Flickwin as a gentleman of unprepossessing aspect, but who had shown him friendship in the gambling-den, and a hint that it would be best to leave when he did.

Mr. Flickwin, in the course of the occupation in which he specialized, frequently took occasion to cultivate the acquaintance of those he followed. It saved trouble in a number of ways. It also pleased his peculiar sense of humour to gain the confidence of those whose lives might be blasted subsequently by his reports. He had been doubly willing to offer his services to show the side stairs which were the nearest way to the street, because he was not sure of his own safety in a place where he was known and unwelcome, and which no sound of shots would tempt the police to enter without Boss Kelly's permission. He had also witnessed the changing of the £1,000 note, with a natural curiosity as to how many more there might be. Had Mackenzie known of the existence of those notes, Flickwin would have been about the last man he would have chosen for this job. But all he had been instructed was that Russell was suspected of some complicity in a London murder, without sufficient evidence to justify his arrest, and that he was to be kept under observation until further orders. Mackenzie's Information Bureau frequently carried out such instructions from Scotland Yard, and had a good reputation for the reliability of the services it rendered. He had thought Flickwin to be the right man for the job.

So he would have been had not the sight of that £1,000 set him thinking of the possibility of a side-line which might be more lucrative. Yet he might have let the temptation go, had he known that William Russell was not only under his own observation, but that of the police, for he valued a whole skin.

But he did not know this, and he learnt, as the meal proceeded, and he gained a gradual confidence, that the prize was great. Even so, he did not think of attempting a personal robbery: it was a matter for Kelly's gang. To introduce such a line of business might be to obliterate the memory of a previous incident which had made him shy of Mr. Kelly's head-quarters. And he would stipulate for five thousand bucks for himself. He saw that they might be won without any great personal risk either to life or liberty. His own part would be of a preliminary kind. Difficult to prove under any circumstances: impossible if the only man who could give evidence against him should be found floating among the jetsam of the East River, which would be the most probable termination of the event.

He knew that if he had Kelly's word for his own share of the spoils, and he did his part in the right way, there would be no fear that the payment would not be made. The transactions of the underworld cannot be enforced by law, and, for that reason, there must be a more absolute confidence, when credit is given, that the need to appeal to it will not arise. Kelly could not have risen to his present eminence had it not been known to all that such bargains were always kept. His career would have ended at a humbler stage with an episode of a one-way ride.

As he faced William Russell across the little white-clothed table that was so commonplace to him, and so unfamiliar to the Englishman, with the delusive liberality of its iced water and pile of small caraway-seeded rolls, of which they might eat as many as they would without any charge being made, he had the memory of his interview with Big Jim Walker (not Jimmy Walker, the Mayor, but a much larger and almost equally important man, being Kelly's chief of staff), less than an hour ago. Big Jim had promised nothing, listening and chewing his cigar in strong prominent teeth. He did this in an aggressive, bullying way, his jaw moving as though he chewed contemptuously the words, if not the persons, of those who laid their petitions before him.

Jim Walker had promised nothing, beyond that he would have a talk to the boss, but he had told him to get busy and find out how much the sap had got, and if he carried it round. That, at the first interview, was as much progress as he had expected to make.

Now Silas led the talk skilfully to the changing of money, allowing Russell to question him upon a topic which was already in his thoughts. Good advice was given, and caution urged. Anecdotes were told of the misadventures of foolish and credulous men. It had been a mistake (might Silas say it without giving offence?) to change a note of such magnitude in such a place. Besides, he was not given a fair value. Not that such a transaction could be carried out without a liberal commission. To attempt that was to invite dishonesty. Hiram Abrahams was the best man to go to where a large amount was involved. He was dear, but he asked no questions, and everyone knew he was straight. Never heard of Hiram? That was because he was a stranger to New York. Everyone knew Hiram Abrahams. He was one of the richest Jews in America.

When they parted it was agreed that Silas should seek out the mythical Abrahams and inquire his terms for exchanging £14,000 of English banknotes for the currency of the United States, and they were to meet again at 6:30 P.M.

Silas Flickwin went back to Jim Walker, who was now ready to deal.

They made terms and plans.

CHAPTER FORTY-THREE

IT APPEARED THAT Hiram Abrahams was a dear man. It was a large amount of banknotes with which to deal; if they had a history it might be difficult, especially as they were of such large denominations. It would have been much easier had it been in fives or tens, even in hundreds— So Silas explained.

William Russell, listening to this talk, was led to anticipate terms which would be impossible of acceptance, even to him. He had a vague idea that the proposal would be in the region of halving the amount. When Silas, with a good deal of hesitation, mentioned ten per cent., he felt the relief of a lifted fear, as it had been intended that he should do. And after all, it was a good sum. Fourteen hundred pounds. It was much to lose. Mr. Abrahams might be well content to make such a sum in a transaction after hours at his own home. For that was what it was to be. Mr. Abrahams lived in a villa in Queens. Such a transaction would be done quietly there.

He would be prepared to change £14,000 of English banknotes at 10:30 P.M., or a larger sum, if desired. He did not mind how large if might be, if he deducted his ten per cent. The rate of exchange would be that which had been quoted that afternoon. He had given a slip of paper with the calculated value of the sum mentioned and the commission deducted, even to the odd cents. Mr. Russell could check the figures beforehand, and the transaction could be quickly completed; when they met. Nothing would move him to abate a cent in the commission which he required, but it was equally certain that he would not pay a cent short. It appeared that he was an exact man.

Mr. Russell was inclined to feel an immense relief. He had given up the idea of going to Canada. Silas had assured him (with truth) that there are many thousands of people in the United States who have no credentials of citizenship, having entered by many illicit ways. Let him go westward to any of the great inland cities, and he would be swallowed up and forgotten. A motor-coach might be a good way to start. People booked on them for long and short distances, and they came and went unheeded by the police.

Mr. Russell intended to lose no time. Tomorrow he would leave New York, and he did not care if he should never see it again. Yet, though he felt confident in the good faith of the projected deal, his caution did not desert him. He inquired shrewdly how Silas was to benefit from it. Silas, as though with a little natural reluctance, admitted that he had not entirely neglected his own interests. He had bargained with Mr. Abrahams that he should have a commission of a quarter per cent for introducing the business. Mr. Russell calculated that in English money. Thirty-five pounds. Quite a good fee, and yet not exorbitant. Not unreasonable in proportion to the magnitude of the transaction, or the amount of Mr. Abraham's profit. The exactness of the accounting gave him confidence in the integrity of those with whom he was about to deal. He was in good spirits when he stood with Silas on the street-kerb that evening, looking for a taxi that he could hire.

He had already signalled to one to stop when he became aware that Silas had attracted the attention of another driver. Silas led the way without looking back. They couldn't have both. What difference could it make which they took? He followed Silas and got in.

CHAPTER FORTY-FOUR

MR. RUSSELL HAD no more than the vaguest acquaintance with the geography of New York, or the situation of Queens, where Mr. Abrahams was alleged to live. It is unlikely that he would have protested had the taxi turned in the direction of Wall Street or of Brooklyn Bridge. But, in fact, it made its zigzag way through the city's centre, as the traffic bye-laws of the moment permitted, very much in the direction which would have been expected by one with a better knowledge.

As they approached the Eastern side of Manhattan they passed through a succession of dreary, ill-lighted streets, and Silas excused a nervousness which had become too apparent not to attract his companion's attention, by saying that he never felt comfortable till he was out of this district, which was a haunt of gunmen, gangsters, and racketeers, where they might be held up at any moment, or hear a stray bullet crash through the glass of the taxi window.

Mr. Russell was too ignorant to question the accuracy of this statement. He did not know that the smallest of racketeers would scorn the idea of residing amid such an environment; nor did it occur to him that those intending to enrich themselves by the holding up of a passing vehicle would be likely to seek it in a less populated and more affluent quarter. Yet he was not seriously perturbed. When Silas called the driver's attention to the fact that another vehicle was behind them, and the pace quickened, he felt that he was witnessing a degree of timidity which he did not share. When Silas asked him if he carried any offensive weapons for his protection, he gave the satisfactory (to Silas) reply that he had never found it necessary to do so. Silas replied that he would alter his mind if he had more experience of New York. He showed a pistol from his own pocket. As though to emphasize his remarks, there came the noise of rapid shooting at no great distance ahead.

The driver listened. He looked back at Silas in an evident hesitation. Silas began to speak and stopped. It was difficult for him to discuss the position with Mr. Russell beside him. An indiscreet word might be remembered against him, and destroy the carefully-constructed screen of innocence which was to protect him from the natural consequences of the crime in which he was taking part.

Big Jim Walker had given him certain instructions that afternoon, and had made it clear that, if he carried them out with exactness, he would not only get his reward. He would be guaranteed against any criminal conviction. But he knew that exact obedience was a condition of that immunity, from which no exception would be allowed.

So far he had done his part in a way which even Jim Walker could not fail to approve. It was at about this place that he was to expostulate with the driver about the direction he was taking, and to receive a reply that the proper road was closed for repairs. That would be the first of the points which his victim, if he should survive his approaching ordeal, would remember in his favour afterwards

They would then turn down under the railway arches, and when they were in that dark stretch which there is no more than an iron rail to guard from the darker river below, there would be another car turned sideways across their path. At the hold-up which would follow, it would not only be the Englishman whose pockets would be emptied. Silas would also surrender the smaller sum his note-case held. It was no part of the programme that murder should be committed if no resistance were offered, but it was a wise precaution to choose a spot where a dead or wounded body could be swiftly flung over the rail.

If the victim should be allowed to live, and should make complaint to the police (which was unlikely enough, for notes which must be changed by such methods seldom bear a history suitable for official eyes) he would himself be a witness of his companion's innocence. Had Silas not lost the contents of his own pockets? Had he not protested when the driver (doubtless a member of the gang), had turned out of his course? Brought before a judge who would be far more in fear of Kelly than of the law of the State, and receiving the major portion of his income from the tribute of the underworld, Silas would have little to fear, even in the improbable event of any charge being made against him.

But he knew, as the driver knew, that exact obedience was the condition of the protection which Kelly was able to give. The man looked back at Silas with an indecision which he would not speak. He could almost certainly locate those shots. The sounds came from beneath the arches under which he was instructed to turn.

He looked forward with an apprehension that something had gone wrong: he looked back to a car which had made no effort to overtake him, but which had hung upon his rear ever since he had left the crowded traffic of the central streets. He went on as he had been ordered to do.

CHAPTER FORTY-FIVE

DETECTIVE PICKLER HAD had in his pocket since early morning a warrant for the arrest of William Trevor Russell, a man who, being of English birth, and wanted by the London police on a murder charge, and concerning whom the question of extradition did not arise, could be sent back immediately that the necessary escort should be provided. He could have executed that warrant at any moment during the day, had he desired to do so, but he had been instructed to delay the arrest until night, for Mr. Russell was serving a very useful purpose, with which the police were reluctant to interfere. He was, in fact, an unconscious bait for the capture of some members of the Kelly gang, which the police desired to lay by the heels as an intimation to that gentleman that certain contributions that they had been accustomed to receive from him at regular intervals were substantially in arrear. They did not propose to proceed to extremities, such as would rouse his allies to befriend, and his political associates to protect, him: it was a mere routine of discipline with which even the Tammany Boss (if it were properly explained) would not be likely to interfere.

They did not desire to arrest any member of the Kelly gang for any more serious offence than that of being in illegal possession of firearms, on which charge they could be held until Kelly had bought his peace with the law: and they saw that to surround them on this occasion, while they lay ambushed for their own victim, would be an almost ideal opportunity for effecting their purpose. They would secure about half a dozen moderately important members of the gang, at a time when they would certainly not be unarmed; and, incidentally, they would prevent a crime, which the efficient police force of New York City is frequently glad to do.

They succeeded in carrying out this programme by a demonstration of force sufficient to secure the surrender of Mr. Kelly's retainers after a mere perfunctory spatter of bullets which produced no casualty, and they had already left the scene with their indignant prisoners when the driver of Mr. Russell's taxi appeared upon it, and looked round for a hold-up which was not there.

He slackened speed. He crawled. He was one of those men who can be relied upon to do exactly what they are told, but who are incapable of independent decision. He would have been less perturbed had he sat passively at the wheel amid the explosion of a dozen guns, had he known that he was fulfilling the orders which he had received, than he now was in the silent shadows of the arches from which no hostile movement came, with his lights showing a clear road ahead, where the expected obstruction should have forced a halt. Suppose he had come too soon? Had mistaken his instructions—or Silas had done so, getting his victim into the car before the appointed time? Had he driven too fast, with the worry of that other car which had hung so stubbornly on his rear? (But there was no sign of that now.) In imagination he tried to face the cruel, contemptuous anger in Jim Walker's eyes, when it had to be told that the plot had failed—because he had been there too soon. He might have to face something more than Jim Walker's anger. What would the boss say? There might be sentence of which he would never know till it came to be executed: against which there could be no appeal. There was no mercy for failure in Kelly's gang.

Besides, where was he to go? Where, and on what pretext, was he to set down his fare? There had been no programme extending beyond that spot. For such a man there could be only one decision. The crawl grew slower. The car came to a halt. He had done his part. The noise of shots he had heard five minutes ago might, or might not, explain the absence of the expected gunmen, but he was not responsible for that. He had done his part. He sat still where he was.

Mr. Russell was a little puzzled, a little alarmed. He supposed a mechanical breakdown. He asked: "What's the trouble?"

Silas Flickwin, a man of quicker brains than the driver, saw that something had gone wrong, and came near to guessing what it had been. He thought that there had been an unexpected encounter with some of the boys of Costelli's gang. That was likely enough, for they were in a district where Costelli ruled, and in which he was known to be jealous of any invasion by other gangsters. Silas saw the prospect of affluence slipping away. He saw difficulties of explanation also. If this taxi had broken down, there were others available to take them to Hiram Abrahams's door. And Hiram was an invention of his own brain. He saw more than that. He saw the sudden prospect of wealth such as he had never dreamt to reach. Why—if he had but a moment's courage, should not the whole sum be his?

He was armed, and his companion had confessed himself weaponless. Men may do many things at the moment's call which they would lack the courage to plan, the nerve to carry through in a deliberate way. Now he replied to his companion's question with a sudden truculence of demeanour, and the pulling out of a gun that he carried, but had never fired. "Hands up!" he said, in the conventional formula that all America knows.

The driver looked round, his arms rising mechanically from the wheel, but he saw that the order was not for him. He supposed that the details of the hold-up had been varied without his knowledge. It was no business of his. His hands went back on the wheel. His eyes looked straight ahead.

Mr. Russell did not raise his hands. Actually it did not occur to him to do so. He was alarmed and frightened, and would probably have surrendered the money had he felt the danger to be acute, but in that first moment of inaction he saw the weakness of his opponent.

Silas was not of the type that can shoot their fellows in cold blood. As William Russell did not raise his hands, he simply did not know what to do next. Courage came to his antagonist as his indecision showed in his eyes. With a sudden movement of his hand he struck up the gun. Whether of intention or by the sudden jar of the blow, Silas fired as it struck his arm. William Russell would never know how close the bullet went to his own brain. He felt confused, deafened, blinded for a moment as the shot burst in his face.

Like an echo, in the next second another shot came from the darkness at the side of the vehicle. Silas sank a huddled heap on the cushions, with a bullet in his own brain.

Detective Pickler pulled open the door of the taxi. He looked at the dead man whom he had shot so promptly in response to the explosion of his own weapon, the cause of which he had not been in a position to see. The event had developed in an unexpected direction He had not thought of Silas as a man of violence, nor (until the last two days) as being in league with the Kelly gang. He looked at William Russell. "Hurt?" he asked, curtly enough.

"No. I don't think so."

Detective Pickler came to the point at once. He introduced himself. He said: "You must get out of this and come with me. I have a warrant for your arrest."

It was, in fact, evident that he would have to get out of that vehicle if he were to go anywhere, unless he would take the wheel himself. The driver had ducked his head even as the detective's bullet had found its mark. Next moment he had slipped out of the further door, and was scuttling away in the darkness along the wall.

Mr. Russell was recovering his nerve, the second shock of this announcement tending to cancel that of the first. He said: "I've done nothing. What's the warrant for?"

"It's no matter of ours. It's London calling this time. Shooting a guy named Marks."

"I suppose it's no use telling you I didn't do it at all?"

"Not much."

"Well, it's the truth all the same."

"Honest?"

"Yes. I didn't do it and I don't know who did."

"Reckon you'll have to tell that where it belongs."

"I suppose—it's not a thing we could square?

I don't mind a fair price.... It won't do you any good sending me back."

"Nope. You'll have to come along this time."

"Suppose we said a thousand pounds? Suppose we said two?"

The detective was tempted, but shook his head. He had a reputation which he valued. He liked to bring in his man. He was also of a standard of integrity which was above the average of the force to which he belonged. He was not of an impossible virtue. He did not attempt to live on his pay. But he was not conscious of enriching himself on the misery of others. In the course of fifteen years' service he had never attempted blackmail, nor to frame a false charge, nor to fake evidence against a suspected man. But if he could improve his banking account without doing harm to any, nor damage to his own reputation—well, anyone but a fool would.

Now he looked at William Russell, as he came reluctantly out of the taxi, and at the dead man, who would never be arrested on any earthly warrant, and, as he looked, an idea came. He reached a hand to Silas's collar, and pulled him roughly out on to the pavement. As he did so, he looked up to say: "You'd better not try that. I'd put a bullet in you before you'd gone ten yards, and it would be the last thing you'd know."

"I wasn't thinking of that."

"Well, don't. Just do what I tell you, and do it quickly, and you may find it a better way."

As he spoke, he turned the contents of Silas's pockets on to the pavement. In reply to his curt order, William Russell did the same with his. In two minutes, a complete transfer had been made. Even his passport was in the hip-pocket of the dead man.

Detective Pickler looked at the contents of a note-case which contained some hundreds of dollars in American bills. He handed the bull; of these back to their owner. "There's no need to let those go." He counted the banknotes. Fourteen, each of a thousand pounds value. He put five into his own pocket. He handed five to William Russell. He folded up the remaining four, and put them into an inner pocket of the dead man's vest, which he buttoned securely.

"Lend a hand here," he said brusquely. "You'd better take his legs." Together they carried the body which had been Silas Flickwin for some distance along the railings. William Russell wondered why they did not throw it over at once, as was its evident destiny, but the detective knew what he was doing. The lower the spot where it was thrown in, the more certain was it that it would be washed into the back-water where he intended that it should be found. It hit the water with a loud splash, and as it did so, Detective Pickler spoke curtly: "Now clear. No, not that way.... You'd better go back, or you won't be let go far.... And don't be in N'York when it's daylight tomorrow. You won't get a second chance."

William Russell vanished into the night.

The detective, conscious of a job well done, walked briskly forward to a point where he emerged again to the level of the upper streets. He found his car, which he had sent on, and relieved the mind of a driver who had been made anxious by the length of time he had waited. But he had had his orders to drive forward and to stop anyone who might attempt to escape at the further end of the lower street. Beyond that he was not to move until Detective Pickler should rejoin him there. He had done his part.

He had stopped a crouching form which had endeavoured to slip past in the shadow of the wall. He held him at his pistol's point. Detective Pickler looked at the man with attention. "Know Chicago?" he asked. The man stared vaguely, and shook his head.

"Then you will tomorrow. And when you leave it, *you'll go west*. Savvy? You'll go west—or you'll go cold if you come back here.... Let him go now.

The man disappeared in the darkness. ...

Detective Pickler reported that he had challenged a man resembling William Trevor Russell, who had leapt into the river to avoid arrest. He had fired at him as he stood a moment on the rail, but whether he had hit him or not, he could not say.... The body was recovered a few hours later, when the tide turned. It was identified without difficulty by the papers which its pockets held. There were notes for £4,000 also, which were handed over, very honestly, to the

Metropolitan Police.... There was a bullet wound in the side of the head. Death must have been instantaneous. Detective Pickler was known to be a good shot.

CHAPTER FORTY-SIX

SUPERINTENDENT WITHERS READ the cable-gram. For a few moments he did not speak. An atmosphere of suspense, of crisis, as though there were subconscious contact with the thoughts in his own mind, held the room in a waiting silence. Then he said:

"Miss Russell, I don't know that you were intimately attached to your brother—I hope you were not, and I don't think you had much cause to be—but I'm afraid I have some bad news to give you; though it may be the best ending that you could have expected to hear.... Your brother's body has been recovered from the East River, New York, under circumstances of which we shall be more fully informed when the mail arrives."

Delia's face went somewhat paler than before, but she made no answer. After a pause. the Superintendent added: "In view of this altered position, do you still persist in saying that you shot Isaac Marks with your own hand?"

There was another silence, which seemed longer than it really was to those who waited for her reply. She looked across at Edward Wilson and the appeal in his eyes may have roused her to the decision which her words implied.

"I suppose," she said, "it doesn't matter what I say now."

Half an hour afterwards Delia Russell was brought before the Magistrate's Court, and formally discharged on the application of the police, their solicitor stating that they did not propose to offer any evidence against her.

Superintendent Withers closed his record of the case with a note that the murderer had been traced, and shot dead in New York while endeavouring to escape arrest. It was a satisfactory ending, removing the crime from the list of those which remain unsolved, of which there had been too many in recent years.

"It's been a queer case," the Superintendent remarked to Inspector Cleveland, when they were back in his own room at a later hour, "but I can't say that you haven't handled it well.... I suppose there's not much doubt that she made that confession to draw us off the right track.... But I wouldn't say that we've had the whole truth now."

The Inspector did not deny that. He had been conscious of a similar doubt, though he had thought that it might be best unspoken. He said: "What shall you do with that money when it arrives?"

"I was thinking of that.... You can let Mrs. Starr know, in an informal way, that there'll probably be £4,000 for her friend to pick up before long. Of course, there'll be some legal formalities to be gone through, but I think that's how it will end up. Whether it was Isaac Marks's money or William Russell's, it seems to have been Delia's mother's at the start.... It's a useful sum," he added, "when you're starting a home...."

Mrs. Starr was on the telephone in her husband's office.

"That you, Ted?" she inquired with a casual cheerfulness. "I'm so sorry! I only got here ten minutes ago.... Oh, nothing much, really. I thought it was when I wrote, but it isn't now. I wanted you to help getting Inspector Cleveland out of a mess."

Delia, in her lover's arms, and in a mood in which tears and laughter contended with no certain victory, was in the process of being persuaded that if she had lost her job at the South Bermondsey Library, there might be other occupation to be found of a happier kind.

"You don't mind," she asked doubtfully, "you're sure you don't mind what I did?"

"No," he said, "I've no doubt you thought it was the right thing."

She sighed a relief which seemed disproportionate to the event, and added: "But, oh, Edward, why did you say you'd done it? You must have known, even if they'd believed you, which they never would, that I'd never have let you—"

"Well, for that matter, why did you?"

"But, Edward, I *did*.... I *did* do it. Oh, Edward, I thought I'd made you understand that...! It wasn't just as I said, because I couldn't say that William had been there.... Mrs. Starr helped me to make up that tale, and then I had to hide when she saw that it wouldn't go down.... I did want to give time for William to get away. I knew they'd think it was he, if they found out that he'd been there.... You know I only went because I was afraid of what he might do.... But he was there first, and it hadn't gone just as I supposed it might. I can't remember it clearly now, it was all so quick, and I was so frightened afterwards.... But when I got there William was threatening him with his own gun.

"I heard Mr. Marks shout as I went down the passage. 'Don't, Will, don't.... Can't you see it's at half-cock?' or something like that. And William said: 'Well, then, the quicker you shell out, the better for you.' And next minute he was coming out of the room with the notes in his hand. He didn't seem to take any notice of me. He pushed past as though he didn't know who I was. I suppose when he'd got the money he only cared about getting away.... But Mr. Marks was just wild when he saw me there. I suppose he'd lost all the nerve he had by what he'd gone through before.... He wasn't on the bed then. He was by the door.... He said what in hell's name was I doing there too, and if we weren't out in ten seconds he'd put a bullet through us both. When he said this, he was between me and the door. I saw the pistol lying on the dressing-table. William must have put it down there when he got the money. That was quite true. I said: 'You won't do it with this.... I'll go, if you'll let me pass,' or something of that sort, and he shouted: 'Put it down, you fool! Can't you see that it's—' something I didn't understand. I had never had such a thing in my hands before. He wasn't getting up from the bed. I think he threw himself back on it, as I turned toward him to go to the door, when he saw how I was holding it.... And then it went off....

"I went and sat in the next room. I was too frightened to think properly, but I knew that if I just walked out and said nothing, everyone would think that William had done it.... And then Mrs. Starr came."

She waited for one anxious moment as her tale ceased for the verdict of condemnation or acquittal which she must hear from her lover's lips, conscious only of the beating of her own heart.

"Well," he said, "he wasn't much loss, and it's over now."

ABOUT THE AUTHOR

SYDNEY FOWLER WRIGHT (1874-1965) penned over seventy volumes of science fiction, fantasy, classic mysteries, historical novels, poetry, and non-fiction, many of them being published by the Borgo Press Imprint of Wildside Press.